This book is for the remarkable Sarah-Jane Reeh

Thanks

With thanks to Jeannie, Alan, Dafydd, Dennis, Jaye Francis, Henry Nissen, Richard Tregear, Richard Revill, John Landau, Kellie Flanagan, Ed Jarrett, Michael Warby, Atli, Belladonna and Ashe. And to all who care for the lost, stolen and strayed.

In loving memory of Sister Connie Peck FM, who even now is giving God a hard time about his negligent care of the widow and the fatherless.

This book is a work of fiction. No character in this book is meant to represent a real person. The City of Melbourne is also an artifact of my imagination.

Chapter One

Four a.m. Who invented four a.m.?

I dragged myself out of bed, slapped at the alarm, thrust bare feet into slipper-wards, stood on what felt like a furry rope and was rewarded with a yowl.

Oh shit. Horatio was waiting politely at my bedside to deliver his morning greeting and I had just begun the day with a bad deed. Meroe would frown at the effect on my karma.

Of course, if Horatio didn't insist on sitting in my slippers it might cut down the number of times this happened, and the consequent karmic debt. I'll probably come back as a mouse, and that would be on my good days.

Suppressing an unworthy thought that he carefully positioned his tail so that I would stand on it and then spend ten minutes apologising to him, I spent ten minutes apologising to him—poor kitty! Did the big fat woman stomp on his innocent stripy tail? I would see if a little milk would assuage his sense of insult.

It did. While Horatio was giving the milk his reverent, devoted attention, I had time to flick on the heater, put on the coffee (without which no baker ever commences the day), survey the squalor of my small stone-flagged kitchen, shiver a bit and drag on some clothes. I tend to dress in the kitchen because there is no heating in my bedroom until the ovens come on automatically at four. I had heard the fans cut in as I shut off the alarm clock.

Not a pretty sight on a cold dark morning, a baker. Long mousy hair tied back ruthlessly. Face entirely devoid of make-up, eyes dark-ringed as a result of waking when all others are sleeping. Thin faces look skeletal at this hour, fat faces like an illustration in a textbook on forensic pathology under the heading 'adipocere.' I'm fat, so it's the adipocere for me. I grin at my reflection, finish washing my face, put on two layers of tracksuit, and toast some gourmet date and walnut bread for breakfast.

Not bad at all. Possibly a little undersweetened. I made a note to add more honey next time I baked it.

I got into baking because I wanted to become an accountant. Bear with me—it makes sense. I was looking for a job which allowed me to attend all my lectures and the local Italian bakers gave me a job as a general hand, hours from four a.m. to nine a.m., which got me to my economics lecture almost on time, though a little floury.

As the years went on numbers became drier and baking more fascinating. It's almost an alchemical process. You combine flour, water and the plant yeast and at the end of the process you get something shiny, crunchy, aerated and delicious.

Four in the morning is a time when the mind has a tendency to run loose. Where was I? Ah, yes. I can pin down the moment when it happened. I was in the middle of a meeting about a takeover and the CEO was talking about currency fluctuations, I should have been fascinated, but all of a sudden there was a click in my mind. I didn't care. There was our client with more troubles than the Jam Tin (aka the Telstra Dome) on a bad grass day and I didn't care. Bastard had too much money anyway.

You can't be an accountant—no, you can't stay an accountant—with that sort of attitude. I left a note about cashing in my superannuation payments on my boss' desk, went home, levered off my uncomfortable shoes, tore off my bloody ridiculous suit with the padded shoulders, dragged on a tracksuit and vowed that whatever I had to do to make a living for me and Horatio, it would never involve wearing a kitten heel again. I joined the bakery full time, completing my apprenticeship. When I left

Pagliacci's, Papa Toni gave me a lump of his own pasta douro dough.

It was still with me, growing happily in its bucket, fed with sugar and kept at the optimum temperature. Yeast must be nurtured. Mama Pagliacci used to talk to her yeasts. Before Horatio arrived, so did I. Now I talk to him and I hope the yeast doesn't feel slighted.

I set up this bakery, Earthly Delights (anyone heard of Hieronymus Bosch? Look at the picture on the wall next to the glass case. It can keep a queue amused for, oh, minutes), in Calico Alley in the middle of the city. I like cities. Even at four a.m. something is always stirring, though around here it is likely to be up to no good. We have a lot of junkies at this end of the city. They are the reason why my bakery has extremely expensive triple locks, bolts and stainless steel security doors. I can't afford the health risk if they break in. I'd lose a whole batch of bread if someone dropped a syringe in my mixing tub.

Yesterday's mail caught my eye, piled on the table. Mostly bills addressed to Corinna Chapman, baker. One was a strange religious tract which appeared to be accusing me of being the Scarlet Woman. Done on a computer—any madman can make a respectable looking tract in these IT days. 'The Wages of Sin Is Death' it proclaimed. Weird.

Horatio, one paw politely on my knee, was intimating that breakfast might be acceptable. I shelved the tract for later consideration. Cities breed madmen. I shook some of the dried kitty food—why do they mould it into little shapes, like fish and hearts? It can't be to amuse the cat. Horatio would eat alphabet cat food that spelled poison as long as he felt peckish. And he'd eat it out of anything. There is no need for a special bowl with *cat* on the side. Who else is going to eat amusingly shaped fish-flavoured biscuits with added vitamins and minerals out of a dish on the floor? Since I've grown up, I haven't any friends who would do that.

I had bread to make. I took my second cup of coffee with me down the stone stairs to the bakery. I could feel the hot air rising. Horatio would join me when he had finished breakfast. He is a gentlemanly cat and considers it impolite to hurry his food. Besides, he needs to remove every crumb from his whiskers before he steps down to meet the Mouse Police, a rough but pleasant pair, far removed from him in elegance.

Horatio is an aristocat. I occasionally feel that I am unable to meet his stringent requirements for suitable conduct in a Lady.

I walked down into the bakery and the lights flicked on, blinding me momentarily. The Mouse Police collided solidly with my ankles in their eagerness to demonstrate that they had been working hard all night and deserved extra servings of Kitty Dins.

As I counted corpses—seven mice and (erk!) eight rats, one almost as big as a kitten—I congratulated them on their excellent patrolling and laid out the food in their bowls.

Allow me to introduce them. Rodent Control Officer Heckle, on the right, a black and white ex-tom of battered appearance, a little light on as to ears and with a curious kink in his tail. A notorious street fighter in his prime, now retired. And on the left, Rodent Control Officer Jekyll, a strong young black and white ex-female who had her litter under the mixing tub and now has no further interest in matrimony. She delivered the best right jab I had ever seen to Heckle when he swaggered too close to her kittens, and thereafter they have a relationship based less on mutual respect than on a balance of terror. I have, however, observed Heckle allowing Jekyll to lick his ears, and I once caught Heckle grooming Jekyll. When they saw me watching they both looked embarrassed. As far as I'm concerned it's meant to be old diggers together.

I got on with the mixing of the first batch of the day to the pleasant crunching of Kitty Dins and appreciative whuffling. Rye flour, sugar, sourdough yeast, water, a measure of white to make it a little lighter, on with the dough hooks and switch on the machine. My rye bread yeast is derived from a certain wild yeast, which is sour. I can sell all the rye bread I make to Eastern European restaurants.

I've got an order for Health Loaf, guaranteed free of fat.

I haven't told the buyer that unless it's a special or sweet bread there isn't any fat in bread. I don't believe that the Trade Practices Act obliges me to do so. Health Loaf is also free of gluten, which means that I need to use baking powder to get it to rise. Gluten is essential in making bread and provides much of the nutritional value as well as the taste. But there it is. The customer, as some capitalist observed, is always right. It's a reasonable deal, I suppose. They get something better than the average sawdust, and I get paid. There's really no satisfaction in making Health Loaf. Without binding elements it's crumbly and without salt, sugar or spices it's flavourless.

I think the eaters would get as much kick out of a handful of unprocessed bran and it would be cheaper too.

I remember delivering a tray of this bread to some healthy function and catching myself muttering, 'Eat sawdust and die, yuppie scum.' I probably didn't really mean it. Right, Health Loaf mixed and into tins and into the oven. Baking powder is a chemical reaction and starts as soon as the liquid is added. Speed is essential. I stacked the tins onto a slide, into the oven, timer on.

Now for the French sticks while the sawdust bricks are cooking. Pasta douro yeast, white flour, a little oil, warm water. Go, yeast. Muffins go in as soon as the sawdust comes out, another chemical reaction. I felt like apple today. Haul out the tin of apple pie filling (yes, yes, I know, but do you know how much peeling I have to do for the potato bread tomorrow?) and reach for the tin opener.

No tin opener. My hand falls confidently onto its place on the shelf and comes back empty.

Damn. I must have taken it up to my own kitchen.

I clatter up the stairs in my Doc Martens (good solid shoes are essential if you are on your feet all day, and at least they never come with a kitten heel), find the bloody thing, clatter down again, remove top layer of tracksuit, open tin.

It's really getting hot now. The ovens are into their stride. Time to open the door and greet the new dawn.

The Mouse Police rush outside with cries of relief, as though they had been trapped for days in a lift with Philip Ruddock talking about border protection. A gust of cold air rushes in. I turn off one mixer and set the rye bread on 'rise.' I prepare the muffin mix, except the milk, and pause to look out at the dawn and stretch my back.

Then Heckle leaps inside as though he had been stung. Something is stuck in his foot, he is shaking his paw frantically and mewing loudly. I grab him and extract a syringe from his paw.

Heckle immediately settles down to allow Jekyll to lick his injury and I stalk out, shaking with fury.

Junkies! Irresponsible bloody junkies. Never mind finding a sharps bin, just drop the syringe in the alley, a waiting trap for an innocent cat. I kick at the wall with a furious foot, a waste of effort, for when they built this building they built it to survive anything short of an exploding volcano. I swear into the chill grey pre-dawn light. Then I see a figure slumped on my ventilation grate. No wonder it got so hot in the kitchen with some vagrant lying on my grate! I stomp over, reach out and grab for the offending shoulder, meaning to give it a good shake and send it on its way.

It collapses bonelessly out of my grasp and falls, flat on its back. A girl, with long matted hair shifting away from her blue face. Not just a delicate azure either, but dark blue like my slate floor.

Not breathing. I run back inside, grab the mobile and call 000, get a bored voice which promises instant attention and instructs me to start CPR. Oh, Jesus Mary and Joseph. My skin tries to crawl off me and find a more compassionate human. This girl is probably riddled with diseases, AIDS, hepatitis A to Z. And she's just wounded one of my cats with her careless syringe. What a bitch life is. It's a punishment for stepping on Horatio's tail.

I still have plastic gloves on and I can use cling wrap on her mouth. I'm shuddering with revulsion as I lay her out on the cold cobbles. I punch a hole in my cling wrap, clear the airway and puff breath into her mouth. I can feel no heartbeat but I don't know where to check. I learned this at school, come on,

Corinna, it's push here and then breathe, count, then push again, breathe again. There are soft lips under the plastic. She feels like a child, all bones, high rib cage, stinks like a sewer. Breathe, count, push, breathe again.

I'm dizzy. I don't know how long I can do this or whether it's working. Breathe, thump, breathe, thump. Both cats are watching me from the doorstep. Horatio joins them, looking quizzical. I see his point. I don't know why I'm doing this either. She's dead. There's not the faintest response to all my shoving and I'm using bruising force.

I can smell singeing. If I don't get those Health Loaves out of the oven in five minutes they'll catch fire. But somehow I can't leave this filthy, childlike corpse, because what would I do if I stopped? Go inside and shut the door?

Hands are on my shoulders. Someone is lifting me to my feet. I stagger up and see, blessings upon them, a pair of ambulance officers who look like they know just what they are doing.

So I drag in a deep breath—I get to keep this one—go inside and haul the loaves out of the oven. They are slightly more crisp than usual but I'm sure the taste-challenged won't notice. I find my cold coffee and drink it and the red mist recedes from my eyes. At school no one told me that CPR required Olympic levels of fitness.

Then I go outside to see what has happened. I don't want to. I just do.

The paramedics have attached an oxygen mask to the girl's face and are injecting her with something. I ask what.

'Narcan,' says one. 'You did a good job, but it might be too late. The respiratory system shuts down, see, and starves the brain of oxygen. We get a lot of brain damage. But narcan cancels out the effect of opiates. Works fast. Right. Back away, lady. They usually wake up cross. Here we go, Jules.'

Julie, his mate, had the girl by both arms, a constabulary come-along-o'-me grip which immobilises quite well. She needed it. The girl came up from her deathly trance screaming and bucking like a frightened beast. It was astounding. One minute she had been utterly still, pulseless and breathless, and the next she was struggling like a fish on a hook. Colour flushed her face. Pink, for a girl, not blue, for a corpse.

'Cunts!' she shrieked in an accent which I'd always heard associated with the best schools. 'You narcanned me! I only had one hit! Gimme back my hit!'

'Could have been your last hit,' said Julie, holding her tightly. 'You took too much. Take a breath, now.'

'They're always like that,' observed the ambulance man, who must have seen how shocked I was. 'You did good there. M'names Thommo. Nice to meet yer.' We shook plastic gloves. He lit a cigarette. I suppose we all have our drug of choice. I took one of his smokes, though I stopped smoking three years ago. It tasted divine. Thommo continued my education. 'Druggies mostly react like this. Don't let it worry yer. From her point of view, we robbed her. Now she's got to go and hustle for another hit. Lucky we're not in the job for the gratitude,' he added. 'You want to come into casualty,' he advised the girl. 'Get a doctor to look at you.'

'Yes, come on,' urged Julie. 'You were pretty close to the edge, you know. Can you tell me your name?'

'Fuck off, cunt,' said the patient.

'Come on,' said Thommo. 'We haven't got all day.'

'No!' screamed the girl, struggling so hard that she broke Julie's grip. She staggered to her feet, unbalanced on one broken stiletto.

'Working girl,' said Julie. 'They don't want to miss out on a paying client by going to hospital.'

'I'm not,' shrieked the patient, hands out, fingers curved into claws.

'Hey, Suze,' said a deep, rich voice, as casually as if he had met her in the street at lunch hour, instead of confronting a screaming hysterical dervish in a back alley at five in the morning. 'What's happening?'

A man had strolled into Calico Alley, walking over the hard damp cobbles without making a sound. He was tall, with close-cropped dark hair, a scar across his forehead, and the most penetrating, bright and beautiful eyes I had ever seen. He was dressed in jeans, boots and a leather jacket lined with fleece.

'These cunts want to send me to hospital!' Suze replied, moderating her tone. I wondered how many of my exceptionally respectable neighbours were even now listening fascinated from their bedroom windows above. Usually the only noise in Calico Alley at that hour was the muted hum of my machines and the occasional squeak as the Mouse Police made another arrest.

'Chill,' advised the man. 'These kind people saved your life, and even if you don't, I think it's worth saving. Now say thank you nicely and come on. The bus stops at Flagstaff tonight, remember?'

To my amazement, Suze turned to us and said, 'Thank you,' in the carefully enunciated voice of a well-behaved little girl who has taken elocution lessons, and followed the tall man out of Calico Alley.

'Who was that masked man?' I gasped, leaning back against the jamb and fanning myself.

'That's Daniel,' said Julie, similarly affected. 'He's the heavy on the Soup Run. You're a baker, aren't you? Then he'll be back.'

'Oh, good,' I said faintly. 'Why?'

''Cos he's on the Soup Run,' said Thommo, nettled. 'Gotta go,' he added, listening to his radio. 'Fry-up on the ring road. Come on, Jules.'

Julie stuffed her equipment into her bag and prepared to follow her partner.

'What's a fry-up?' I asked as she walked away.

'A burning car,' she said. 'Nice work. You saved that girl's life. 'Bye,' she said.

I went into the bakery, made my muffins and my French bread, threw in a few twists with the leftover dough, all the time trying not to think. The terrible colour of the girl's face. The feel of her bones under my hands. And the cruel ungrateful strength of her reaction, which had not surprised the ambulance officers at all.

It was only when I observed Horatio examining Heckle's foot that I was recalled to my own duty of care to my dependants.

Heckle, uncharacteristically, allowed me to feel over the injured foot. I could see a small puncture in the hard pad of his weathered paw. It had been bleeding freely, which, in view of what might have been in the syringe, was good. I bagged the syringe and put it in my drawer, meaning to take it with Heckle to the vet. Could cats catch AIDS? There was a feline version called…what was it called? God, I was so tired, and so cold…

Heckle, who is basically an old softie, was purring rustily under my absent-minded caresses when there was a knock at the open door and the rich voice asked, 'Can I come in?'

'Why not?' I asked, feeling weak.

He drew the door closed behind him. Horatio, contrary to his usual practice, walked towards him, tail straight as a taper, uttering a polite greeting. Daniel of the Soup Run dropped to one knee, holding out a hand. Horatio was graciously pleased to allow his ears to be stroked and his whiskers smoothed.

'What's your name, ketschele?' he asked.

I found my voice. 'He's Horatio. This is Jekyll and this is Heckle, and I'm Corinna.'

'Delighted,' he said to all of us. 'I came to thank you,' he added, taking the other chair. Jekyll planted herself firmly on his foot. She is a cat who makes her intentions plain.

'It was nothing,' I murmured. 'It bloody nearly was nothing, too. If those ambulance people hadn't turned up…she was as blue as this floor…'

I hadn't realised how upset I was. Daniel dislodged Jekyll gently, took off his coat, wrapped it around me, and ferreted around in the stockroom. He came back bearing a bottle of brandy which I used for making fruit loaves, poured me half a glass and put it in my hands.

'Nothing like that ever happened to you before, did it?' he asked quietly. 'Do you want water in your brandy? It's all right. You're shocked. You'll get used to it.'

'I hope not,' I said, sipping. I don't drink a lot of neat spirits and I choked a little. Daniel patted me on the back. He was so blatantly, physically attractive that even without the shock I doubted if my knees would have held me up. He had the same lithe, graceful movements as Horatio. No wonder they approved of each other. His jacket bore his scent, a clean male smell with a hint of sweet spice; cinnamon, maybe. He also had eyes one could happily drown in. And that wreck of a girl had been transformed into a good child under his influence. A magician. Meroe, the witch next door, would say he had great mana. He seemed to be considering my answer, which didn't deserve any great consideration.

'True. One should never get used to human suffering. But it is inevitable if you do this kind of work.'

'What kind of work?'

'I'm on the Soup Run,' he said simply, as though this explained everything.

'What's the Soup Run?'

His eyes widened into trout pools. I had amazed him.

'But you live in the city. You must have seen us. The pink and green bus? We stop at four locations in the city. I'm on the late shift, ten p.m. until four a.m. I've just finished.'

'Of course. You're a social worker.' I had certainly seen the bus, and remembered the shrieks of outrage from Keep Melbourne Clean when they used to stop outside a McDonald's near the station. The pink and green bus attracted the homeless and the junkies like bees to Solomon Islands honey. I found it hard to imagine this cat-like spunk as a social worker. He saw what I was thinking and smiled.

'Not really. I'm not trained in social work. The Soup Run has to deal with the wounded ones, the ones like Suze, as well as the hungry and the cold and the lost. Sometimes the clients can be physically threatening. We've got a nurse on board, you know, and they always think she's got drugs. So the Soup Run always has one heavy, to deal with any physical trouble.'

'And that's you,' I said lamely.

'That's me. Daniel Cohen, at your service. Being on the Soup Run is a mitzvah, a blessing,' he said. 'And grandfather always said that the reward for a mitzvah is another mitzvah.'

He grinned. I was warm enough now to give him back his coat and drag on my discarded tracksuit top. Brandy danced in my veins. My tired brain finally made the connection between my profession and the Soup Run. What goes with soup? What always goes with soup?

'Tell me, Daniel,' I said, 'does your Soup Run need some bread?'

Chapter Two

I rang the vet, who assured me that no human disease was likely to be spread by a needle to as tough an old campaigner as Heckle. My vet is Irish. There is something extra reassuring about being reassured in that buttery God-love-you accent.

I got dressed in respectable shop clothes, a pair of trousers, a shirt and a vest. Ten o'clock and I was still thinking about Daniel. This was more amusing than thinking about the shop and definitely more amusing than worrying about how I could possibly engineer another meeting with him. He would come for the bread, he said, or send someone, and I didn't want him to send someone. I wanted him to come himself, and if that sounds like a Freudian slip, it isn't.

Absolutely no reason why that gorgeous man should find me attractive and I stomped firmly on the idea before it made me unhappy with myself. I can't afford to spend days in self loathing as everyone expects fat women to do. Self loathing eats your life. Being fat isn't my fault or even my sin, despite what all those TV ads say. I was myself and that was what I was and the matter could safely be left to a reasonable assortment of whatever gods happened to be paying attention to my shop on this bright morning. They might easily be visiting Meroe at the Sibyl's Cave next door.

I love autumn in Melbourne. The nights are cold and the days are sunny and the temperature is just right for someone who spent her whole adolescent Beach Baby phase sitting under a tree, trying not to melt. The sun was now slanting down between the buildings and the morning rush was over. The poor huddled masses, clutching their coffee and thinking of their overextended finances, had bought muffins fresh from the oven, croissants au beurre, pasta douro rolls with cheese inside and bacon-topped flat rolls as a substitute for what the civilised world calls breakfast. I watched them scurry away, from Gucci to Armani, heels tapping, briefcases under one arm and expressions harried. I was meanly and profoundly glad that I was no longer part of the Gadarene rush to get to the office before the boss got in. Poor bastards! They would have to stay there until the day was all gone and the boss finally went home. Whereas I got to close after lunch and tonight I had a possible assignation with a gorgeous man. Things were, indeed, looking up.

Horatio was, as usual, sitting in a dignified posture next to the cash register, which he likes because I pat him every time I make a sale. Or possibly he is lurking. It is hard to tell with cats. Some ailurophobe complained to the health inspectors about him, but the man who came to check him out spent half an hour telling him what a fine, what a very fine cat he was, yes indeed (although Horatio knows that, he does like to be told again and again), and dismissed the complaint. As long as he doesn't stretch out for a snooze on the actual bread I think we are safe. At least with that inspector.

The rush had died down and I could leave the shop to Kylie (her mother was a fan, poor girl), my shop assistant of the day. Kylie and her friend Gossamer (another victim of a fanciful parent) live one floor above me in 2A, an apartment belonging to Kylie's father. They are nice girls, most of the time, though they do have a tendency to appear tipsy in the evening. This is, I ascertained, due to their discovery that they could only stay as thin as Kate Moss or whoever is the latest highly paid anorexic by giving up either drinking or eating.

I fear daily for their metabolisms and live in hope that they finally do get that major soapie part for which they are hanging out. One which requires them to gain two stone. That would about bring them up to a human weight.

Until that happens, Kylie and Goss help out in the shop and since they confine their drinking to evenings and I have an electronic cash register which tells you how much change to hand out, they are very helpful. And at least they won't eat the stock. Also, Horatio likes them and they adore him. And sending them along to a corporate lunch with the Health Loaf makes all the yuppies eat up the nice sawdust like little lambkins, hoping thus to look like Kylie and Gossamer. They wish.

I made up a nice basket of different rolls and went back inside Insula, my apartment building. It was built in 1920 by an architect who had either studied the classics or was, as Professor Monk suggests, completely insane. He decided that what the city of Melbourne really needed was a Roman apartment building, which is what Insula means. And in the best materials and with great attention to detail, he built one. All eight storeys of it. It is covered on the outside with peacock blue tiles. We have the *tesserae*, the tiled mosaics of various gods and goddesses, on both walls and floors. We have the *impluvium*, an indoor pool with goldfish in it, beside which Horatio likes to sit and meditate—and, incidentally, drive the fish crazy. We have an entirely un-Roman elevator, though it does have Medusa-head bosses all over the ironwork. We have a roof garden which is open to all tenants, where we can sit in the shadow of the glass towers and drink a gin and tonic at three in the afternoon, aware of the massed envy from every office window. Every apartment has the name of a Roman god embossed over the door. And like the Roman original, the bottom floor houses shops, stores and my bakery.

I came here because I loved the place the moment I set eyes on the artfully censored Priapus next to the *impluvium*. It has a strange, mad charm. Also, the apartments are big. In the twenties an apartment was the size of a small house. There are only two to each upper floor. My apartment is tucked into a corner so I am on two levels, the bakery and shop underneath and two bedrooms, a parlour, a bathroom (with dolphin frieze) and a kitchen above. The Professor's flat on the third floor is probably the nicest in the whole building, because his furniture is also Roman.

When he retired and his wife died he probably felt like curling up and dying too. But instead he found himself a flat in Insula, sold his house and most of his possessions and had suitable furniture made. He is a darling and the sexiest seventy-six-year-old I am ever likely to meet.

Just now he is laid up with a bruised leg from falling down the authentically hard Roman steps. At his age one has to be careful so I am bringing him bread, Kylie does his shopping and Goss has gone to the Athaeneum to change his books. He gave her a long list which I hope and trust she just gives to the librarian. She may be able to sing all the lyrics of any Justin Timberlake song but she is not, I am confident, going to be able to pronounce Suetonius without serious tongue damage.

The elevator goes up. It's one of those ones with folding metal doors. Medusa stares into my eyes as I fold them back to get out. So far I have not turned to stone. I never learned all this stuff at university. Living in Insula is a real education.

Professor Dionysus Monk, it says on the door, and I knock. He got this particular apartment because the tesserae over the door shows us Dionysus, god of wine, leaning on a convenient leopard, cup in hand and lecherous eye contemplating a couple of nymphs retreating into the middle distance. One senses that they are not intending to run fast—at least only fast enough to be caught by the softest available moss. I suspect that in his youth the Professor took after his namesake. He still has a gleam in his eye.

The door was open and I went in and paused. It really was lovely. The walls are painted in ochre and terracotta and have prints from Pompeii on them. The tables are low, with carved animal legs, and the couches are covered with throws and cushions. Even the light fittings resemble oil lamps.

Professor Monk was reclining on his (Roman, naturally) couch with his bruised leg elevated on a red cushion. An entirely anachronistic television set sat on a stand in front of him and he clicked it off as I entered. He had ruffled his thin white hair and I noticed that both his book table and his glasses were out of reach.

'Corinna! Sweet nymph!' he declaimed. 'Seconds before I expired of ennui. How people can watch television for hours I cannot imagine.'

'Why were you?' I asked. He ruffled his hair again so that it stood on end like a cocky's crest. His blue eyes looked sad.

'That nice district nurse came in this morning to settle me for the day and wheeled the wretched thing up and I really didn't feel I could protest, when she had gone to all that trouble,' he said. 'And if this leg is to get better I really mustn't move unnecessarily. I was watching the oddest thing,' he said. 'A women's program. Her name was…Oprah, I believe. The things that people were saying! It was most indelicate.'

I resolved never to tell Dionysus Monk about Jerry Springer or Jenny Jones.

'I've got bread and you have breakfast,' I said. 'Tea?'

'If you please,' he said hungrily. I cursed that nurse. Feeding her patient TV instead of breakfast seemed to show that her priorities were in entirely the wrong order. The Professor caught my thought, something he does which is occasionally unnerving. He chuckled.

'Panem et circenses,' he said. 'Bread and circuses. I think I would rather have the bread than the circus. And perhaps you could move that table closer so that I can get to my Aristophanes? It's been beckoning to me for hours, poor thing.'

I did as he asked then took my bread with me out of the parlour. His kitchen is modern, thankfully. I warmed the rolls, found the butter and the Oxford marmalade he favours and made a big pot of weak tea. Why was I doing this? When I first came to Insula I was lonely. I had broken up with my husband James and there seemed to be nothing in the world for me but work (and cats). Professor Dion had taken me out to dinner at amusing little cafes, lent me books, and listened to my woes without saying a word about his Aristophanes translation cooling on his desk. I owed him, as Kylie would say, big-time.

While he ate his breakfast I told him about the junkie in the alley and Daniel of the Soup Run. He smoothed marmalade over a crust and remarked, 'Juvenal knew a lot about wickedness in cities. Let me lend you his *Satire III: On Rome*. This Daniel sounds like a good man. What do you think?'

I muttered something about handsome is as handsome does and he gave me a very knowing look.

'Ah,' he remarked and ate the crust. 'That was really an excellent breakfast,' he added. 'Thank you so much, nymph.'

I left him with all his papers within reach and collected a copy of the Satires from the big bookcase which lines one wall.

On the way down in the lift I found I was blushing.

I haven't done that since I was a teenager. Must be hormones. Early onset peri-menopause. Or something.

My shop was not busy when I got back to it so I decided to take some good-morning bread to my neighbour and co-tenant, Meroe of the Sibyl's Cave. She is a Wiccan witch and was going to call the place The Magic Box, but after what happened to all the proprietors of the Magic Box on *Buffy*, she decided to take Professor Dion's advice. Anyway, call a place the Magic Box and you run the risk of customers who are looking not for inner enlightenment and oneness with the goddess but whoopee cushions and plastic dog turds with which to Amaze their Friends, should they ever find any. Not the right kind of ambiance at all.

The Sibyl's Cave sells anything you might need for casting spells: crystals, dream-catchers, chi-enhancing exercises, visualisation CDs and fresh herbs. (But not voodoo dolls; Meroe says that practitioners of voodoo are just going to have to sew their own.) If you want to make an oracle from a sheep's shoulder blade, mix up a love potion, consult the spirits by any one of eleven fortune-telling methods or buy some very pretty postcards, the Sibyl's Cave is your shop. Here you can register for any form of magic training, purchase fresh motherwort and fern seed, and catch up on the occult news with a copy of *Wiccan Times*. The shop is small and cramped and stuffed with things, all of them fascinating. I believe in absolutely nothing except yeast and the inevitability of politicians, so Meroe and I have agreed not to discuss it. Thus we have stayed friends.

As always, I wondered about the little model of a woman enclosed in a bottle, hung up by the door. It was marked 'A Present from Cumae' and it always made Professor Dion laugh. One day I must ask him about it.

I knelt to greet Belladonna, Meroe's cat (or as she says, familiar). Belladonna is entirely black from nose to tail-tip, as befits a witch's cat. She is a dignified, slim, very beautiful creature. Meroe says that she brings Meroe luck by reposing gracefully among the junk in the window, occasionally batting at a hanging crystal with a languid paw. I think that she brings her more customers by lying there being so decorative that people stop to look at her and are then lured inside by the astounding eclecticism of the stock. Meroe herself matches the shop. She wears, usually, a long skirt and a loose blouse, and then throws over it some length of embroidered silk or fine wool. With her long black hair and dark eyes she can appear perfectly uncanny. Also, she has an unexpectedly deep voice for a woman. I have never asked how old she is and I really can't guess. Sometimes she looks no more than thirty, especially when she laughs. On days when the cold wind whistles down Calico Alley and she wraps her shawl around herself, she could be a hundred.

Today she was wearing a length of yellow Chinese silk patterned with dragons and her hair was loose on her shoulders. I offered my bread and she gave me a hand to stand up. She has thin hands, elegant and strong.

'You looked like an Egyptian making an offering to Basht,' she said in her deep voice. 'Come in, have some tea.'

'What sort?' I asked with deep suspicion. I do not approve of herbal tea. If I want to stew weeds, there are plenty in the garden.

'English breakfast,' she said. 'Will that do? Come in, Bella. Nasty cars out there.'

Belladonna gave her a scornful look, shook the paw she was about to place on the threshold, and poured herself up onto the back of Meroe's fortune-telling chair. It is considerably shredded. Meroe says that it adds to her credibility and Bella lives for the day when she can scrape down to wood. She stropped her claws busily as we sat down. The tea was definitely real tea, and I sipped, breathing in the steam. Meroe sliced the date bread and nibbled at it.

'Good bread, as usual, Corinna, thank you. So, what's the news?' asked Meroe comfortably.

'I thought you would already know,' I teased.

'You summoned an ambulance at five this morning for a young woman dying in the alley,' she said in her low tones. 'Then you met a tall dark man of mystery. More I cannot tell you.'

'How did you know?' I asked.

'The cards do not lie,' she said. I spotted the logical flaw.

'But did you consult them?'

'No need. We do not use magic unless we have to use magic,' she said, grinning. 'Kylie told me when I nipped into your shop for a cheese roll. Who is this tall dark man?'

'His name is Daniel and he's on the Soup Run,' I told her. 'Do you know about the van?'

'Surely. A friend of mine used to work on it—he was a nurse. So Daniel's the heavy. Hmm. Looks like fate is taking an interest in your life at last, Corinna. And about time, I might add, though the ways of fate are inscrutable. I do wish they weren't. I spend my whole life trying to make them more scrutable. With only a little success.'

'Any peep into the future is bound to be a bit fraught,' I sympathised, hardly at all.

'I've been looking into the crystal ball,' she said soberly, all traces of a twinkle vanishing from those disconcerting black eyes. 'This is the second overdose in a week. None fatal so far.

But there will be another. Something horrible is happening in the city.'

I could have told her that. It's a city. It stands to reason that something horrible is happening in it somewhere. I sipped in silence. Meroe was not waiting for me to respond. She was just sitting. She has a gift of stillness which is very attractive. If she hasn't anything to say, she doesn't say anything. She has no small talk, which for such a dedicated gossip is surprising. Like the Patrician of Ankh-Morpork, she considers that a person who does not know the word on the street before it hits the street is just not trying.

I stroked Belladonna as Meroe sold a divining rod to a person who looked like a stockbroker and a bunch of note-cards to a heavily moussed teenager, giggling at her own effrontery and courage in going into a shop called the Sibyl's Cave. Then two Goths wandered in to examine the heavy silver jewellery and I got up to go. More than three people in the shop and one needs permission to inhale.

I waved to Meroe and squeezed past a man in a black velvet suit with a ruffled shirt. He had long blond hair and amazing, almost black eyes.

'I'm a vampire,' he said politely. 'My gift is death.'

'That's nice,' I replied. It was going to be an odd day.

I privately assumed that the vampire called himself Lestat or Armand and was clinically insane. But I got out unbitten and went back to Earthly Delights, spacious by comparison.

Kylie had been replaced by Gossamer. It was no use trying to describe either of them by mundane things like hair or eye colour. These could change overnight. At the moment Gossamer had greenish hair and bright green contacts. She looked rather like Professor Dion's nymph. A tree nymph.

A dryad, that was it. This morning Kylie had had pink hair and her own eyes, which are blue. Or so I believe. The only way I could be sure about their identity was their navels, which were always on display. Kylie had a silver ring with a blue stone in it in hers, which is round and flat. Gossamer has a gold ring in hers, and it tends to have a lip on the upper rim. I checked. Gold and lip, Gossamer. Otherwise they really could be twins.

'I got the books,' she announced. 'Some of them were in Greek! And Kylie's gone for the shopping. Poor old Prof. Did you hear the goss? Another junkie's OD'd in the lane.'

'In the alley?' I asked, feeling like Lady Macbeth. 'Oh woe, alas, what, in my house? Twice?' Gossamer scorned this comment.

'As if! The lane, Flinders Lane. Outside the leather place. Ms. Dread was real upset.'

I could not imagine this. Mistress Dread ran a select studio selling leather garments to the discerning customer and what she had seen in her shop should have insulated her against anything. She lived in 2B (Venus), opposite the girls. It was always a shock meeting Mistress Dread in plain clothes. She preferred quiet country casuals and expensive shoes. I had no idea if she was a man or a woman, biologically speaking, and it was none of my business. In her tweed skirt and brogues she looked like an English countrywoman out for a ramble—one looked for the Labrador and the green gumboots. When she was dressed in her leather corset and fishnets, fully six inches taller, she was terrifying. Even without the whip.

Calling her Ms. Dread was either Gossamer's attempt at sly humour or a sign of profound stupidity. I could never decide which.

'Is the junkie dead?'

'Dunno. They took him away in the ambulance. The cops have been round asking questions. They want to talk to you about the one this morning. Isn't this exciting?'

I decided. Stupidity. But she is very young and I should not be judgmental. I was definitely an idiot when I was eighteen.

I mean, I fell in love with a drummer in a garage rock band.

A drummer, I ask you. It is always possible that Gossamer may grow a brain and, anyway, they do say that prolonged starvation lowers the IQ.

'Did the policeman say when he was coming to see me?'

'She's here,' said a voice from the door.

Oops. I turned around. A neat, uniformed, middle-aged woman was not smiling at me. I toyed with the idea of explaining that my speech patterns had been formed at an age when policewomen didn't exist and then I decided not to. This was just business.

'You want to talk to me? I'm Corinna Chapman. What can I do for you, officer?'

'My name is Senior Constable White. I understand that you called an ambulance this morning to an overdose? Can you show me where it happened please, Ms. Chapman?'

She laid an emphasis on the Ms. which I did not miss.

'This way.' I waved at Gossamer to keep selling bread and led her out of the shop and into Calico Alley, where I unlocked the bakery doors.

'Nice locks,' she approved.

'We need them. Come in, please. I opened the door at five a.m. to let the cats out,' I explained as the off-duty Heckle and Jekyll blinked up from their pile of flour sacks. I tried supplying them with those dinky kitty beds and they sniffed them politely before going straight back to the empty sacks. In winter they will accept a sheepskin to lie on. 'Then Heckle came back with a syringe in his paw. I went out to yell at whoever had left it there and found this girl collapsed on the hot air vent.'

I swallowed, remembering that slate-blue face. Senior Constable White motioned me to a chair and sat down on a stool. 'That must have been a shock for you,' she murmured conventionally.

'Yes, it was. I called an ambulance and gave her CPR until the paramedics came. They gave her a shot of something and she came out of the Valley of the Shadow, screaming.'

'Narcan,' said the police officer, writing in her notebook.

'Then the ambulance left. The Soup Run heavy, Daniel Cohen, came and calmed the girl. Then he calmed me. Then he left and I got on with the baking.'

'Did Mr. Cohen seem to know the girl?'

'Yes, he called her Suze.'

'And did you keep the syringe?'

'Yes, as it happens, I did, it's in a plastic bag in that drawer. I was going to take Heckle to the vet but when I rang him he said there aren't any diseases a cat can catch from a dirty human needle so I should just watch and see if he was limping tomorrow and he isn't even limping now,' I said, aware that I was babbling.

Senior Constable White rose, walked over to Heckle and coolly took his paw. Even more surprisingly, Heckle let her and did not pull away or scratch. She had great authority. Then she came back, opened the drawer, and examined the needle through the clear plastic. Then she snapped the elastic band back over her notebook, took the plastic bag, and thanked me for my time.

'No, wait,' I said. 'There was another OD outside Mistress Dread's just now. What's going on?'

To my surprise, she answered me.

'One of two things. Either someone is supplying hot shots to drug addicts with the intention of killing them. Or someone has added an extra ingredient to their heroin—usually it is cut with glucose but someone may have decided that Ajax or Die, Rat, Die! gives it that extra kick—and is killing them by accident. At any rate, someone is killing them. Keep your doors locked, Ms. Chapman. Thank you for your cooperation. If you will come down to St. Kilda Road at your convenience, someone will take your statement.'

She gave me her card and walked away. I grabbed Heckle and hugged him. Being hugged occasionally is in his job description. I didn't like this at all. Life had seemed so ordinary when I woke up.

Chapter Three

The day was getting on and the lunchtime rush would be starting soon. I put Heckle back down with a handful of kitty treats to comfort him (and a handful of kitty treats for Jekyll in the interests of justice) and went back to the shop. I booked an order for ten loaves of seven seed bread, a speciality of mine, for the next day, and more rye bread for a German restaurant. Then the health bread freaks demanded more crumbly stuff, and the Greek restaurant asked for extra pasta douro for a banquet. I was going to have a busy morning.

I decided to ditch the planned potato bread and make fresh herb rolls instead. Life is too short to peel potatoes, I agree, but bread made from real potatoes does taste better than the stuff baked with commercial potato flour. My customers pay me for the extra taste. I am what is known as a niche marketer. Which generally translates as ignored by all government departments unless they want (1) bread or (2) money.

And, for the shop, olive bread with all those plump, beautiful kalamata olives which Karen the caterer had given me. Turned out that the chairman of the board was allergic to olives and she had bought the best. Poor woman was almost in tears. Ours is a disappointing profession sometimes. With a batch of muffins that would make up the shop's supply for the day.

Herb rolls meant I had to send Goss to Meroe right away to get a collection of whatever fresh culinary herbs she had left before the witches bought out the shop. Meroe's herbs come from an organic farm (probably by broomstick, I can't imagine how she gets them into the city so fast otherwise) and they taste wonderful. The herbs have to be robust to survive baking.

I gave Goss her orders. 'And make sure you say "kitchen herbs,"' I said, forcing her to repeat it. It had never happened, but I didn't want any of the other plants to wend their way into my bread. Entrancing as the idea of turning some customers into toads might be, I couldn't imagine trying to explain it to a sceptical police officer like, for instance, Senior Constable White. *L White*, her label had said. Lynn? Louisa? Lepidoptera? She looked like a Lepidoptera.

A strangely forthcoming Senior Constable Lepidoptera White. She had told me a lot. Had she been giving me a message? Had she just been up all night? Had her mother taught her that a civil question deserves a civil answer? These were deep questions.

Meanwhile a line was forming of people anxious not to spend their lunch hour trying to buy lunch and I snapped out of my daze and into sell mode. The cash register rang cheerily, Horatio purred, and the money rolled in as the bread rolled out (sorry). I began to wonder whether I was going to have any bread to spare for the Soup Run when the door clicked closed and suddenly the place was empty. Two p.m. on the dot and only the poor office assistants and shopkeepers, who had drawn late lunch, were likely to come in now.

Goss returned, having lingered fondly outside Black Flower Boutique, where her next dress lived until she could earn more money. Her Goth friend Carol Holland would make sure no one else bought it. It was a daring dark purple number with a peekaboo front to show her navel. I wondered again, what was this thing about navels? However you look at them, they are not aesthetic. Also, no one with my figure likes present fashions. One does not want one's cardigans skimpy or one's skirts short, and one definitely does not want to show one's navel or any points adjacent. What happened to breasts? I like breasts. I'm fond of mine. Goss is as flat chested as a ten-year-old boy.

Goss thrust a big parcel of herbs into my arms. The scent was heavenly, the essence of green growing things. I identified thyme, parsley, basil, rosemary, coriander, tarragon and a stick of bay leaves with that dark oriental smell.

'Yum,' I remarked.

'That lady cop was at Meroe's,' giggled Goss. 'Going through the herbs. Meroe isn't happy.'

'I bet she isn't,' I agreed.

'Especially since she called Meroe "Sibyl,"' said Goss, stroking Horatio.

'Oops.' I was not the only person to be making linguistic mistakes today. Although, I admit, Basil Fawlty's wife was called Sibyl, the original sibyls were powerful witches who spoke oracles. I hoped that Meroe might take it as a compliment but decided that she probably wouldn't. I don't know where Meroe came from, she's never said, but it was a place where they really didn't like the police.

With the world in the state it is that could be just about anywhere…

'Did Ms. White say what she was looking for in the herbs?' I asked.

'MJ,' said Goss, going off into a fit of the giggles. Marijuana? In the Sibyl's Cave? It was funny. Meroe is sternly against all drugs. Except, I suppose, flying ointment and essence of night-shade. She has been known to threaten smokers with eternal karmic backlash and doesn't even approve of my gin and tonic when I finish work for the day.

It dulls the chakras, apparently. I told her that I liked them dull. Senior Constable Lepidoptera White was doomed to disappointment, and probably a lecture on chakras as well.

'Time to close up,' I said, fastening the door and pulling the shutter across. Goss loaded the remaining bread into my sack while I put out the stuff I could resell at half price into its rack. That left me with a good load. I paid Goss and let her out the back way and sat down to total my cash register receipts, count and bundle the money, and make out the deposit slip for the bank. Then I put the cash float in the drawer, allowed Horatio to precede me into the bakery, and sighed. Another day past and I was pooped.

I walked down to the bank on the corner and deposited the takings, then I re-donned my trackies and began to clean the bakery. This involves a lot of scrubbing and I find it soothing. Big bakeries employ scullions, but I did it myself. Horatio always removes himself to the parlour when water sloshes across the floor, my last task. There. I wrung out a track suit leg and straightened my back. I had cleaned and dried all my cutlery and pots and mixers; I had tidied my own kitchen and washed my own dishes; the cat dishes were scrubbed, the cat litter was changed and the floor was scrubbed and it was me for a bath. I flung the tracksuit into the washer and set it going.

I love baths. I ran one and sprinkled in Body Shop bath milk with a liberal hand. No, with a generous hand. The original meaning of that word has been lost. By the time I finished my eleven-hour day I was always filthy. I lay there feeling like the Queen of Sheba. Dark blue dolphins danced along my frieze. Horatio sat on the edge. He balances beautifully. Vaughan Williams' 'The Lark Ascending' was playing. Bliss.

The CD finished and I finally arose from the foam, dried myself and put on my favourite garment. It is a floor length house gown of heavy dark purple silk figured with chrysanthemums, the only present I ever liked or kept among those my ex-husband James brought back from his travels. Though I sort of regret throwing out those toys from the sex museum in Amsterdam. Who knows what that strange object did when filled with warm milk as the directions suggested? Probably nothing good. I loved this part of the day. With my Esky in one hand and my cat in the other, I ascended to the roof garden like a goddess.

The roof garden design has remained unaltered from the original, partly because when the building was unfashionable, someone had chained the entrance and the vandals didn't know it was there. It has gazebos. It has pergolas. It has bowers. Horatio led the way to the rose bower, his favourite. I sat down on the wicker love-seat, concocted a gin and tonic from my Esky, added ice, and leaned back contentedly.

No one here, except Mrs. Pemberthy and her little doggie, Traddles. I don't like dogs very much. They have no self control. But Horatio had obligingly taught Mrs. Pemberthy's yappy little mop-dog a measure of healthy fear and he usually never came near us. Mr. Pemberthy was talking to Trudi near the lilac trees. A light shower of rose petals fell down on my dress as a starling landed on the bower. Horatio watched interestedly. The starling eyed Horatio. I drank my gin and tonic.

The city was full of people who were working hard, and I wasn't one of them. It is a lovely feeling. I closed my eyes for a moment. Horatio climbed onto my knee and curled up into a loaf shape, paws folded under. We drifted off into a light doze.

When we woke someone was kneeling in front of us.

I jumped and spilled the drink and Horatio, in keeping his balance, stuck a few claws into me. Every cat owner knows that this is not malicious. Which doesn't mean that it doesn't hurt.

'Sorry,' apologised the kneeling person. I blinked myself awake. Trout pool eyes looked into mine.

'Daniel? How did you get in?'

'I met one of your girls, the one with green hair, in the street. She let me in and said you were up here. What a lovely place,' he said.

'Isn't it? Would you like a drink? I've only got one glass,' I said.

'We can drink it sip for sip. You look very different in that gown,' said Daniel, sitting down beside me and holding the glass while I poured the gin.

'My ex brought it back from China. It's my favourite dress.'

'I can understand that.' Had he stiffened a little when I said 'ex'? I poured tonic and offered him first sip. He accepted.

He sipped very neatly. His chin and jowl were darkened. I wondered how often he shaved.

'I didn't realise you had such unusual eyes,' he said. 'That's the trouble with dawn, there are no colours. They're grey, really grey.

Sea-grey eyes,' he said, handing me the glass. Our fingers met. I couldn't think of anything to say. His fingertips were calloused, as though he worked at a manual trade. I didn't know anything about him. But who cared? He began, 'Would you—' and just at that moment the starling dropped down to the grass, Horatio leapt off my knee and swiped at it and Mrs. Pemberthy's bloody dog decided to join our little conversatione. The world was suddenly full of yapping (the dog), squawking (the starling), hissing (Horatio, who had quite lost his composure) and yelling (me and Mrs. Pemberthy). It took some time to sort out the mêlée and after that the moment, if it was a moment, had passed. We sat down again. Horatio washed. I refilled the glass.

'What brings you to Australia?' I asked lamely enough.

'I was born here,' he said, taking a healthy swig of the drink. 'I went back to Israel with my parents and joined the army, and then I came back here. I work on the Soup Run for fun. I've always been nocturnal.'

'Like Horatio,' I said, pointing out my fearless hunter, who was sitting with his back to us, washing in a very thorough fashion. One got the impression that Horatio would have blushed, if he hadn't been a cat.

'Cats and lovers love the dark,' he said, which sounded like a proverb. 'What about you? You didn't start off as a baker, I can tell.'

'How can you tell?'

'Trade secret,' he grinned. He had very white teeth. I still didn't know anything about him.

'What trade?'

'That would be telling,' said Daniel. 'There, we've finished our drink. I'd better collect the bread and get going.'

'Start by collecting the cat,' I said, feeling frumpish and cross. Daniel went over to Horatio and said something, and Horatio climbed onto his shoulder and draped himself across the leather-clad neck. He looked like a very elaborate fur collar.

My apartment is called 'Hebe.' It shows a rather curvy girl in a slipping tunic pouring out nectar for a series of reclining gods. The builder decided that the shop apartments should be dedicated to the attendant gods. Thus we have the Pandamus family, who run the Cafe Delicious, living in Hestia, goddess of the hearth. The software company Nerds Inc. live in Hephaestus, smith of the gods. And Meroe lives in—I swear—Leucothea, the white goddess, who is also called Hecate, Queen of Witches. She says it was Meant. With a capital letter. And it probably was.

I let Daniel in and went to my kitchen to fetch him the bag of bread. This was not how I had foreseen our next meeting. Also, I had stinging puncture wounds across my thighs from Horatio's abrupt take-off. That cat can accelerate upwards like a Harrier jump-jet. I sat down heavily. I folded back the silk to inspect my wounds and Daniel came in, soft footed, and caught me.

He contemplated my half-naked state, drew in a breath, and went into the bathroom. When he returned he sat down on his heels and smoothed anti-sting into each little puncture. It was one of the sexiest things I had ever felt and I shivered.

'You're beautiful,' he said. Then he stood up. 'I must go,' he said. 'Can I come back tomorrow?'

'For more bread?' I asked. I let the dress fall and stood up before him. He was tall. My nose collided with his second shirt button. I smelt that elusive spice scent again. My body seemed to be magnetically attracted to him.

'That too,' he said cryptically, took the bread, and went.

'Someone thinks I am beautiful,' I told Horatio. He gave me a measuring look, went to his dish, and suggested dinner. That was another problem. I had to go to bed at eight or before. Did I have enough energy to get dressed and go down to Cafe Delicious for an early dinner of luncheon leftovers, or was I going to settle for free range boiled eggs and toast soldiers? No contest.

I fed Horatio and the Mouse Police and ate my soldiers and eggs. They were very good. I read the *Wiccan Times* absently as I wondered about Daniel. He was gorgeous, yes.

I was not, that also was true. But he had said that I was beautiful. He wouldn't be saying that just because of the bread. I moved my thighs. I could still feel those warm, sure fingers shifting over my flesh. Flesh that was awake and alert and suggesting that there were lots of things we could do with Daniel that did not involve bread. I knew that. I told my flesh to pipe down until I could get Daniel into a space which did not contain anything other than human mammals, excluding all cats, birds and dogs, and read on.

This really was an odd newspaper. It had an article on Wiccan men which made them sound extremely desirable. There was the sacrificial consort, who seemed to be the summer king from Arthurian legend. One elected a monarch in spring and when the year began to fail, one killed him and got another next spring. I suppose it saved feeding him over the winter. Which made for a short reign but an extremely merry one, as the summer king would probably pollinate himself to a state of collapse if he was to die in autumn. Lot to be said for a willing sacrifice. I had already heard the definition of an ideal lover: one who turns into a pizza at three a.m. That sounded sacrificial to me.

There was Poseidon, god of the sea—we had an apartment called Neptune, the Roman form of Poseidon. Occupied by Jon, a travelling exec who only stayed a week or so, distributed strange sweets and trinkets marked, e.g. Made in Cambodia, and went off again. He worked for some aid agency and could tell riveting stories if you caught him between assignments. Kylie thought he was wonderful and had hopes of an affair, but whenever she steeled herself to seduce him, he wasn't there. This rather put a damper on the whole thing, but the article said that Neptune was cyclical and would be back with the tide. Then there was Pan, the old god, master of woods and darkness, father of goats. He sounded agreeably rustic and rather dangerous. But you always knew where to find him. Just follow the goats.

I finished my supper, cleared the table and read the last of the article with my nightcap, a cup of Ovaltine, the sleep drink of my childhood. Osiris, lord of the dead, father of occult wisdom, dark and mysterious, who came by night.

I closed the *Wiccan Times* and took myself off to bed. Horatio was already reposing next to my pillow. I have a bed big enough to sprawl in and I sprawled, stroking Horatio and thinking, as I fell asleep, that Osiris and Daniel might have had a lot to say to each other...

I didn't wake until the alarm clock exploded at four a.m. and the fans came on. In my sleep I had crooked an arm around Horatio and was holding him close. He was bearing this like a good cat but the moment I woke he removed himself and jumped down. My arm was stiff. I must have been hugging poor Horatio all night.

I got up and did my exercises. I do these when I wake up feeling stiff. I managed to get my elbow uncreased and restore the blood supply to the fingers which held the coffee cup. Then I put on my trackie and went down to start breakfast and the usual routine of the day. I had forgotten to keep any bread for myself so I ate biscuits and marmalade with my coffee and turned on the TV for company.

Not a good idea. All the international news was as bad as expected and I am, personally, sick of being stuck with a government which gives not one flying...er...fur for the opinions of the people. It's not as if I voted for Mr. Goodcardigan (Leunig's description) and his band of merry warriors. But he ignores me just as if I did.

Nothing like a healthy dose of mistrust to start the day off with a bang. I went downstairs moodily. I gathered the ingredients for my olive bread and set the mixer going. Heckle and Jekyll arrived at their usual pace, shoulder to shoulder like players in that strange sort of American football where they wear armour. Gridiron, that was it. I checked the night's harvest. Four mice and three rats; we might be getting the rat problem under control at last. I checked the cats over for rat bites, rewarded them, disposed of the corpses, washed my hands, and began making seed bread.

This is my secret recipe. You need seven kinds of seeds; I use kibbled wheat, oats, poppy seed, dill, fennel, caraway and coriander. It's a basic rye bread dough and the extra seeds are poured in while it is mixing, so that they are evenly distributed.

The final result is a dense, chewy bread studded with seeds and terribly good for you. Or so I am told. What I find attractive about it is the taste, which is divine, especially with blue cheese. But the proportions have to be exact. I measured and poured carefully. By the time the olive bread was coming out of the oven, the seed bread was ready to go in and I heaved a sigh of relief. The rest of it was easy. I did the usual pasta douro for the Greek restaurant, made double for the shop, and was peacefully mixing Health Loaf by six a.m. Then it was just the rye bread, which I can make in my sleep (and often have) and the muffins.

They are curiously easy to make and have largely replaced most other cakes in general consumption. Fashion is a strange thing. I used to have to throw my carrot cake into the pig bin, because although it was succulent and moist and had a very tasty yogurt icing, no one would buy it. Make the same mixture into a muffin and the shelf would be bare by ten a.m. Odd. 'No accounting for tastes, the old woman said when she kissed the cow' as my grandmother used to say. Come to think of it, that was an odd thing for her to say…

Nearly done. I opened the door into Calico Alley very carefully, in case there was another junkie on my grate, but there was no one there. Heckle and Jekyll strolled out to sniff the air and perhaps walk along to the Japanese food bar, which often had scraps of fish left. Which they would donate to a poor hardworking feline if he sat there looking winsome enough. It is hard for Heckle to appear winsome, what with his street-fighter 'I could beat you with a steam iron tied to my tail' air, but for raw tuna, I have seen him manage it. I stood at the door, inhaling the dawn. Bakers see a lot of dawn. I was glad that I had changed my profession. I like sunrise.

The Japanese cafe rises early to get to the fish market. Kiko waved at me from there, putting out a plate of scrap fish on which Heckle and Jekyll dived as if they hadn't been fed for a week. I don't feed them fish more than twice a week, it isn't good for them, but a treat is good for everyone. 'A bit of what you fancy does you good.' I was quoting Grandmother Chapman a lot this morning.

I was grateful to her because she had taken me in when my parents had finally taken leave of their senses. She had just come and collected me one night when I was five and they hadn't tried to stop her. 'You're not fit to have a child!' she had said. She was right. They had no idea how to look after a child. Grandma had to teach me how to use a knife and fork, how to wear shoes, how to switch on an electric light. My parents had believed in going back to the land, and that meant candles. And an earth-closet. Oh, that pit toilet, how it stank. And no shoes, even in winter. When I thought of them I only remembered being cold, always cold. They were still in Nimbin and I devoutly hoped they stayed there. I was a great disappointment to them, which was fair enough, because they were a great disappointment to me.

Gloomy thoughts for a shining morning. I went back in to remove my health loaves to their cooling rack and put in the rye bread. I then stripped and chopped all the herbs except the bay leaves. My chopped herbs went into a Swiss-roll style casing of pasta douro. The scent made me more cheerful as I rolled and sliced and slid them into the oven.

My muffins this morning were raspberry. They object to a lot of mixing, muffins. They come out tough if one mixes them too much. Fine with me. I put them in the oven too and went back into the street. Heckle and Jekyll were ambling home, licking fish off their whiskers. I heard a whistle. Seven a.m. and here came my newspaper. I was making such good time that I could have another cup of coffee and some seed bread and cheese while reading about the latest doom and mayhem. The paper boy, who was known for his reckless use of plastic-wrapped papers as missiles, flung it to me as he passed. I fielded it. Heckle and Jekyll split to either side of Calico Alley as the bike passed. They were used to the paper boy. They came back to flank the bakery door like small stone statues, noses lifted to the morning smells.

I left them there as I shut the door and locked it. They could get in through the cat door, carefully placed so that not even a really adroit thief could use it to reach a lock. I wandered up to the bedroom to get dressed and then down to the kitchen for more life-giving caffeine. I shed the tracksuit, noticed that last night's cat-claw wounds had almost vanished, put on my shop clothes and sat down with another cuppa and the first loaf of seed bread. It tasted just as I remembered. Really, really good. Sliced beautifully. Dense and rich.

I struggled with the plastic-wrapped newspaper until I managed to peel it. I have taken hours to do this on bad days. Well, it would have been hours if I hadn't lost patience and taken to the sandwich wrap with a breadknife, a girl's best friend. Mine has been sharpened so often that it has a rather elegant sickle moon curve in it. Druids could use it to gather mistletoe. Horatio floated to the table and sat down on the paper for a leisurely wash. I read around him.

'Another heroin death,' said the headline. 'Is there a serial killer in the city?'

Now there was a question to which I didn't want to know the answer. I read all of the story which wasn't covered by tabby fur. It was so interesting that I actually slid Horatio sideways onto the sports section. (Four heroin addicts had OD'd in the city within three days. Three had recovered, one had died.) Name and story followed. But every one had been a regular visitor to the soup van, which was actually mentioned. Senior Constable L White was quoted as saying that inquiries were continuing and that the respectable portion of the city had no need to worry. Well, that made me feel a lot better. I did not like junkies, no one did, they were a major pest, but where did Lepidoptera get off implying that they were expendable?

I scanned the rest of the news, which was all bad as usual, folded the paper and tried the crossword. No luck. Time to go to work. I could hear the girls opening the outer shutters of the shop. The city was on the move. More cars, the clang of trams, the scurrying of feet. Lights came on in the glass towers. Melbourne was facing another day.

Chapter Four

I had an ordinary morning, sending off the bread orders, arguing with the carrier, checking the carrier's account, showing where he had made a mistake in his arithmetic and watching him trundle off, wondering if he was going to drop the bread in the gutter out of spite. I was a victim of my own success. I used to just trundle the bread along on a hand cart, and I never had this sort of hassle. I resolved to get another contractor as soon as I could spare a moment to find one. I was just folding the account and stuffing it crossly into the drawer when someone who compelled attention marched into the shop.

She was six feet tall in her stilettos. She was wearing a red leather corset and fishnets. She had a head of straight dark hair which fell to her waist and a spiked collar around her shapely neck. This matched the spiked armlets around her shapely wrists. The only thing missing was the whip. She was, of course, Mistress Dread from the leather shop and she was furious.

'Have you seen what they've painted on my wall?' she screamed in a full throated alto which made me wonder if she had ever studied for opera.

The customers had forgotten all about bread and that, for me, is a bad thing. Various mouths, both male and female, had dropped open. I nodded to Kylie to take over and got out from behind my counter. Horatio raised an eyebrow. This was not the behaviour he expected in a respectable lady. But I needed to get Mistress Dread out of the shop.

'Show me,' I said.

Without a word, she turned and strode out. I had to run to keep up with her. She took me into Flinders Lane and stopped me with a hand on the shoulder. She was strong. It takes a lot to stop me in my tracks like that.

'There!' she declaimed.

It was noticeable, all right. Someone with a can of red paint and a sense that the end justified the means had sprayed 'WHORE OF BABYLON' in letters a metre high across the whole frontage of the leather shop. I couldn't think of a thing to say but, 'Oh shit,' which was, I admit, weak.

'Is that all you can say, Corinna? What I want to know is, did you see who did this?'

'No,' I said. Her red-lipsticked mouth was only centimetres from my neck and I was fairly sure that she would bite. I pitied the poor idiot graffitist if she laid her hands on him. 'I came out as usual at six and I looked down the alley and I didn't see anyone. You might ask Kiko. She gave my cats some fish, she might have noticed,' I added.

This was unkind. Kiko was a friend. I shouldn't sic this virago on her.

'And have you had the letter?' demanded Mistress Dread.

'What letter?'

'This one, the scarlet woman one,' she yelled, thrusting a piece of paper at me. I recognised it.

'Oh yes, the wages of sin is death. Yes, I got it yesterday. There may be no connection,' I said. 'There must be more than one lunatic in the city.'

'There may be hundreds,' snarled Mistress Dread. 'But I'm putting that cop onto this.'

Good idea, I thought. Mistress Dread might prove an education for Lepidoptera White. Though, on second thought, if she'd been in the police force for long, Mistress Dread wouldn't be in the top one hundred weird things she had seen.

'And you're going to see the Lone Gunmen,' she told me.

'I am?' I hadn't seen Nerds Inc. for a week. They didn't come out much in daylight.

'Yes. Ask them if they can identify the print, what sort of computer was used, that sort of thing. Or would you rather I went?' she demanded, her voice dropping to a throaty low E full of menace.

'I'll go,' I volunteered. Nerds Inc. were nice boys and they might not survive a visit from Ms. Dread. She was too much woman—or something—for people who conducted most of their human relationships at at least one remove. Either SMS or email. Though they might just fall to their knees in devotion, of course. They are, at least technically, male.

Mistress Dread stalked off down Calico Alley to strike terror into Kiko's heart and I went cravenly back to the shop. It was far too early for Nerds Inc. to be awake. They usually surfaced around noon, when the day had been thoroughly aired. And it was no use taking them bread. They subsisted entirely on pizza, takeaway chicken, nachos and cheese Twisties, to deduce from their rubbish. However, a few bottles of their favourite drink would be welcome. They liked those pre-mixed drinks with names like Arctic Death and Russian emblems on them, and I sent Kylie for a supply while I served several hungry office workers and the man with the horse and cab. It is a very well tended horse and while Bill likes my bread, his noble steed loves my muffins and gets one a day. I wished him good morning. He looked worried.

'What do you make of this talk about a serial killer?' he said. 'That's going to be bad for trade.'

'I think it's nonsense,' I said bracingly. 'Anyway, do a lot of junkies hire your cab?'

'None,' he said.

'Well then,' I said. 'Here's a nice muffin for Dobbin and I hope he enjoys it.'

Bill went out but he had me worried. I did all my trading during the day, of course, and most of my bread was spoken for; I didn't really need the shop, I just liked having one. A serial killer might have the same effect on Melbourne tourism as SARS had

had on Hong Kong as a pestilence-free holiday destination. Still, nothing I could do about it. Kylie came back with the drinks and let me in on the latest gossip. How that girl does it I do not know. All she has to do is stand still and gossip enters her skin by some sort of osmosis.

'The Prof's doctor says he's allowed to walk around with a stick,' she announced. 'His nurse told me. I told her to tell him to take it easy, I can do his bit of shopping after two. Not as though there's much. I can take his bread up then too. Make sure the ditz hasn't left him with nothing to watch but Oprah. I mean, he might end up watching Jerry Springer and then…I don't know what Jerry would do to the Prof…'

'Neither do I,' I said frankly. 'We might never get him down off the curtains.'

'Like Horatio that time the wolfhound came into the shop,' she giggled reminiscently.

I recalled the incident. Not only had Horatio reacted entirely by instinct and scaled the highest curtain, but he was so embarrassed when he came down that he didn't speak to any of us for two days. There was now a large sign on the door saying 'No Dogs Except Guide Dogs.' I exempt guide dogs from my general loathing of the canine species. They are self-consciously Good Dogs. You can practically see the little halo above their ears. And they never, never, never notice cats, much less chase them.

Grandmother Chapman had a failed guide dog as a pet. He was very clever but easily distracted. One can imagine that this would disqualify him from work with the blind, but he was very good with the unhappy. I hadn't thought of him in years. His name had been Ebony, a black Labrador.

I shook myself alert. Kylie had more gossip: 'Then someone painted—'

'I saw it,' I said. 'That's what Mistress Dread came to talk to me about.'

'If she gets her claws into him he'll be sliced and diced,' commented Kylie. 'Did you see her nails? All silver. I reckon they're those glue-on metal ones.'

'More like talons,' I agreed.

'Do you think Mistress Dread's a man?' she asked in a whisper.

'I've never liked to ask,' I replied. 'There are six-foot women with size twelve feet. In any case it isn't our business. She's a good neighbour. And she had one of those strange letters.'

'Scarlet woman letters? So did Goss and me,' said Kylie. 'I thought it was a joke.'

'Some madman leafleting all letterboxes with a female name on them, I expect,' I said. 'Don't worry about it. I'm going to see the nerds this afternoon to get some information about the letter. Have you still got yours?'

'Tossed it,' said Kylie. 'You going to see the Lone Gunmen? Ask them if they're testing any good games. Then Goss and me can come down and play with them.'

'Have you done that before?' I asked.

'Couple of times,' she said. 'They're all right. Not interested in sex.'

I found this hard to believe. Not interested in housekeeping, for sure. Not interested in the outside world. When I asked, in passing, what they thought of the Coalition of the Willing invading Iraq, they asked me who published the game. Political consciousness was not their main skill. Taz had once told me that the city was a lot cleaner these days and it was all down to that good bloke, our premier Jeff Kennett.

I hadn't the heart to disabuse him of this notion. But Taz, Rat and Gully were quiet, didn't have noisy parties and ran their business well enough to pay their rates, so I had no objection to them. They might have done the graffiti. Their names sounded like tags to me. But I couldn't imagine them either knowing what the whore of Babylon was or having the nerve to paint it across Mistress Dread's shop and thus risk incurring her wrath. Wrath which would also descend on me if I didn't come up with some information on that letter, of course.

We were interrupted by a rush of customers. The herb rolls danced off the trays. I grabbed one to save for my own lunch and another for Meroe. Once you get used to the concept of a thing which looks like a coffee scroll but tastes like essence of green, you'll find one isn't enough. You'll want to eat another. A satisfactory amount of olive bread was passing out of my hands as well. It isn't the money...well, it isn't just the money. I like to see people eating my bread. The rush died down. Everyone who was going to work had got there. Now there would be a lull until morning tea.

I slipped out to give Meroe her herb roll before I got tempted to eat it myself. She is a vegetarian, of course. Which doesn't mean she isn't picky about her food. As I squeezed into the Sibyl's Cave I saw that this was not going to be a cheery morning with tea. Dressed entirely in deepest black, Meroe was concocting something in a mortar and pestle and muttering under her breath. Every time she pounded the pestle down she gave a small, terrible smile.

I had been given the lecture about the threefold return and had taken it with a pinch of salt. The theory was that a witch had to be careful what she did, magically, because she would get it back threefold. This meant, effectively, that she couldn't curse anyone, because the curse would rebound upon her at triple strength, like those washing powders advertised on TV. I hadn't quite believed it at the time—no one could be that virtuous—and now I didn't believe it at all. I put the paper bag down on the counter and fled.

I wondered who she was cursing, for she was certainly cursing someone. I hoped that it was the graffitist and not the cop. Lepidoptera was only doing her job. Someone had told me that the Witchcraft Act had been repealed. I hoped it was true.

After that, serving in the shop had a certain charm—there was little chance of being turned into a cockroach and stepped on. We kept selling and Kylie kept gossiping. I hadn't heard the half of it.

Mrs. Pemberthy had complained about me and Horatio to the council, the residents' committee and the police. The council were used to her and said that they would investigate. The police were unlikely to bother. The residents' committee might be a problem. Mrs. Pemberthy and her husband were both on it, and so was Joe Pandamus, who didn't like cats though he got on all right with me. But so was the Professor, who did like cats, and Taz. I didn't know how he had ended up on the committee and quite possibly neither did he, but he might be a valuable ally. Not going to have surfaced yet, though.

Kylie continued, telling me that Jon the exec was back and she was going to ambush him tonight. I wished her luck. She was worried about what to wear. I said that her pink dress was ravishing. She was about to go into a major sulk—Kylie can fling a sulk the length of the whole room—when she brightened.

'You like the pink dress?'

'It's terrific.'

'Is it hot?' she demanded, her blue eyes pleading.

'Boiling hot.'

'Good,' she said. 'He's about the same age as you, so if you think it's hot so will he, don't you think?'

'Most likely.' The pink dress had a skirt fully ten centimetres long, more of a belt, really, and a slashed neckline. I could not imagine any man holding out against it for any length of time. I spared a moment to try to remember what I had worn when I was eighteen, sighed, and reflected that the world might be in a terrible state but at least the reign of the bubble skirt had been mercifully brief.

'Don't worry,' said Kylie, patting my hand. 'You had your time, didn't you, though you're old now?'

I was about to tell her that thirty-eight wasn't actually pensionable age when I remembered how old thirty had seemed when I was eighteen. I just nodded. Besides, yesterday someone had told me I was beautiful. And sounded as though he meant it.

An odd thing happened. The phone rang and when I answered it was my ex, James. I hadn't heard from him in months. While we weren't actually friends, we hadn't split with great bitterness. Just loathing. He was a high flyer, I was a low flyer, if not actually earthbound. He liked merchant banking and I liked baking. He wanted me to stay home and look after his children and soothe his furrowed brow when he came home from a hard day's accounting, and I didn't. We were not a match made in heaven and I couldn't, offhand, think of anything we had in common now. That had always been the problem. But he sounded just the same as he always had. In a hurry.

'Hello, James, this is a surprise—' I had got as far as that when he cut me off.

'I know. You still running that bakery? Come to dinner on Saturday night? Meet you at the Venetia at seven thirty? My treat. Want to talk to you.'

'But—'

He cut me off again. I had forgotten how angry this habit made me and I was about to refuse to go anywhere with him. But my curiosity got the better of me. Me and Kipling's mongoose, Rikki-Tikki-Tavi, whose motto was 'run and find out'. It's got me into more trouble.

James went on. 'Can't talk now. Waiting for a call from Singapore. Seven thirty, right? The Venetia. Bye,' he said, and hung up.

Well, the food would be good. The Venetia had been specialising in Italian food long before the days of frozen pre-cooked supermarket lasagne in every freezer. Though mentioning the latter in the Venetia would probably get you turfed out into the street as a peasant unworthy of their food. I not only couldn't afford the Venetia, I couldn't justify spending that much on feeding myself when there were bread and eggs in the world. But if James was paying, then why not? And what on earth did he want to talk to me about?

That would have to keep. The morning tea rush had arrived.

When it was over, leaving the shop considerably emptier, Kylie informed me that she had seen the person who had bought apartment 4A, Daphne. It had a picture of a woman turning into a bush. Next to her was a very annoyed Apollo. One saw his point. All that trouble to lay hands on a recalcitrant nymph, and just when you've got her she has the nerve to turn into a tree. Heh, heh.

'What was this person like?' I asked.

'I don't know,' she confessed. This was a hard thing for Kylie to say. She has the insatiable curiosity of a magpie. 'It was a man, about the same age as you. Blue suit, pretty tall, bit bald. He only had one suitcase and a lot of boxes. I suppose he must have bought old Lady Diana's furniture. I liked her.'

'So did I.'

Lady Diana was a kindly, witty old lady with a strong British accent who had broken her hip months ago and not recovered properly. Her heirs had moved her tenderly to one of those well-staffed, five-star nursing homes on the Mornington Peninsula, where she spends her days watching the sea and skinning the other old ladies at bridge. I was sorry to see her go. I had never forgotten her reaction to viewing Mr. Pemberthy's new 'undetectable' hairpiece. 'What has he done with the rest of the sheep?' she wondered, for my ears alone, and I nearly split a gusset trying not to laugh. Unavailingly. Mr. Pemberthy had been most offended.

'Well, he must have registered with the residents' committee, we can ask them. But not at the moment. Horatio defended himself against Traddles yesterday and Mrs. Pemberthy is a bit upset.'

'Good Horatio,' cooed Kylie, stroking the noble ears. 'Would the beautiful kitty like a bit of cheese?' she asked, slicing open rolls and putting cheese in them. The beautiful kitty graciously accepted a bit of cheese, and then another bit, before Kylie was finished with the cheese rolls. I did the ham ones. I just do ham. Or cheese. If you want avocado and turkey, go to Cafe Delicious where they will compound you a sandwich out of any ingredients whatsoever. Except possibly cement. Then again, if you had the money in your hand and asked the Pandamus family to make you a cement on rye, no butter, they would probably do it. They believe that the customer is always right. Samantha says that the strangest one she ever made was Vegemite, fetta cheese and cranberry sauce. I'm not sure that I believe her.

I decided that tonight I needed some solid food and would dine with the Pandamus family. By about five they were down to leftovers but their grandmother did the cooking and whatever was left over was sure to be—as the name said—delicious.

Time for me to collect my alcoholic bribe and go and rouse the Lone Gunmen. I left Kylie with the lunch crowd and went into their shop. It was open, which argued that one of them was awake, or perhaps 'conscious' might be the right word. Or maybe 'sentient.'

The walls were painted black just like every nerd's bedroom, and were layered with posters for each new video game. I would bet that somewhere right against the paint there would be an ad announcing Pacman. Someone was lurking behind the counter, trying to stay out of direct sunlight and reading William Gibson. Taz. I was in luck.

They named themselves after three characters from 'The X-Files,' though Rat had a rat's tail haircut rather than stringy yellow hair and Gully had possibly heard of the concept of a suit but would certainly never have (1) owned one or (2) worn one if he had. Byers is never seen without his suit. And Frohike is a slob, whereas Taz…well, there were some similarities. Taz didn't look up as I came in.

'New magazines come in tomorrow,' he said. 'Go away.'

'I'm not a customer,' I said. 'Though if that's how you treat them I'm amazed you can pay your rates.'

He looked up and dropped the book, bent, tried to retrieve it from under the desk, couldn't reach, grovelled, got the book, and hit his head on the way up. Taz is a person whom one cannot imagine walking a tightrope.

'Hi, Corinna,' he said, rubbing his temple. 'Ouch,' he added. 'I didn't know it was you. I thought it was Del Pandamus. He's hanging out for the new Livewire mag. I've told him a hundred times it doesn't come until tomorrow. Sorry.'

'Not to worry. I have a task for you,' I said, laying the scarlet woman letter on the table. On, I could not help noticing, a pile of invoices, a sheaf of receipts and a pizza box. 'What can you tell me about this letter?'

'It's addressed to you,' he said.

'Yes,' I said. 'I got that far all by myself.'

'And it says nasty things about you.'

'I got that too. So did Mistress Dread.'

Taz turned a paler shade of soap. Though I would not call him unwashed—he smelt quite acceptably of shower gel and chili sauce, which argued nachos for breakfast, yerk!—he is a slob. He habitually wears three t-shirts, one over the other. As they get stained, he peels them off and replaces them. I assume that someone's mum comes over and collects a huge wash and brings them back all clean and possibly ironed, for the ungrateful little ratbags to crinkle and spill chili sauce on again. If it isn't someone's mum, I can't imagine how they keep up the supply of t-shirts. Some of them are witty, though, and some are nostalgic. The top t-shirt was a satirical one. It read, in the famous Nike script, 'Pike. Just do nothing,' a sentiment of which I could approve. Unfortunately Taz was living up to his t-shirt at present.

'Perhaps I can find ways to motivate you,' I said, aiming for Darth Vader and probably achieving 'woman with bad cold.' I put the six-pack of Arctic Death on the counter. Taz's eyes lit up.

'Yes, my Lord,' he said, in character. 'This letter was written in Calypso on an iMac running Appleworks. Good computer but the laser printer is a bit off. See? The text doesn't sit straight on the page.'

'Could you identify the printer?'

'Negative, Master. The guy might have just put the paper in crooked. If he straightened it up for the next page it'd be straight. He uses too much bold,' said Taz, examining the letter critically. 'Bad design. Too many capital letters.'

'Not someone used to setting out announcements, then?' I asked, grasping at straws.

Taz explained with weary condescension. 'Corinna, every school-aged kid could do better than this. Most school computer courses teach design and layout. This guy is an amateur with—by the look of it—shit for brains. If he did send one of these to Mistress Dread.'

'Not only that, someone painted "Whore of Babylon" on her wall and across the glass,' I said, wondering how he would react. His pale brow wrinkled in thought.

'Whore of Babylon? No, I don't know that band. What are they, death thrash? They're in big trouble. Satanic revenge won't mean jack to them when Mistress Dread catches up with them. That is one scary lady.'

'Oh, I do agree. Well, thanks, Taz. Oh, by the way. Kylie asked if you had any new games. I gather she and Goss like playing with you.'

'Oh? Er…tell her not. They're a bit…'

I had to know. 'A bit what?'

'They scream a lot and then they drink the drinks and want to get snuggly. And we like the games, see. Not the girls.' Taz was wriggling uncomfortably. Kylie had been right. Whatever the Lone Gunmen did with their hormones, it wasn't sex.

I looked in on Meroe on the way back. She had put her potion aside. She thanked me for the herb roll. Then she fell silent. She didn't even speak as she sold a pink crystal to a young woman and then filled an herb order for a middle-aged man who didn't look like a warlock to me, but if he wasn't, what did he want with all those strange plants?

'Meroe has a great gift for silence,' he told me. I agreed and went away until she felt that she had a need for speech.

That visit to Taz had been a waste of six bottles of Arctic Death. All he could tell me was that the man was an amateur and probably, by inference, over about twenty-five. Younger than that and he must have encountered a computer. The trouble was, there were a lot of people over twenty-five.

I went back to my own shop and there was Daniel, and suddenly the whole day improved. He was wearing his usual jeans, loose shirt and leather jacket and he looked tall, dangerous and beautiful. I took a mean pleasure in greeting him warmly in front of the enraptured Kylie.

'You're up early,' I said.

'I've got to go and see the cops, so I can't share your gin and tonic today,' he said. His hand was on my shoulder and it warmed me all the way to the bones. 'But come out with me on Saturday night? You don't work Friday or Saturday night, do you, with the shop closed for the weekend?'

'Of course not,' I said, and remembered James. 'But I've got a dinner engagement.' I wasn't going to call meeting James a date.

'Later than that,' he said. 'I'll come for you at midnight. I want to take you out on the Soup Run.'

'All right,' I said. He bent and gave me a modified hug, and then walked away.

'Wow,' said Kylie weakly.

'He has the same effect on me,' I agreed, sitting down.

'You're going out with him?' she asked, with the sort of emphasis that could have got her sacked if her employer hadn't been thinking about other things.

'Yes,' I said.

'Wow,' she said.

That did appear to sum up the situation rather well.

Chapter Five

Without the promise of Daniel's company afterwards, the scrubbing began to get me down and it was the last straw when someone bashed on the bakery door. I hefted my pail of soapy water and staggered over to open it. If this caller was that carrier, telling me that he couldn't deliver some bread because he couldn't read the address or remember where Collins Street was, I was going to be really cross. And in need of a new carrier, while he would be in need of a towel, an ice-pack and a referral to a good dentist. My back hurt and my knees were wet and I had had enough.

I threw open the door and came face to face with a scared stripling who looked like he was about to run away terribly fast.

'Sorry,' I said. 'I thought you were someone else.'

'I'm glad I'm not him,' he said. Cheeky boy, eh? I looked him up and down. Sneakers which had seen better decades. Track pants which hung on him in folds and a meagre t-shirt which had once belonged, according to the legend, to Folsom prison. Thin as a lath. Scrappy pale hair and weak blue eyes.

I felt like I had kicked a stray dog.

'What can I do for you?' I asked.

'Got any jobs? I could scrub the floor for you,' he said, seeing my bucket. I doubted he could but I felt like a sit-down.

'Ten dollars,' I said. 'Here is your bucket.' I handed it over. 'And here is your mop. Get into all the corners.'

I sat down on the stairs and watched someone else mop my floor, a strange experience. The boy put a good deal of effort into it. It was clear, however, that he had never mopped a floor before.

'No, wring it out,' I said. 'You put the string part into that clamp on the top of the bucket and then press the pedal. Yes, like that. The less water the better. Good. That will do. Mop yourself over here.'

He came close and I gave him the ten dollars. 'And then mop yourself out and empty the bucket in the drain. What's your name?' I asked.

He looked up at me from his housewife's crouch. 'Jase,' he said.

'And who sent you to me?' I asked, knowing the answer. The boy bridled, which is a difficult thing to do with an armload of mop.

'No one sent me. I saw you talking to Daniel so I thought you must be all right,' he said. 'Thanks for the job.'

He went to the door, emptied the bucket into the drain, rinsed it under the tap and put the bucket and the mop inside.

'If you come back tomorrow you can do it again,' I said, rather surprising myself. This kid was going straight out to spend that ten dollars of my hard-earned cash on drugs. I had seen the scars on his arms. Jase squinted up at me from the door. He may have nodded. But then he closed the door and was gone.

I dropped a duster on the floor, slid across on it and locked and bolted my doors. Jase might be a charity case, or he might have been checking out the locks. With that bolt, all the lock picking in the world was not going to let him in to my bakery.

Oddly cheered, I went upstairs for my bath. Lily of the valley today. And when I ascended to the bower with Horatio to drink my gin and tonic, Mrs. Pemberthy and her rotten little dog were not there. In fact, the roof was empty.

No little dogs, no starlings, and—regrettably—no Daniel. I took a little stroll around the garden, noticing that Trudi, the retired gardener of 8A, who gets a contribution from all of us to care for our little piece of Eden, had already put in lots of bulbs for spring. Little spears were starting through the earth in the raised terracotta tubs. The roses were blowing and Trudi's own import, the linden tree, was growing well. A few more years and we would be Unter Den Linden.

Horatio strolled nonchalantly ahead of me, sniffing at the occasional bloom in the condescending manner of a lord mayor at a local flower show. One almost looked for the elaborate gold chain around his furry neck. While he was deciding to give Trudi a second prize for her impatiens, I perched on a wicker chair and looked at the city.

I have always loved Melbourne, except for the times when I have hated it (mostly at four a.m.). The towers have never grown exceedingly tall, not like Hong Kong or Los Angeles, where walking on the street is like being a forest dweller in a huge planting of sterile trees. I hate that feeling of scurrying about under those monstrous structures, with me mouse-sized by comparison and feeling, obscurely, that I ought to watch out for a plummeting hawk. Only a few parts of Melbourne are like that. Mostly, it is still a city built by humans on a human scale. Frequent overbuilding and consequent bankruptcies and crashes do help to keep the builders in check. Mother Nature's little way of keeping her balance among the capitalists.

To celebrate I made myself another gin and tonic and raised my glass to a poor office peon who was staring at me with his tongue hanging out. Make your own destiny, I said to him. Even if it leads you into very strange places.

He, of course, did not reply. Presently the sun went in and Horatio and I descended to our apartment. It was only four, so I decided to go down and ask the Professor if he needed me to bring him some dinner and—oh, yes—I had to visit Mistress Dread to report. Or else she might visit me and that was not a nice thought.

Just as I was leaving the garden I found that someone had augmented one of Trudi's painted pots with a slogan. I had to stoop to read it. This one said: 'Thou shalt not suffer a witch to live.'

I stood for a moment looking at it. I fought down the urge to wash it off or cover it up. The handwriting might be identifiable. There might even be fingerprints. Perhaps they could test the paint. It was in the same red as the 'Whore of Babylon' on Mistress Dread's shop, and the same sort of unformed childish hand.

I found a tarpaulin which Trudi must have left and draped it artlessly over the legend. This was bad. This was very bad.

I had to see Mistress Dread and add this to her police report and that seemed to be the most sensible thing to do first, after I warned Meroe that she had an enemy and he had access to our building.

I returned Horatio to our apartment, checked my own locks, and dived down to the Sibyl's Cave. Meroe was still sitting there in silence and I lost my patience.

'Someone has painted an anti-witch slogan in the roof garden,' I said angrily. 'Meroe? Snap out of it, this is important.'

'Is it? They slaughtered us in droves in the Burning Times and witchcraft survived,' she said in a dreamy voice. I could have shaken her. I fear that my vibrations were all of a jangle.

'I don't care about whether witchcraft survives,' I snapped. 'I care about whether a certain witch survives. Pay attention! What are you going to do?'

'Nothing,' she said. 'I have locks and wards. There is no shortage of madmen who want to burn any woman with skill and intelligence—even now. He'll have to get in, and then...' She looked up at me and her eyes were bleak. 'Then he'll be sorry.'

'I'd rather find out who he is and get him sent to a nice safe loony-bin,' I said. 'Did you get the scarlet woman letter?'

'Yes,' she said. Some of the ice was melting in her manner.

'So did I,' I said. 'So did Goss and Kylie. So did Mistress Dread and they've painted "Whore of Babylon" on her shop. This isn't just aimed at you. But the slogan on the garden pot says "Thou shalt not suffer a witch to live."'

'Exodus 22:18,' she said helpfully.

'And I'm going to the cops,' I continued.

'No. Not on my account,' said Meroe firmly. Now she was definitely with me.

'No, on my own, and for the girls,' I said loudly. 'Who were you cursing this morning? Don't tell me you weren't, I know a curse when I hear one.'

'Not a curse,' she said. 'I was preparing a…learning experience.'

'A learning experience? What was he going to learn? Dying for beginners? I saw your face when you were making that potion and you looked like you came straight from Endor with an armload of wolfsbane and a direct line to Hecate.'

She almost smiled and began to explain, gesturing me to a seat. I noticed Belladonna in her usual posture, working her way through the underlay.

'The only circumstance in which a good Wiccan is allowed to use strong methods against someone is if the person will learn something life-enhancing from the experience,' she told me in her normal voice. 'If, for instance, their habits are set or their mind is clouded. And they need, say, a shock. To jolt them into a more harmonious mode of thought.'

'Harmonious,' I said.

Meroe nodded. She had shed the black shawl and her wrap was of scarlet, a little too close to the colour of blood.

'So they aren't going to wake up without legs, or find that their mouth has healed up overnight?' I asked. 'Or be transformed into a toad?'

'Not unless that would be educational,' said Meroe sweetly.

'And you have designed this educational experience for whom?'

'The man who sent the letter, and the one who wrote the slogan. They may be the same person, of course. I went up to the garden early this morning,' she said. 'I saw it then. I don't like witch-burners.'

I pounced on the one piece of information she had given me. 'So it's a man?'

'Pendulum never lies,' she said complacently. I could have argued with that, but we had an agreement.

'So how shall we know this guy?' I asked. 'Will he turn conveniently blue or go bald or something?'

'Oh no,' she said. 'But all that he does will go amiss. That was a good spell, that one. My mother taught it to me, to be used against burners. I can already feel it working.'

'Oh, good.' I felt strangely at a loss for words. I promised more herb rolls for tomorrow if she could sell me some more herbs and left with my highly scented parcel.

Sometimes, I admit, my friend Meroe gives me the creeps. So it was a bit of a relief to find Senior Constable Lepidoptera White talking to Mistress Dread when I went into her shop.

I had never been inside before. I had expected the usual sex shop stuff, but it looked like the salon of a very expensive designer, all cream leather and gold brocade curtains. The only sign of the Mistress' preoccupation was a stack of books, like pattern books, on a low glass coffee table.

'Hello,' I said to the senior constable. 'I'm afraid I've found another slogan.'

'Did you ask the Lone Gunmen about the letter?' asked Mistress Dread.

'Yes, they said the layout was lousy, that it was done in Calypso on an iMac with a laser printer and that any schoolchild could do better. So we look for someone over twenty-five, and that isn't very helpful.'

'Another painted slogan?' asked the police officer. She looked neat today, and tired as well. Perhaps that was how she always looked. One thing. She was not at all fazed by sitting on a very low leather couch with a person of indeterminate sex, who was wearing a red leather corset and smoking a cigar in a holder. That took style.

'Yes, I'll show you, if you like,' I said. Ms. White heaved herself to her feet.

'You may have the offensive words removed,' she told Mistress Dread. 'We have photographed them and tested the paint. It's spray paint, as you might have guessed. If you find a spray can lying around, bag it. It might have fingerprints. Now, Ms. Chapman. Show me your graffiti.'

I led her up to the roof garden and removed the tarpaulin. She sat down on her heels to examine it.

'Exodus 22:18,' I told her.

'Looks like the same paint,' she said. 'Same biblical obsession too. Have you spoken to your friend the witch?'

'Yes,' I said. 'She's put a curse on him.'

Ms. White actually cracked a smile. A tired one, as might be expected.

'That might be better than anything I can do. How did he get up here? Isn't there a security code on the main door lock?'

'Yes, but there are people in and out all day—nurses and cleaners and people delivering things. If anyone rings the bell someone in the building will usually buzz them in if they say it's a delivery.'

Ms. White tutted. 'This close to the station, you ought to have a doorman. Still, that's people for you. Give them the best lock in the business and they'll leave the door open. This looks like the same loony. Same paint, same religious problems, same writing. Look at those weak loops! He's probably left-handed and he might have paint on his sleeve'—she pointed to a smear —'but apart from that he could be anyone. This porous surface will never take a fingerprint. Have you noticed anything else lately?'

'No,' I said. 'But ever since the junkie nearly died on my grate it's been all go.'

'You be careful of that Daniel Cohen,' she told me, straightening up.

'Why?' I asked. Daniel seemed to be the nicest thing that had happened to me in…well, ever. 'What do you know about him?'

'Nothing,' said Lepidoptera White. 'In my job, that's suspicious. Why does he go on the Soup Run? Hasn't he got a job? He doesn't even have a car registered in his name and no one seems to know where he lives. He's often seen in company with prostitutes, so maybe that's his interest.'

'Maybe,' I said, disliking her. 'But your computers would have told you another thing and I bet you checked.'

'What?'

'Has he got a criminal record?' I asked.

Her silence lasted all the way down in the lift and out to the door.

'No,' she said at last. 'Not in Victoria. Not in Australia either. But you watch your step,' she warned me, and went.

I thought about it as I retreated to the lift and arrived at the Professor's door. He answered it, leaning heavily on a handsome gold-headed stick.

'I sent out for a Roman one,' he said, 'and I got Egyptian, but it will do.'

I explained my errand. He suggested that I buy two portions of whatever Pandamus' grandma had left over and come and eat with him. That sounded like a really good idea, so I complied. I added to the moussaka and green salad with pine nuts a bottle of my favourite red wine and we had a very pleasant meal. We ate in his kitchen. I asked him about witches in the ancient world.

'My dear, the place was rife with them,' he told me, wiping his moustache fastidiously with a spotless napkin. 'Satirists had a particularly hard time with witches. One cannot read, in Petronius' Satyricon, of a witch treating a young man for impotence without wincing. The only bit of her treatment which I can bring myself to remember involved thrashing his private parts with nettles. One would think that this would remove any sexual inclination he might ever have had, at least until the blisters healed.'

'Ouch,' I agreed.

'But, of course, there were sibyls,' said Professor Dion. 'Very wise women. Prophets. My favourite is the story of the Sibylline Books. Do you feel like a story?'

It had been a tough couple of days and I nodded. I would love to hear a story, preferably one not about doom, fate, curses or pain. I filled his glass and my own.

'An early Roman emperor heard that the Sibylline Books were for sale, and he wanted to buy them. He would have been a fool not to, they contained a complete prophecy of the whole history of Rome, in twelve books. So the king went to the sibyl as she sat by her fire, and asked, how much? And she said, a hundred talents. An enormous sum of money.

'A talent would buy you a boat, or a racehorse. The king temporised, a very unwise thing to do. The sibyls were great ladies, not to be trifled with. She looked at him as he bargained for a lower price and threw half of the books on the fire, just like that. Then the king asked, how much for the remaining six, and she said, a hundred talents. He said this was unfair as she had burned six of them, and again she threw half on the fire. How much now? screamed the king, and she said, a hundred talents, and he thought he saw her hand move, so he said done, and paid a hundred talents for three books when he could have had all twelve for the same price.'

'That's an interesting allegory to tell a businessman,' I said. 'I'll tell it to James on Saturday night.'

'James? He is your ex-husband? Do I scent a budding re-romance, if that could be called a word?' he twinkled at me kindly.

'No, you don't. He wants to talk to me for some reason, why I can't imagine, and he's paying. Besides, he has a doting wife now and I believe that she is pregnant.'

Professor Monk poured himself some more wine in such a pointed manner that I got the hint.

'Don't be silly. He likes them thin and drooping, something I never was. Either thin or drooping. He's up to something. James always is. And then I'm going on the Soup Run with Daniel.'

'Tell me about him,' the old man suggested. 'But first, help me to my couch, will you? The thing I never imagined about Roman furniture, before I had it made, was that it was so comfortable.'

I arranged him in a supine posture and fetched the little table with all his things and put it within reach. Then I reclined on the facing couch. He was right. It was very comfortable, once you got used to the strain on the left arm.

Then I realised I didn't have much to tell. I didn't know a lot about Daniel. I could practically see Lepidoptera White folding her arms and nodding at me. I dismissed her as an unpleasant vision.

'He has a grandpa who told him that the reward for a mitzvah is another mitzvah,' I said. 'He used to be in the Israeli army. He's gorgeous.'

'Sounds like a good beginning,' prompted Professor Monk.

'He has a lot of personal…well, Meroe would call it mana. He told a screaming addict to be a good girl and she became one.'

'*Auctoritas*,' said the professor. 'It works on dogs too. Or so I am told. I've never had it.'

'And I'm going out with him on the Soup Run on Saturday night and I'll probably learn a lot more about him,' I added, sounding a bit defensive even to myself.

'I'm sure you will,' he said. 'Nothing like women for gathering information. I've always thought it was supernatural. The things your young lady was telling me about our neighbours would have made my hair stand on end, had I any left.'

I made a mental note to tell Kylie to tone down the goss for Professor Dion.

'She's failed in one mission, though,' I said. 'She doesn't know anything about the man who's moved into Lady Diana's.'

'I met him in the lift,' said the Professor. 'Do you mean that I know something that Kylie doesn't? I am pleased. His name is Holliday. Retired. Something in the city, I would have said, he was wearing a suit which had once been very fashionable. About five years ago, perhaps. No children, no dependants, no wife and no pets. He seemed sad. Perhaps he has lost his wife. I remember what that felt like,' he added. 'He asked several questions about who lived here and I referred him to the residents' committee, who will tell him more than he needs to know.'

'What was your impression of him?' I asked.

'Tallish, balding, usual number of eyes and ears, I suppose. The situation wasn't rendered more comfortable by Mrs. Pemberthy getting in at the fourth floor and telling me about the sins of your vicious cat. She was also complaining that Mr. P spends a lot of time in the garden, which I find unsurprising. How is the delightful Horatio, by the way? Give him my best regards.'

'Time for me to go,' I said. 'Can I turn on your TV?'

Professor Dion shuddered. 'Just find me my glasses,' he said. 'Thank you for a lovely evening, my dear.'

I found his glasses and let myself out. I returned to feed Horatio and the others and put myself to bed after checking that all the locks were secure. I hadn't done that since the day I came to Insula and it was a little disappointing. That might account for the fact that I woke bright and early at two a.m. and spent the rest of the night on the couch with Horatio, watching a very old horror movie. The whole building was silent. Insula was built with thick walls and internal partitions so unless someone is having a very loud party or a very loud fight, you wouldn't know there was anyone else in the place with you. At least, I reflected, it was now Friday. After I did this morning's baking I got two days off.

It wasn't worth opening on the weekend in my bit of the city. Most of the action moved across the river to the huge Southbank complex, with its gambling halls and restaurants and street theatre. I was in the working district and only the workaholic, the junkies and the wandering madmen came here on the weekends. And they didn't buy much bread.

It had been a wise choice for my own sanity. Baker's hours are too unsociable to do them all the time. This way, once I finished on Friday, I at least got to sleep in two mornings and didn't need to do the Monday baking until Monday morning. When Grandma Chapman had been alive I used to visit her every Saturday. Now I did some gentle shopping, visited a gallery, saw a movie. I had largely lost all my friends when James and I broke up two—no, nearly three years ago now.

I didn't really miss them. I would doubtless make more friends when I needed to. At the moment Horatio and I were rather enjoying being alone.

Though not at three a.m. on a very dark night. Watching a very spooky movie. The vampire's mouth opened and he had two thin teeth like hypodermic needles. He had no hair, cat's slit pupils and fingernails like a Mandarin. Very scary. I was making Horatio nervous and he was making me nervous and finally I got up and gave us both a nice drink of milk. He had his in a saucer and I drank mine, microwave-heated and Ovaltined, from a cup.

'Perhaps *Nosferatu* was not a wise choice of movie,' I said to Horatio. He licked up the last of the milk and blinked in agreement. 'Even if it is a triumph of German Expressionism. In fact, since I am sure I just saw something dark flick past that window, I vote we go back to bed and pull the covers over our heads,' I said to him.

He beat me to it. Four paws are faster than two, especially if the two have loose slippers on. We fell into an uneasy doze until the alarm clock alerted me to the fact that Friday morning had officially arrived.

Chapter Six

I baked, I fed, I washed, I did all the usual stuff. I didn't feel very imaginative so I made lots of French knots, plaits, twists and baguettes. My muffins were blueberry. I hacked up the herbs for the herb rolls and made the large order of rye bread for the restaurant. Saturday is always a restaurant's busiest day. If it isn't, the restaurant is not going to be there for long, so eat while you may. I remember one very experienced restaurant owner talking about her children. She fervently hoped that they didn't follow in her footsteps. She wanted them to have a nice job, like lawyer or teacher or labourer or gardener, where they had scheduled meal breaks and they got to sit down occasionally. Selling food for a living, she told me, was a mug's game. And she was right, but it does have its compensations.

Strangely, when it was time, I didn't actually want to open the street door. It must have been a leftover from that movie. I wondered if something dark and horrible was waiting outside. But the valiant Mouse Police were bouncing up and down, eager to seek for prey, or possibly fish, so I dragged the bolt and undid the locks and they shot out into the alley.

I followed slowly. The sun was rising, which was always a good thing, and a ray fell on my face. I looked around. No bodies on the vent. Kiko's brother Ian was sweeping. The sound came clearly down the alley in that silence which precedes the roar of traffic. No paint on my wall. Just a quiet sunny morning. Just what an underslept baker needs.

Then someone screamed. Not loudly, but it was a scream and I went around the corner of the alley at a sort of fast creep. I wasn't going to rush into the middle of anything and if that was Jack the Ripper round there, there was a sporting chance he wouldn't see me, busy with his latest victim as he would be, as I raced back inside, locked all the doors and called the police. I am not the stuff of which vigilantes are made, as you will have noticed.

But there was no gore—at least, not yet. What I saw was a large man in a suit and sunglasses—at this hour!—preparing to cuff my floor-scrubbing scarecrow of the day before. Again, to judge by the way Jase, yes, that was the name, was cowering against the wall with his hand across his face.

This I could handle. I retreated a little and then came around the corner yelling, 'Heckle! Jekyll! Puss, puss, puss!' and then stopped dead as I saw the threatening little tableau. A picture of innocence, I was. To add to the impression, Heckle came skidding up behind me in case I really meant it about the cat food. A gust of baking accompanied me.

The big man released Jase, said something to him in a low voice, then marched into Flinders Lane. I let him go. When I was sure he had gone, I beckoned to Jase and he limped into Calico Alley, spitting out something white. It was a tooth. Oh dear.

I let Jase sit down on the doorstep—after all it was clean, he had scrubbed it himself—and fed Heckle and Jekyll some kitty treats, since they had come promptly when I had called. Cats are not trainable by any method other than always—always, without fail—rewarding the behaviour you want. If there's invariably a kitty treat in it for them, they will come when they are called, unless something really much more interesting is happening. Miss one reward and all that training goes the same way as a John Howard election promise about Medicare. They whuffed appreciatively as I drew some hot water, found a cloth and sat down to have a look at the poor boy's face.

He scooted away from me, whining, 'I'm all right!' but I ignored this as he clearly wasn't. As honorary first-aid monitor at a tough girls school which went in for hockey like other people went in for hard drugs—ferociously, mindlessly—I was used to this sort of injury. I mopped off the blood and found that Jase had a cut lip and a missing tooth which must have been loose, because there was not a lot of bleeding at the empty socket. His mouth was already ballooning up.

It isn't like this in the movies, I know, but in the real world the victim of a beating looks like they have put a compressed air nozzle into their mouth and turned it on. They look ridiculous which, since they are always in considerable pain, seems unfair. There wasn't a lot of Jase's face and now it was going to be all lip.

'I'll get you some ice,' I told him. 'Then maybe a nice cup of coffee. I suppose you aren't going to tell me what that was all about, are you?'

He shook his head and winced. I checked and found a bump on the back of his skull. His hair was filthy. He probably had lice. Or not. Only a louse which liked slumming would live in that hair. I had an idea.

When the bakery had been designed, someone had put in a small bathroom, just a toilet and a shower. I didn't use it because I lived upstairs. I left Jase and went up to find a bottle of shower gel which was supposed to make me feel focused and which was still almost full. Aromatherapy is a good idea, everyone likes nice smells, but I didn't care for the scent of ginger on my skin, preferring it in gingerbread. I also grabbed a towel and a worn but clean dressing gown which had belonged to James and which I kept in case I had to do any painting. I also found some old thongs.

Jase was still sitting on the step when I came back, which rather surprised me. I thought he would have run as soon as I turned my back. I helped him to his feet.

'In there,' I told him, 'is a shower. Go. Wash yourself. Wash your hair. Especially wash your hair. I will wash your clothes. Then you can sit here in the warm until the dryer spits them out and then you can go. By which time the bloke in the shades will have moved on. All right?'

I expected an argument but he just murmured, 'Thanks,' and took the garments and the gel. Soon some frightful trackies were poked through the door and I heard the shower running. I slung his revolting clothes into the washer, set it on 'soiled' because it didn't have a setting for 'filthy' and continued with my bread.

I was almost finished when a terribly clean Jase came out of the bathroom on a puff of steam. He was at least two shades lighter and revealed as a blond. I gave him an ice-pack to hold to his mouth and slid the last loaves into the oven.

'This is a nice place,' Jase almost said. 'Warm.'

'It's nice now,' I said. 'It's hell in summer.' I took a look at him. His eyes were no more dilated than usual and he seemed to know where he was. As far as he ever did.

'Jase, where do you live?' I asked.

He extricated his hand from the folds of James' dressing gown and waved it. 'Here and there' he seemed to mean. I really wasn't going to get anything out of him and it seemed cruel to press. So I just got on with the bread and the washer got on with its sacred duty and Jase sat on my chair, watching me work.

He seemed interested.

'Wha's tha'?' he asked, pointing at my prized bucket of yeast mixture.

'That's mother of pasta douro,' I said. 'A mixture of yeast and warm water and it has to be fed every day with flour and sugar. Some bakers call it a starter. Yeast is a plant,' I said. 'It has to be looked after like any plant.'

'No flowers,' said Jase. 'Just flour.'

This was a witty observation. I looked at him. He was huddled in James' dressing gown, which went around him twice. He would weigh maybe only forty kilos and he looked as frail as a reed. But he must share some attributes with the city's indestructible sparrows, who made a living any place they could and somehow were always there when anyone dropped anything edible. Most of my motherly feelings are for cats, so maybe Jase reminded me of an underfed, scrawny kitten that some heartless fiend had shut out in the street.

When the washer completed its ministrations I put the track pants and underwear in the dryer, but the act of washing had removed so much dirt and chili sauce and various disgusting human fluids from the Folsom t-shirt that it had fallen to rags. Jase looked stricken.

'I'll give you another,' I offered.

'One of yours?' he asked. I nodded. 'Sweet as,' he enthused, hissing through his missing tooth. 'That has to be nice and loose. Homey. I mean,' he added hastily, 'I'm real thin, and you're—'

I stopped him before he could dig himself into an even deeper pit. 'What sort of shirt would you like?' I asked.

He expressed a preference for something with long sleeves—all junkies, I guess, would prefer long sleeves—so I found a dark red skivvy which had rather shrunk in the wash. It would still hang on Jase like a shroud.

We drank our coffee and he asked me several other things about bread. Intelligent questions. As long as I stayed off cross-examining him we could have a conversation. I found I was quite enjoying it. No one really cares about bread, not like I do.

Finally, I had finished the baking and Jase's clothes were dry. He dressed again in the bathroom and, without asking, put his dressing gown in the washer.

'Thanks,' he said. 'Bye,' and he was gone. He looked quite respectable in the skivvy, but he was still going to find eating hard for a while. Still, junkies don't eat a lot, I imagine.

The day began with me deciding to find a new carrier for Monday, recognising Goss from her golden navel ring, and noticing that the shop needed a really good scrub. It was clean enough for the most difficult health inspector but the grime from the city floated in all the time and after some time it became ingrained in curtains and rugs and even in the polish on the floor. Gossamer told me that Kylie had gone to an audition. Meroe had made charms for both of them and I was hoping that they would begin to operate some day soon, before they died of malnutrition.

It was an ordinary morning. For some reason there are more shoppers in the city on a Friday as people often take the day off. I've done the same thing myself, made a firm resolution to see that film or visit that sale and then found, suddenly, that I was running out of week. I sold out of the herb rolls before lunchtime, made a killing on the fancy bread, but rather struck out with the blueberry muffins and ordinary baguettes. I ate a muffin myself (it was no use asking Goss to taste test anything with starch in it) and it was fine. Just the peculiarity of the passing trade, which today had its stomach set on spiced apple. In a way it was good. A sackful of baguettes and muffins would do for the Soup Run tomorrow night.

I wasn't feeling too sure of myself after my little encounter with Jase and the man in sunglasses. There was a violent undercurrent in the city which I really didn't want to have anything to do with. I hate violence. I hid my face through half of *Lock, Stock and Two Smoking Barrels* (though the ending was brilliant). I avoid going to Terminator-type movies and I don't even enjoy comic-book level violence like James Bond. Also, I bruise easily. While the Soup Run existed to help the poor and homeless, that didn't mean the staff didn't get abused, or why would they need a heavy?

Lust has got me into some strange situations, like the time I woke up and found a rock band asleep on my living room floor (with the bass guitarist in the bath, covered in ghee—I never did find out what that was about). Or the time I found myself handing out how-to-vote cards for—no, I can't say. Lust had once caused me to buy a baby-blue apron with ruffles when James' boss, who had a 'Bewitched' fetish, was coming to dinner. In the cause of lust I have hitchhiked to Adelaide, watched seven games of basketball, caught cold sitting in a garage listening to a variety of mind-fracturing sounds and bought Tupperware. Lust made me agree to talk to a secondary school food technology class.

I felt a little better. I had paid my dues. I could take it. The Soup Run couldn't be more violent and dangerous than that food technology class.

Lunch cleaned out most of the remaining stock. I decided to shut early, paid Goss and sent her to close the shutters.

I heard them come down with their usual metallic rattle and then a squeal from Goss. I caught up the broom, with which I had been sweeping the floor. See previous comments on lust. I was in a militant mood.

But outside I merely found Daniel. Goss had narrowly missed braining him with a shutter and she was now apologising in several different positions.

'Sorry!' she squeaked. 'I didn't see you! I didn't mean to!' Then she got a good look at those trout pool eyes and the leather jacket and squealed, 'You must be Corinna's Daniel! Nice to see you! Kylie was right about you!'

Before she embarrassed me any more, I invited Daniel inside and shut Goss out, where I could still hear her squeaking. Daniel went straight to greet Horatio, who rose onto his paws and accepted the accolade, lowering his head.

'You close early on a Friday,' he said. 'You aren't Jewish, are you?'

'No, I'm tired,' I said tartly. 'Are you coming up? If so, grab the bread. I'll cash up later. Horatio and I watched a horror movie last night and we scared ourselves.'

'You'd think a gentleman cat would have more sense,' he said, ruffling the regal whiskers. 'I'll take the cat and the sack, if you please. What do you have to do now?'

'The scrubbing,' I said. 'But I've had some help with that lately. Possibly he might come back so we can leave the floor to him.'

'Who?' asked Daniel. I really liked his voice. It was a calm, rich tenor. What with Meroe and Mistress Dread, there were a lot of deep voices around Insula these days.

'He says his name is Jase,' I told Daniel, shutting the door to the shop and locking it. 'He came in yesterday and scrubbed the floor for ten dollars. And he came in this morning for a shower.'

'A mitzvah,' laughed Daniel, putting down the sack and allowing Horatio to stalk along his arm to a convenient shelf. I started running the hot water.

'Are you staying to help?' I asked, surprised.

Daniel took off his leather jacket and rolled up his sleeves. He had forearms like Shane Warne. 'Least I can do,' he said, and seized a brush.

Two people working in the same space can make light work or they can continually get in each other's way until the party of the first part begs the party of the second part to please sit down on the steps and let her get on with it. This had been the case with everyone I had ever worked with. But not Daniel. He seemed to guess what I was going to do before I even knew I was going to do it, and was never in the way when suds cascaded or liquid squirted. In fact, we ended up with a very clean bakery and he didn't have a damp spot on him, whereas me and my trackies were sopping. He joined Horatio on the steps as I opened the street door to mop the floor and there was Jase. His bruised face had begun to darken. Daniel was across the floor in a moment, cradling the sore jaw in one big, very clean hand.

'Someone got you,' he said to Jase, who nodded. 'Gonna tell me who this dude is?' he asked, and Jase shook his head. Daniel sighed and let him go.

'Do the floor?' asked Jase.

'Go to it,' I said. It was already clean, but Jase needed the money.

I joined Daniel on the steps. This time Jase did a much better mopping job. I liked sitting on the steps, my shoulder against Daniel's (I was sitting on a higher step) and Horatio behind me, supervising the staff.

'Tomorrow?' asked Jase.

'Closed tomorrow and Sunday,' I said. 'Come back Monday.'

He didn't protest, but took the money, ducked his head at Daniel, and went.

'You're handling him just right,' approved Daniel, allowing me to precede him up the steps to my apartment.

'I am?'

'Yes. Firm. Junkies are like—like crusaders. They've been pursuing their quest, deaf and blind to anything else, for years.

They haven't had any rules for living because of the little voice in their head which just tells them, your mission in life is to get a fix, get a fix, a fix, a fix. That's all they think about. That's all they can think about. Then there's a heroin drought, like now, and they detox, perhaps in a police cell, perhaps in a squat somewhere. Now they're back in the real world and they don't know how to live in it. You didn't give him money he didn't have to work for because the bakery won't be open and you're sorry for him. By the fact he came back, I bet you didn't ask him a lot of questions. Not even, where are you going to sleep tonight? Did you?'

'No, I don't think that question and answer makes a conversation. We were talking about bread. It's a very interesting topic,' I said. 'Do you know anything about Jase? A large man in a suit and sunglasses, reminding me irresistibly of the Blues Brothers except not funny at all, was beating him up this morning in the lane. I just happened to come round the corner and the guy went away.'

'A blue suit?' asked Daniel.

'Certainly. Day had dawned, I could see colours.'

'That's not so good. The only Blues Brothers suit I know of is inhabited by not a very nice man at all. I wonder what Jase has done to him? I wouldn't have thought Jase was important enough to attract that sort of attention.'

'You aren't actually going to decode your previous speech, are you?' I asked.

'No,' he said equably. 'What do you usually do now?'

'I have a bath and change my clothes, then a little lunch and a gin and tonic. Want to join me? You could watch if you like.' I asked, trying to keep hope out of my voice. The bath was big enough for two.

'I'll stay here and amuse Horatio,' he told me.

Rats. I took a quick bath and came back to find that Daniel and Horatio were both staring out the parlour window, contemplating the pigeons on the sill. Those pigeons had a death wish, or else they knew all about the fact that cats cannot reach through glass and were teasing him. Never a good idea with Horatio, who, if he caught them, would tear them wing from wing in revenge for past taunts.

I left them to it, slashing some baguettes to pieces and laying out butter, pickles, a packet of ham, some red English cheese and a bunch of Meroe's organic salad, the most delicious leaves in the world. She says that they aren't actually picked by the pixies and wafted to her shop on a pinch of fairy dust, they just taste like that. That was all I had in the fridge, apart from a couple of emergency frozen chicken breasts and a lot of cat food. I usually do the shopping on Saturday. Daniel didn't seem to mind. He accepted a glass of chateau collapseau (rouge) and ate bread and cheese with what looked like relish.

Of course, I should have thought, anyone with a grandpa who talked about mitzvahs was probably not going to eat ham for lunch.

'I shouldn't have offered you ham,' I said. He raised his eyebrows. They were straight.

'You can offer whatever you wish,' he said. 'That just shows your generous heart. It is up to me whether I accept or refuse. In the case of ham, I refuse. In the case of…'

He leaned forward and took my hand. He lifted it to his lips and kissed my work-worn knuckle very gently. I dragged in a deep breath.

Then my bell began to ring frantically, Horatio jumped onto Daniel's shoulder, Daniel let go of my hand and I swore.

'Shit! Now what?' I went into the parlour and pressed the intercom button.

''S'me, Goss, you locked me out and you got my mobile, I need it,' said a fast, angry voice.

'Can't you do without it?' I demanded.

'Spend a weekend without a mobile? Duh,' she sneered.

It was true. Goss was as wedded to her mobile phone—her whole social life revolved around it—as Tom was to Jerry, Marge to Homer, or Princess Leia to Han Solo.

'Go to the bakery door,' I sighed. 'I'll come and let you in.'

'Whatever,' she snarled, which meant 'yes, and this is all your fault for making me put the phone under the counter while the shop is open. If you let me carry it in my hand this would never have happened,' which is quite a lot for one trisyllable to carry. It managed. I turned to look at Daniel and Horatio, who had come to the parlour door.

To my surprise, Daniel was laughing. He had a pleasant, infectious chuckle and I found myself laughing too, despite wondering how long it would take to wring Goss' neck and where I could conceal the body. Horatio, who would never allow himself to smile, seemed gently amused. Well, I hoped it kept fine for them.

I clattered down the stairs to the bakery, clean and sweet smelling, into the shop, unlocking as I went. I found the wretched phone and opened the bakery door to discover Goss jumping up and down with impatience. I thrust the phone into her hands and she clasped it to her bosom (such as it was) with a gesture that would have been considered overdrawn on 'The Bold and the Beautiful.'

'I might have missed a call!' she complained, giving me an accusing look. Then she saw Daniel behind me. Her mouth opened and I knew that she was about to make a declaration as to why I had shut her out of the shop. I reminded her that she had calls waiting, closed the door, and leaned on it.

Then I looked at Daniel and he looked at me and we started to laugh so hard that we ended up sitting on the steps, clutching each other and practically crying. Every time I started to regain some control he would make a most endearing snuffling noise and set me off again. We sat there for some time. Horatio, confronted with the essential irrationality of humans, had mounted to the parlour and was enveloped in slumber.

'We're alone,' said Daniel huskily.

'Alone at last,' I agreed. 'We had to resort to sitting on cold stone steps but we did it.'

'So before someone else rings the doorbell, calls out fire or reports a landing of Martians on the roof garden, I am going to kiss you,' he declared, and did.

He was strong and tasted spicy and his mouth was softer than silk. I had to pull away to draw breath. I was close enough to notice that his eyelashes were fringed and absurdly black. Beautiful Daniel. And with all the thin gorgeous girls in the world, he was kissing me.

And doing it damn well. Important parts of me were melting when we finally drew apart. I could feel his handprints on my back. My whole body protested when I was no longer in contact with him.

'Well,' he said pleasantly. 'That settles that question.'

'Which question? You never asked a question,' I mumbled.

'Do you kiss as well as I thought you would?' he said. 'Not possible to answer without empirical data. Can we stop sitting on the steps now?'

'I think we should,' I said, and led the way upstairs to the parlour, beyond which was my bedroom with a bed quite big enough for two humans and Horatio…

But now it came to it I couldn't. Not yet. I didn't know enough about him, just that I wanted him. I knew that I wanted him badly, but I hadn't had a lover since James and I split, and I had what was either a sudden failure of nerve or an attack of common sense.

Daniel sensed that I had backed off and just sat down with me on the sofa. It is a large overstuffed sofa and very comfortable, though after a few hours one has to be extracted from it by crane. He held out his arms again.

'Not rushing into anything, ketschele,' he said quietly. 'I haven't had a lover since Sarah died and I don't even know if I can remember…'

'How long ago?' I asked, snuggling back into his em-brace. His skin, under the shirt, was hot against my cheek. This man would have been in great demand in the cave during the Ice Age.

'Four years. A suicide bomber took her with him. In Tel Aviv. I wasn't there and they wouldn't let me see her when I returned. Then I came back here. I like Australia. What about you?'

'Not since James. We split and I sort of lost confidence. And I was busy. Bakers don't keep disco hours, if I ever went to discos, which I didn't. I'm sorry about your wife.'

'I was only married a couple of months. We didn't ever get to know each other. It would have been nice, getting to know her,' he said.

I didn't reply but cuddled closer. This was the first real hug I had had since so long ago that I don't remember. Grandma Chapman hadn't gone in for physical affection much.

Presently we got up and finished lunch. Then Daniel went away and I put Horatio and me to bed for the rest of the afternoon. It had been an emotional day, and emotion makes me sleepy.

Chapter Seven

On Saturday morning I woke promptly at four and then did one of my favourite Saturday things. I turned over and went straight back to sleep. Below, the city might wake and the Mouse Police pursue their avocation, but Horatio and I were fast asleep and firmly remained so until about ten a.m., when we felt that we had slept all that we could usefully sleep and got up in search of some breakfast and maybe a little look at a novel. I was giving up news for Lent. If it wasn't Lent, I was giving it up for Passover. Or something. I had had enough of the world. It could go its way and I could go mine and we just wouldn't notice each other, like two cats on the same roof.

Besides, I had the grocery shopping to do, a little light housework to complete, and—eek!—clothes to choose for the evening. What on earth was I going to wear to dine at the Venetia with James? I'd ditched all my office clothes with cries of relief. A nice quiet suit with a flamboyant scarf or pashmina was the right thing to wear, and I didn't have them. I owned a good collection of t-shirts and track pants, and it was almost worth wearing them to the restaurant in order to catch the maitre d' as he fainted, but I am not a cruel woman.

First, the breakfast of apricot jam, cafe au lait and someone else's croissants (the French artisan boulangerie in Little Collins Street makes the best) and a few chapters of the newest Jade Forrester. Romances with a twist. She specialises in heroes who are small, blond and ugly, and she makes them desirable. There is a lot to be said for tall, dark and handsome, however. The Mouse Police came upstairs for a conference with Horatio and they all adjourned to sleep in the sun on my balcony. Nothing is more soothing than watching cats sleep.

I had a very comfortable morning.

I was hauling home the grocery shopping (cat food weighs a tonne. I have pointed this out to the cats and they are not at all grateful), thinking of Daniel and approaching my own front door when Meroe caught up to me and relieved me of a canvas bag. Before I dropped the lot. It's a matter of balance.

'What have you been buying? Lead shot?' she asked.

'Cans of Kitty Dins,' I said, opening the door. 'A couple of packets of kitty meat and a big box of dry food. The rest of the stuff is for me,' I added, stepping inside.

Then I skidded on something, dropped an armload of stuff, and landed hard on my backside. With the noise of my fall, or even before, all available cats had vanished with a whisking noise. I greatly admire the way that they are never there when anything happens. I recall watching Mistinguette, the aged grumpy grey cat who preceded Horatio, walking along the mantelpiece and deliberately edging a big mirror towards destruction—just because she felt like it (as I said, grumpy). I actually saw that mirror fall and when it hit the ground, the lounge room had shattered frame, shards of broken mirror and seven years' bad luck in it, but a complete absence of cat. She emerged later from the kitchen, claiming that she had been there all the time, waiting for her inefficient staff to bring her afternoon milk, and was far too old to climb mantelpieces even if she should wish to do so. Which she didn't. It was the most barefaced piece of cheek I had seen before or since, apart from the children overboard affair.

And that was politicians. I groaned, sat up, rubbed various parts of my anatomy and started to gather up my scattered shopping. Meroe, luckily, had the eggs, the milk and the frozen peas. Frozen peas spread like lava and you keep finding them only after they unfreeze.

What had I slipped on? I retrieved a tin of pineapple from under a chair and found it, a flat sheet of paper, which on my polished tiles had acted like an ice-skate.

'Prepare to meet thy doom, unchaste woman!' the paper said. 'Corinna Chapman, you must die!!'

I handed it to Meroe without a word. Now it was personal. And our very own pet lunatic knew where I lived. Meroe produced one which said 'Witches must burn! Prepare to die, Miriam Kaplan!!'

Meroe, my stalwart Meroe, was actually shaking. I had a cold hollow where my stomach used to be. Immediate measures had to be taken. It didn't matter that it was only four in the afternoon and the sun had not even approached the yardarm.

I sat Meroe and me down in the kitchen, that ancient female refuge, and poured us both a large glass of brandy. And wonder of wonders, the woman who lectured me on my dull chakras lifted the glass and downed the spirit in one gulp.

'He knows where we live,' she said in her dark brown voice, coughing a little. 'And he knows my real name.'

'You're Miriam Kaplan?' I asked, coughing over my brandy in turn.

'I haven't been Miriam Kaplan for years and years,' she said. 'Twenty years, at least. Meroe is my craft name and I don't know anyone now who even knows that my name was Miriam. How did he find out? Who is this creep?'

'Maybe the curse will kick in,' I suggested, a little disconnected by the brandy.

'It has,' she said firmly. 'It's working. Everything he does will go amiss. Therefore these are clues which may lead to his undoing and we ought not be so scared.'

'I'm not feeling any better for hearing you say that,' I told her.

'But you're an unbeliever,' she answered gently, pouring another shot of brandy. 'I ought to have faith in my own karma,' she said, sipping rather than gulping. 'I do have faith,' she added. 'But I'm scared, all the same.'

'Hey, me too. Gimme that bottle.'

I put the groceries away. Routine is calming. Meroe and I began to talk about ordinary things, to give ourselves time to recover a little. I wondered aloud why the makers of the stoutest and most admirable cat food container made the cat food that Horatio will not eat. She wondered whether cats could be weaned onto a vegetarian diet and I riposted that this would merely cause them to regard their owner as either (1) a large carnivore who was meanly keeping all the meat for themselves or (2) dinner.

Horatio and the Mouse Police crept back into the kitchen, looking wary. Was I going to do that again, in which case this kitchen was no place for a delicately nurtured cat (or even those who had been dragged up in the gutter, like the Mouse Police)? If I was not intending to do that again, considerable cat food was required to assuage the shock of seeing one hundred kilos of woman and shopping hitting the floor without warning. The Mouse Police rushed to Meroe with cries of greeting and allowed her to stroke their nibbled ears and their heaving flanks. Horatio levitated onto the table, sniffed my glass, curled a whisker and returned to the balcony, where the last rays of sun were still warming the tiles.

'We need to tell that police officer,' I said. 'We need to check with Mistress Dread in case she's got one too. And, oh God, what about Goss and Kylie?'

'I'll go and talk to them,' offered Meroe. 'You get Mistress Dread.'

'She gave me her mobile number, I'll ring her,' I said, unwilling to leave the bright kitchen with the sun on the balcony. Meroe went out and made me lock the door behind her. I rang Ms. Dread and found that she had also received a letter though she was strangely unwilling to tell me about it. It sounded the same as ours, with escalating exclamation marks. Sure sign of an unhinged mind, my old English teacher used to say. Not a comforting thought at this juncture. Senior Constable White had been contacted and was expected soon, and told us to try not to handle the letters (some hope!) and to keep them in a plastic folder. I fetched one from my desk and slid both letters into it. Meroe's also had been slipped under her door without an envelope.

Meroe came back to tell me that both the girls were out but she had managed to slide their letter from under their door and with luck they would never know about it. I added it to the plastic sleeve. It said the same as ours: 'Gossamer Judge and Kylie Manners, you are unchaste temptresses, you will die!!!'

Three exclamation marks this time, and both full names. Meroe sipped some more. She had dropped her shawl and was staring into space. Then she began to talk, without prompting. The brandy was loosening my abstemious friend's tongue and she plunged straight into biography.

'I was born at the fairground in Geelong,' she said. 'My parents came from Poland. No one cared for us, everyone persecuted us, from Hitler onwards.'

'You're a gypsy?' I asked quietly.

'Half gypsy. My father rescued my mother from a border guard who was going to rape her. Her family was dead. She was trying to get out of Poland and that was frowned upon. He was an Australian aid worker. These Australians, they are everywhere. Walk into any pub in the world and there's an Australian behind the bar, my father said, nice blokes and good sheilas, work hard, and always go home. Boomerangs. They still call Australia home, eh? So my father came home with my mother and he tried to live like a gypsy but he couldn't, poor man. Too hard, too bare, too dirty. My mother really loved him so she went to try to live like an Aussie; too soft, too clean, too distant from the earth and the road which was always calling her. So they split and I lived half the year as a good little schoolgirl and half the year as a barefoot gypsy.'

'That must have been hard,' I said, wanting her to keep talking.

'Yes, but good. Most gypsies don't know another life, most Aussies don't either. I knew both so I could choose. And here I am. Neither. If you're a witch you have to find your path yourself; it isn't either your father's or your mother's. For me it was Wicca. I knew some of the old spells, some of the old rituals, I knew about tarot because a Romanian woman taught me to read cards when I was twelve. The old magic is self limiting, just a crude attempt to manipulate the world in accordance with will, as Crowley said. But Wicca isn't all that old. Gardner largely invented it in the nineteen twenties. It is wholly of the light. Some of Mamma's magic goes back a lot further than that, and some of her rituals belong to the dark.'

'And you belong to the light?' I asked.

'Not by preference,' she said, grinning suddenly with her white teeth. 'I am a daughter of darkness and I know I'd be good at the left-hand path, so I don't usually do it. I don't even do the small, mild curses which most Wiccans allow themselves. When I was mixing up Mamma's All Things Amiss spell, I could taste its potency, I knew that it was gaining power through me. It's still gaining power.'

'Good,' I told her. 'In this case I think you can make an exception. This guy has it coming.'

'So do lots of people,' she said, her gaze dropping to her hands clasped around the glass. 'I shouldn't have done it. I was afraid that this would happen. I'm really, really good at curses.'

'If I can give up smoking you can give up curses,' I said. 'I loved smoking. It was lovely. I'd pull the smoke down into my lungs and feel an instant effect; cleverer, more focused, less tired, less hungry. I still miss it and I don't do it, so neither will you.'

'You still have the occasional cigarette,' she told me.

'And you can do the occasional curse, when it would do most good,' I riposted. 'Now, are you going to tell the lady cop about the curse?'

'No,' said Meroe.

'Then let's talk about this stalker. He's got access to the building so it has now become officially serious. Let's analyse. He's using a lot of biblical quotes,' I began.

'Yes. A fundamentalist Christian, perhaps,' Meroe agreed.

'You could say the same of Savanarola,' I said.

'Yes, and he deserved a curse as well,' argued Meroe. I felt cheered. She must be feeling better about her dark side.

'And he hates all unchaste women and witches,' I said. 'So far it's just the unchaste and the occult, right?'

'Assuming that Mistress Dread is considered an unchaste woman.' Meroe sipped more brandy. I wondered how much she was going to drink and where I was going to store her while I went out to dinner. She would probably enjoy the couch and the cats would enjoy having a nice unconscious body to repose upon. But she still sounded perfectly coherent, while I was deciding to knock off the spirits or I wouldn't enjoy my very expensive dinner.

'Any more unchaste women in the building?'

'Mrs. Pemberthy,' she suggested. We both went into what can only be described as a giggling fit about Mrs. Pemberthy's chances of unchastity, especially since Traddles would take grave exception to anyone approaching her.

'Probably not,' I said.

'And so far all he has done is send letters,' said Meroe. 'We'll just have to keep the doors locked and stay alert.'

'And alarmed,' I agreed. 'But I need your advice on a far graver matter.'

'Which is?' she arched an eyebrow.

'What am I going to wear to dine at the Venetia tonight?' I wailed.

Having someone else sort through your wardrobe is always humiliating. She will find, for instance, your Robert Smith t-shirt, the three pairs of jeans with holes in the crotch, the lime green dress you unwisely thought might look less ghastly in sunlight, the red jacket which doesn't fit anymore but is never-theless the very jacket in which you began university, the shabby black you wore during a brief period of being cool, and the but-tonless, zipperless, damaged clothing which lurks pathetically in the basket for me to have a sewing binge. Which I do every six months or so.

But Meroe was in a mellow mood and in any case not one of fashion's most notable victims. She sorted out a pair of respectable black trousers and flat black leather slippers, a kurta, still in its packet, which my mother had sent me for Solstice, and an outrageous purple chiffon wrap (with sequins) which I had found at an op shop and had meant to make into a cushion cover. I protested at the combination, but Meroe just told me to try it all on and it looked—well. It looked chic. I am not used to being chic. The Indian shirt was soft black cotton, not too hot, and it hung loosely over the trousers. It was a combination I would never have come up with in a thousand years.

But Meroe was not finished yet. She found me small silver earrings and dragged my hair up into a very sophisticated knot, secured with a silver slide which someone had brought back from Greece. Then she painted my face, very swiftly and surely, with such cosmetics as I had, and my eyes were dramatic and my mouth was purple and, really, I felt like Mistress Dread, someone masquerading as someone else. But it was perfect.

'You've done this before,' I accused.

'Four younger sisters,' she admitted. 'Are you going to make a night of this dinner date?'

'No,' I said. 'What, with James? You jest. I will be back by about ten.'

'I must go home, Bella will be fretting,' she said. 'You look lovely! Ring me when you get in. I think we had all better take more care of each other.'

'Even Mrs. Pemberthy?' I asked.

'Her too,' said my witch, and told me to lock the door after her. And I did.

Then, since housework was out of the question in my beautiful clothes, I read some more Jade Forrester until it was time to gather my bits and start walking towards the Venetia. James was the most unpunctual person I knew, in personal matters (he never missed a conference or a client), but I liked being early. I have observed that those who consider that ten minutes is enough time to get across Munich and catch the train for Italy and those who know all the neighbourhood dogs because they spend so much time walking around the block, having arrived an hour early, always marry each other. It must be some sort of cosmic joke.

The city was waking up for the weekend as I walked at an even pace, hands in pockets, towards the bulk of the Town Hall and along Swanston Street, before turning uphill. Unlike, say, Sydney, where the only flat spaces are on railway station platforms and cafe tables, Melbourne has one hill, but it's quite steep. I prefer to stroll slowly, pausing to take in the view and remark on the passers-by, rather than rush up it and miss the beautiful buildings. Also, I was not going to arrive at the Venetia out of breath. It was a balmy evening. My clothes felt comfortable. The leather slippers moulded to my feet. The kurta was loose and did not catch under the arms. And my chiffon wrap was a hit. Several passing people looked at it and one undeniable punk, green mohawk erect in display like a cockatoo, said, 'Cool!'

Also, I was finding Insula uncomfortable, what with having our very own madman, and it was nice to be out. I hadn't been out on a Saturday night for years and now I had two dates. One, admittedly, was with an unpleasant person but the food would be good, and I could prepare myself for the Soup Run when I got home, dined and, with any luck, wined. Unless James had entirely changed his spots.

That didn't seem likely. I paused to look in the window of an excellent bookshop and checked my watch. On the dot.

I squared my shoulders and mounted the stairs to the piano nobile, where I would find the Grand Dining Room of the Venetia. Where, in all probability, I would be snubbed by a head waiter and spend the next half-hour crumbling bread and drinking water, if James was on form. I was all prepared for both of these things—I had my Jade Forrester in my bag and my icy stare in stock—so I was surprised to find the head waiter very polite and James already seated, glaring at a menu as though it had done him an injury.

He gave a start as I came into view. 'Corinna!' he said. 'You look…you look very good, really very tasty,' he said as the head waiter seated me. I looked at James. I had slept next to him for years. I knew exactly how to stop him snoring (though my last resort, decapitation, had never been used).

I knew what he ate for breakfast. Or at least, I had known. Now he looked like a stranger, and a not very attractive stranger at that. He was always a tall stringy ex-basketball player. Now he had filled out more than a bit. The tailoring was straining over his corporation and he had lost a lot of hair. Also there were dark shadows under his eyes and a little tic by his upper lip. The suit would have cost thousands and I bet the shoes would be equally pricey, but this was not a happy or contented man.

'Nice to see you, thank you for coming,' he said with the studied insincerity of the merchant banker on the make. 'So baking suits you,' he commented.

'And how are Yvonne and the baby?' I asked. He puffed out his chest so far that it almost preceded his stomach. At any moment he was going to produce baby pictures. Poor James, I thought, as he fumbled for his wallet. I really did take you out of your comfort zone, didn't I? Me with my weird parents, and us not being either Dharma or Greg. I dutifully inspected the sheaf of pictures. Nice baby. Looked like Winston Churchill, which is what all babies look like to me. Nice wife, wearing—I swear—an identical blue ruffled apron. I must have left it behind when I walked out. Good call, Corinna.

The waiter came with another menu for me. It was roughly the size of a small tablecloth and contained enough food to feed Baghdad. I gave it back with a sweet smile.

'You order,' I told James. I had no idea what any of the Italian names meant and a show of deference might get James to tell me what he wanted with more ease and less personal abuse, to which he always resorted when I disagreed with any of his plans. He didn't call it personal abuse. He called it a robust discussion. And, at that point, I always called it off.

James and the waiter went into conclave. Terms like tortellini and bottarga and involtini were tossed and caught.

I was very tempted to read my book but I was being polite so I looked around.

The Venetia was an old restaurant. Families occupied most of the big tables. It was such an institution that grandparents were dining with their grandchildren, all of whom had once cowered under the severe eye of that apostolic maitre d' and his shining glasses. The tables were crowned with snowy linen, all the cutlery was heavy silver, and a man going past with a shoulder-mounted rocket launcher proved just to be a functionary with a pepper grinder.

The walls had been frescoed some time ago—about 1930, I would have said—by someone who had had Piero della Francesca described to him but had never actually seen one of his paintings. They were pleasant, however. The Venetian theme was supported by several near-Canalettos and a huge model of a gondola in silver wire. I was running out of things to look at, so I turned back to James and the waiter. White smoke should have been issuing from the chafing dishes. They had made a decision. They both mopped their brows. Then the wine waiter made a suggestion, which James refuted hotly. Just as I was about to ask if either of them would like a carving knife, they came to an agreement. Seconds before my patience wore through. This continual fuss about the minutiae of a menu was one of the things, I remembered suddenly, that I had hated about James.

But now he was pleased and the waiter was bringing the entrée.

'This is ravioli,' he announced. 'Shredded duck and mushroom ravioli with a pomegranate and duck reduction. And I have scallops agnolotti. With it a glass of a nice white.'

I was flattered. A nice white cost more than fifty dollars a bottle. A very nice white was over a hundred. I cannot understand spending that much on wine, because to appreciate it you have to drink it and when you have done that, it is gone. But the ravioli was very tasty. I said as much.

'So, what can I do for you, James?' I asked as they took away the plates and poured us a glass of red wine. I knew this one. It was Chianti, but not the red ink I had drunk as a student. It was a light, fresh wine, a bit like Beaujolais nouveau. I liked it.

'Can't I just ask my ex-wife out to dinner?' he grumbled.

'Well, yes, I suppose so,' I agreed. 'But usually not to the Venetia.'

He did not reply and the waiter brought the next course. Quails for me. Yum.

'Quail with sage and ham stuffing, a brandy and redcurrant jus on a bed of polenta,' announced James, as proud as though he had shot the quails himself. 'And I have roast pork with Sicilian mint and brandied apples.'

A waiter delicately, reverently, placed various vegetables on our dish; tiny broccoli, itsy-bitsy squash and prenatal potatoes roasted with rosemary. This was a very good dinner and I did not want to quarrel with James yet. With him, there is always time. I tasted the quail. Gorgeous. The flesh was still pinkish and moist and the bite of the brandy was taking off the oiliness of the ham and sweetening the sage. Superb. I could talk a lot of small talk for a meal like this.

So I talked to James of many things, none of them of any consequence. I remarked on the warmth of the weather and the dryness of the season. I talked about the people in my building. I discussed the economic climate (no worse than usual). I asked after various ex-friends and we got into some gossip.

'Tom has left that dreadful woman,' he told me.

'What, Marielle? The French one?'

'No, she's after your time. He left Marielle after she hit him with the salver. At a work function. Scattered petits fours all over and nearly lost him his job. She went off with some artist, back to France. No, this was an Italian, I think, her name was Elizaveta.'

'What did she do?' I asked. I had loathed James' old school friend Tom. Not only was he an amazing wine bore—whole bodies of water had been put to sleep by Tom discoursing on

Burgundy, the navy could employ him to calm storms by talking to them about les grands vins—but he had tried to kiss me in the kitchen, and then told James that it was my idea. So I could understand Marielle belting him with a handy salver when the time was right. He did have a fascination with violent women, though. His first wife had chased him out of the house with a fish gutting knife at the end of a four-hour monologue on champagne and he hadn't stopped running until he found Marielle, who said it with salvers, so what had Elizaveta done?

'She soaked the labels off all his bottles of wine,' groaned James. 'And then she left.'

I was about to laugh and then realised how pretty a revenge this was. Most wine bottles are the same shape and size. How to tell the Grange from the Jamieson's? By the cork? All right for the old bottles but modern ones are much of a muchness. I supposed it would give Tom more time alone with his wine collection. I warmed to Elizaveta.

'Too bad, poor Tom. Whatever happened to Holly…no, Hollance—you remember, the entrepreneur who quoted George Bush saying the French don't know about entrepreneurs, they don't even have a word for it, and didn't know it was a joke?'

'Holliday,' said James. 'Strange you should mention him. He had a bit of a tragedy. His daughter ran away. Just vanished into thin air. Split up his marriage. He's gone to live in your building, that stupid Insulate.'

'Insula,' I corrected. 'And I like it there. It's an eccentric building, and it suits me.'

'You always were difficult,' he mumbled.

'Poor Holliday,' I said. 'No wonder he doesn't seem to be very friendly.'

'Used to be a big man in redevelopment too,' said James with a measure of sympathy. 'No firm'll touch him now, of course. He's a drunk. Used his super money to buy that place and his wife got the rest. As wives usually do.'

This was a dig at me and not true. The money to buy my apartment had come from my own funds and from a loan which

I had laboriously repaid. By, as it happens, the sweat of my brow and all by myself. I said so and James grunted.

Dessert was being served. Zabaglione for James, who loved its sweetness, and a selection of gelati for me. It was wonderful gelati, bearing only a family resemblance to that brightly coloured ice you buy from wandering vans in summer. An orange so orangey that it was definitive, a very creamy hazelnut and a sharp red raspberry. Somehow the chef had filtered out all the seeds and kept in all the flavour.

I supped and sighed.

'All right, James, tell me,' I said when I had scraped the plate and munched the little almond wafers. I was well fortified by a glass of muscat and a cup of cafe negro. James let out a waistcoat button and leaned forward, looking into my eyes.

'If you sold that apartment you could free up a lot of capital,' he said.

'True,' I agreed.

'I'm working on a Singapore deal and I'm willing to let you in on the ground floor,' he urged. 'We're taking over a Singapore bank. An amalgamation which will supply us with a lot of available money and allow us an entrée into a lot of areas.'

'James—' I temporised, but he never did let me finish a sentence.

'Property market's about to crash,' he said. 'That will be the time to invest in some buildings which are no longer functional and build new ones. Then we'll be in at the beginning when it swings up again.'

'And in the shit up to the neck if it swings down further,' I said. 'Sorry, James. No. Thank you for dinner,' I said, getting up.

'At least look at the prospectus,' he said, thrusting it into my hand.

'I certainly will. We must do this again sometime. Good night, James,' I said, and walked out with a large glossy folder which I intended to place neatly in the next bin I passed. James must be losing his grip. The idea that a smaller company can do anything but weep silently as a larger company has its way with its assets is ridiculous. And hadn't James learned that if a smaller player—like Australia—buys into, say, a big English insurance company, the person who is going to be taking in washing by New Year is not going to be the big English company. Asymmetric information. They know more about you than you know about them. The legal term, I believe, is 'screwed.'

I found that I had walked home still holding the prospectus so I dumped it on my table as I greeted the cats, changed my clothes, rang Meroe and reported all safe, and sat down to wait for Daniel.

Poor Holliday! What a terrible thing. I resolved to go and at least say hello to him tomorrow. To have a child die was bad, but to have her disappear—that must be appalling. I was very sorry for him. I didn't even know his first name.

Chapter Eight

Somewhere in the back of my mind was a line of poetry which went with something Daniel had said. 'I'll come to you at midnight.' I rummaged in the books until I found it. A worn poetry book from school. 'I love Duran Duran' on the cover. I flipped through it until I found the poem. I had loved it as an adolescent, for its black, romantic tragedy.

'The Highwayman' by Alfred Noyes. 'Look for me at midnight, I'll come to you at midnight, though Hell should bar the way' said the highwayman to his lover, and when it all went wrong and Bess had warned him with her death, they 'shot him down on the highway, down like a dog on the highway, and he lay in his blood on the highway, with a bunch of lace at his throat.'

Unexpected tears burned the back of my throat. Something was happening to me. I had felt more, and more mixed emotions in the last few days than I had in years.

I closed the book and put it away. I thought I could feel—Meroe would be able to tell me how—the raised level of tension in the building. One man mourning a lost daughter. Meroe and me worried about a madman. The usual troubles of young women from Kylie and Goss. I wondered how they were getting on with seducing Jon. Was that Kylie's project? I couldn't recall. I hoped Daniel was going to turn up soon, because I was falling asleep. I wasn't used to being awake at this hour.

He buzzed exactly at midnight and I went down, carrying the sack of bread. I had reverted to overseas travelling style and was wearing my keys and my money in a money-belt—so much easier than a purse and nothing to snatch. And it is always useful to have both hands free.

Daniel hugged me. I would never get used to this. I gave him the sack and he led me down the lane to where a bus was parked. It was larger than an ice-cream van, though it had the same sort of servery window, and seemed to contain a lot of people. Several of them were cutting up bread so I joined in. We appeared to be making good thick cheese sandwiches. The woman with the cheese smiled at me. She was wearing a blue uniform and had on a blue veil. A nun.

'I'm Sister Mary,' she said. 'Nice to meet you. Your first time?' she asked, sliding a pile of perfectly sliced cheese over to me.

I slapped the sandwiches together. I had made a lot of sandwiches in my time. I admitted it was my first mission.

'Everyone gets soup and a sandwich,' she said. 'Anyone who wants to talk to the lawyer, that's Phil.' A young man in a 'not in my name' t-shirt grinned at me. 'The nurse tonight is Mrs. Palmer.' A stout old lady gave me an assessing look. She was wearing a nurse's uniform as though she had been born in it. Upside-down watch and all. I would put my diagnosis in her hands any day. She was the sort of nurse that young doctors pray for, rely on and, if they have any gratitude, buy chocolates for. She radiated certainty.

'Our social worker and miracle worker is Jen,' continued Sister Mary. 'She can wedge a client into a lodging house with pure force of character. And the grace of God, of course. You and I are the hander-outers. Finished with the cheese? I've a whole plate of corned beef over there. Don't forget the pickles. Oh! You must be the baker!' she took my hand in both of hers. 'You make very good bread,' she told me. 'And to feed the poor is one of the corporeal works of mercy. God is watching and will reward your charity,' she added, and picked up a long ladle to stir the soup.

Jen was packing sandwiches into greaseproof paper and then into paper bags. She smiled sideways at me.

'If God is watching, so is the city council,' she told me. 'We have to be very careful where we stop and for how long. Keep Melbourne Clean would love to put us off the road. They've already tried to deregister the bus, claiming illegal modifications. That didn't work. Then they letterboxed all the businesses on our route trying to make them ban us from stopping. Then Phil told them that this was a public thoroughfare and therefore they couldn't stop us.'

'The old Queen's High Road argument,' said Phil. He seemed very young to be a lawyer. 'As long as we are keeping the peace and not causing a public nuisance we're in the clear.'

'The key to that being "public nuisance,"' put in Sister Mary. 'Our clients are, by nature, people with problems, and they do tend to drop litter and make noise. So we have taken to the back streets and we always go around with a garbage bag and clean up before we move on. So far, we've survived.'

'All ready?' asked Daniel at the wheel.

'All secure,' Sister Mary sang out. I wondered how old she was. It was always hard to tell with nuns. She was plump and rosy and clear skinned. Forty, perhaps?

The bus moved cautiously out of the lane and made a quiet left-hand turn. Apart from steadying the soup urns, everyone just sat still. Eyes were closed. Everyone was gathering their strength. It was like watching soldiers being transported into battle, without the CNN commentary. Daniel drove very nicely for someone trained to drive by an army.

We stopped in a byway just behind Swanston Street and there were already people waiting for us.

What shocked me most was how normal they looked.

I expected homeless people to look like—well, Jase, thin and dazed. I handed out my first cup of soup and a sandwich to a man in a flannel shirt who said, 'Ta, love,' in a strong English accent and who could have lived next door in any suburb where people garden or repair their own cars. The next was a thin girl on teetering heels followed by a sullen teenager with bad skin and blue hair. A young man took two sandwiches and two cups of soup and then the bundle on his back stirred and cried and I realised it was a baby.

Then they became a blur. Just hands; thin hands, pale hands, dark hands, old hands. I supplied them all. Some sat down in the little square to eat and drink and come back for a refill. Some walked off quickly, away from the crowd. One boy in a hat made of kitchen foil talked, all the time, to someone I couldn't see, begging to be allowed to eat. 'Come on, just a bit of soup, just a bite of sandwich?' he pleaded. 'I'm so hungry,' he said. I looked at Sister Mary.

'Poor boy,' she said. 'He's schizophrenic and the voices won't let him eat.'

'Why isn't he in hospital?' I asked.

'No room,' said Sister Mary. 'Most of them have been closed down and the land sold for apartments. The last government said that the mentally ill would be cared for by the community. Well, dear, this is how the community does it.'

'What about his parents?'

'He's big and strong and violent and they're afraid of him,' she said matter-of-factly. 'He's all right if he takes his medications but they make him feel slow and stupid so he doesn't take them and then he gets into this state. We'll see if Mrs. Palmer can help. She knows him.'

Mrs. Palmer called from the van: 'Kane?' and the boy in the shiny hat came to her as though drawn by a string. Mrs. Palmer looked at him severely through her glasses.

'Your medications?'

The boy fumbled in his pocket. Mrs. Palmer took the bottle and shook out several tablets. She held them on the palm of her hand as I had once held sugar for a nervous horse.

'Take them,' she ordered. 'Now. And your soup. Eat your sandwich. Then there will be chocolate.'

The voices, it appeared, liked chocolate. The boy gulped the tablets, drank the soup and ate his sandwich. Then Mrs. Palmer gave him a lump of honeycomb chocolate. He did not thank her but wandered away. She shrugged a shoulder.

'Sometimes it works,' she said. 'If they have had a stern authority figure in childhood. If I can catch him for the next few days we can stabilise him. The chocolate is a very useful gift. Donated from the manufacturers. So kind.'

'And tax-deductible,' I said. Once an accountant, always an accountant. Mrs. Palmer patted my shoulder. 'You're going to fit right in,' she told me.

Several people were waiting to talk to Mrs. Palmer and three wanted legal advice from Phil. In this street lighting, he looked about fifteen. I must be getting old. I made myself useful, going around with the garbage bag and collecting litter. We wouldn't want Keep Melbourne Clean to cavil at the mess we made feeding the homeless, would we? I didn't like them already.

The young man with the baby was talking to Sister Mary. A young woman was slumped against him. Her eyes were unfocused. 'We've been on the emergency list seven months,' he said. 'She's getting worse.'

'Book her in for a detox,' said Sister Mary gently. 'You can't keep sleeping in a car. It isn't good for the baby. What happened to the last money you saved for a deposit on a flat?'

The young man didn't reply. Sister Mary went into the van and handed over a big packet of nappies and a shirt. 'Wear the shirt to see the housing office,' she said. 'Better let Nurse look at the baby. See you next time, dear.'

'It's outrageous that he can't get somewhere to live,' I exploded. Sister Mary grabbed me and drew me aside.

'Not as easy as that,' she said. 'God help them. The wife is a heroin addict and will do anything for the man. He also uses drugs. Every time they get close to having enough money for a deposit, one or other of them spends it on a binge. If he books her into hospital to detox, he'll lose the money he gets from her prostitution. And if the welfare authorities notice that both of them are addicts and sleeping in a car, they'll take the baby into care, and the baby is the only thing—apart from drugs—that they care about.'

'That's disgusting,' I said. My righteous indignation vanished and I felt as if I had missed a step.

'Don't make hasty judgments,' she said severely. 'Take one case at a time, and never lose faith.'

'Yes, Sister,' I said meekly, quite out of my depth. I picked up more papers and we set off again. Some of the people waved. Most of them didn't. I didn't know what to feel so I sliced more bread and made more sandwiches as we chugged gently up the hill to the next stop, the Treasury Gardens. Home of the Big Day Out.

This was a Bad Night In. Someone was lying on the grass. Several people were gathered around him. Mrs. Palmer moved with that deceptive speed that nurses learn in their first year. They aren't actually running but they'd pass Cathy Freeman on the flat. I saw her shake her head.

'Nothing,' she said. 'Cold. Anyone know him?' she asked the crowd, who were melting away fast. Some were even running for the trees.

'Move the van around to the other side of the gardens, Daniel, or we'll lose all our clients,' said Sister Mary. 'I'll stay here and call an ambulance.' She hopped down, alone in the middle of the night, with perfect confidence.

'Would you like me to stay with you?' I offered.

She turned her blithe face to me. 'No need, dear. Nothing will harm me. And perhaps I can get in a few prayers before the ambulance arrives.'

When I looked back I saw her, kneeling down beside the dead man, folding her hands in prayer. What a woman. Jen shook her head.

'She's amazing, especially when you consider that she's nearly seventy,' she said. 'Here we go. I'll help with the soup. Quite a crowd tonight,' she said. 'They'll all be hyped because of the death. Stay calm,' she advised.

We were mobbed. People were yelling and someone was screaming. The bus actually rocked on its wheels. Daniel got out of the van and walked along until he was exactly in the middle of the crowd.

Then he slapped his hand on the side of the bus, so hard that there was an echo, and silence fell.

'We've got soup and sandwiches,' he said, loudly and slowly. 'And we've got advice. We'd love to help. But we can't hear you when you yell and there's always another place we can be. You are not the only hungry mouths in Melbourne tonight.'

The silence held. I handed out food and soup as fast as I could and Daniel marshalled the fed away from the hungry. An old man brought his sandwich back.

'It's got pickles,' he said. 'I can't eat pickles, they give me wind.'

'Cheese?' I asked.

'It gives me gripes,' he said.

'Sorry. It's cheese or corned beef, or just bread.'

'Gimme some cheese,' he grumbled.

My next client felt he had to apologise. 'Don't worry about him, Miss, he's always going crook,' said a middle-aged man. 'He was a doctor before the grog got him, they say. Ta,' he added, and took his food away.

It was horrible and fascinating and after a while it did begin to blur. Was it Flagstaff where I saw the two children, wrapped in the one blanket, asleep beside the doting father who had kidnapped them? Or maybe Treasury. A garden, certainly, which also had a camp of men brawling around an illegal fire, drinking something out of a can which reeked of methylated spirits. And why were so many of the homeless so young? Didn't they have homes to go to? What had happened to their parents? Didn't they care where that skinny trio, boys who could not have been over thirteen, spent their nights? Where did they spend their nights? And could I cope with the answer to that question?

And all the time I was watching Daniel as he moved among the lost and strayed, talking, comforting, giving out chocolate and hugs. The skinny girls loved him and would fall into his embrace as though he was the teddy bear which they should still have had. In three hours I was worn out, body and soul, when the van drove back into the side street to meet the next shift.

Daniel parked the bus and gave the keys to a bright, affable Maori some three metres tall with no neck, hands like hams and a blindingly white smile.

'This is Ma'ani,' said Daniel. 'Somehow there's never any big trouble on his shift. Mind you, we've had to reinforce the suspension,' he said. Ma'ani shook hands, engulfing my arm to the elbow. I assumed I would get the feeling back in the arm in due course. Of course there was no trouble on Ma'ani's watch. He would just sit on it.

'Come on, ketschele,' said Daniel. 'You're exhausted. Lean on me.'

'What about Sister Mary?' I asked, remembering we had left her with a dead body and just driven off.

'Cops'll take her back to the convent,' he said. 'Everyone knows Sister Mary. This way, Corinna. One foot in front of the other.'

That was all very well for him to say. By leaning heavily on Daniel I managed to get to my own building, key in the code, and go inside. There I slipped and would have fallen, except Daniel bore me up and turned my face into his chest.

'Just lean against the wall for a moment,' he said in a tightly controlled voice. I leaned. I opened my eyes. I was standing in a sea of blood. It was too much. I couldn't move. Horror really does root you to the spot, by the way, though I felt no urge to scream. Why scream? What had been killed? Where was the body? I couldn't see anything in the lobby but blood, which was dripping into the impluvium. It would kill the fish, I found myself thinking. And on the wall there was a legend, in that same unformed primary school writing. 'Death to the unchaste.' Blood was coagulating and dripping from the letters. Pure horror movie.

Daniel had crouched and stuck a finger into the red fluid. Then he sniffed.

'It's tomato sauce,' he said. 'Not blood, Corinna. Don't you faint on me now. Someone must have used a catering pack of the stuff. Let's go in through the bakery so we don't tread it all over.'

'What about the fish?' I asked idiotically.

'In the bakery,' said Daniel, leading me outside and round the corner, 'is a mop and a bucket and I am quite good at swabbing. And you will be quite good at sitting still until you feel a bit better. And then you can tell me what is going on in here. You've gone as white as milk, kitten,' he said affectionately. His affection was suddenly very important to me. 'Most people don't do that when they see spilt condiments.'

'It's the madman,' I told him.

I unlocked the shop where all was quiet. Daniel took a mop and bucket and after I had collected my thoughts I took another and joined him. We mopped for a while. Tomato sauce is ideal for mopping because, unlike milk, it doesn't leave a greasy afterstain. So much easier to deal with on tiles than, say, Aubusson rugs.

'The vinegar is probably good for the tiles,' he said, scooping the mess into his bucket. 'It's bringing the pattern up very nicely. Not much has gone into the pond and the fish seem to be eating it.'

'A new taste sensation. Tomato sauce flavoured fish food! Tell all your fishy friends!' I said, feeling much better and rather ashamed of myself. With a two-mop squad we got the hall clean and shining and Daniel was right, the tiles did look brighter.

'A perfect end to a perfect evening,' said Daniel as we emptied our buckets down the drain. I suddenly liked him very much.

We went up to my apartment, greeted the cats, and put on some Ovaltine. There are days when Ovaltine is the only answer. Horatio and the Mouse Police were occupying the fluffy blue mink blanket which I bought for myself and Daniel gently dislodged them and wrapped it around me.

'Now,' he said. 'Tell me about the madman.'

I began with Mistress Dread and proceeded through the Lone Gunmen, the increasingly specific letters and the use of the real names, even of Meroe who hasn't used her birthname for twenty years.

'Hmm,' said Daniel. 'Temptresses and unchaste women and witches. Not a man who has much time for the female sex, eh? Knows far too much about the tenants of this building. Older than twenty-five, owns an iMac with a wobbly feed in his printer and a serious down on all women.'

'There must be thousands of them,' I sighed.

'At least,' said Daniel. 'Now I understand why you nearly fainted when you saw all that tomato sauce. This lunatic is in the building and you must feel unsafe here. Drink your Ovaltine,' he instructed. I drank. It tasted lovely. I yawned. He noticed. 'Therefore, with your permission, I shall trespass on your couch for the night. I need to talk to you, Corinna, but it can wait until morning. Go to bed, now, ketschele,' he said. 'I'll be here.'

I managed to brush my teeth and wash my face and release my hair from its clasp. Then I did as he said. I climbed into my voluminous nightie and I went to bed, and the last thing I saw was Daniel tucking me in and kissing me on the cheek.

I woke up feeling wonderful. Horatio was purring into my ear, always a charming sensation. I was in my own bed and I had had a nightmare about blood. Probably due to that Polish film festival I had gone to years ago. They had a film called *Blood*. And another called *Snakes*. I can't now recall why going to them seemed like such a good idea at the time. But they had marked me for life.

Then I remembered. Not a dream. The Soup Run, the dead man, the blood all over the lobby. Except it was tomato sauce.

I needed to get up and find someone rational to talk to, rather than myself. I wasn't making anything like enough sense. I got up and, escorted by Horatio, made it to the bathroom (he always sits politely outside as he does not care for shower spray). I dried myself and dressed in a tracksuit and went into the kitchen, because I could smell coffee. If anyone wants to test whether I am actually dead, let them brew coffee near me. Strong espresso coffee, for preference. If there is not a twitch or a moan, if there is no reaction at all, then they should order the wreaths and book the gravedigger.

The kitchen contained not only coffee, but Daniel, who had gone out to buy croissants and had even taken the butter out of the fridge. I nominated him for sainthood on the spot and grabbed for a cup of the life-giving fluid. He did not say a word but smiled at me and pushed over the apricot jam.

That's when I knew I was in love. I had never met anyone who preferred silence in the morning. Morning was the time James always chose for his robust discussions. It's amazing I stayed with him as long as I did, really. Daniel took his coffee out onto the balcony where Horatio was discussing a saucer of milk. Not a sound apart from a faint lapping. I ate and drank and recovered my sanity.

After half an hour, I said, 'You can come in now,' and he did.

'I don't like mornings,' said Daniel, sitting down and pouring more coffee. 'I thought that you might feel the same.'

'You are unique, and also you make good coffee,' I told him. 'Did you sleep well?'

'Until I woke unable to breathe and found that I had Heckle on one side of my blanket and Jekyll on the other, pinning me down. They are surprisingly heavy, cats. I struggled out and sent them down into the bakery to do an honest night's work. They have presented me with three rats and seven mice and I have rewarded them with Kitty Dins,' said this paragon among men. 'Naturally I also fed Horatio, who ate his breakfast and retired again. Then I thought that we could do with a reward as well and went out for some croissants. I hope you like them au naturel, rather than au beurre.'

'My favourite,' I said, truthfully.

'Mine too. I used to get them from an artisan boulangerie in the Quartier Latin. A beautiful girl used to serve in his shop. If she hadn't been so cheerful at that hour I would have tried to further our acquaintance. But she was, so I stuck to just buying her grandfather's bread, which was very good. I got quite friendly with him. He was an absolute bear in the mornings.'

'Do you have to do anything today?' I asked.

'We have to talk to your police officer about the tomato sauce,' he said. 'Or you do, perhaps. It might be better if you left me out of it.'

'Yes, she doesn't seem to be one of your biggest fans,' I remarked. 'Any idea why?'

'She thinks I am a suspicious character,' he said. 'And so I am. No car registration. No previous connections. No house purchase. Not on the books, and that always makes police-men edgy. You also need to consult your residents' committee's books,' he added. I decided not to pursue the mystery of why Lepidoptera White didn't like Daniel.

'I do? Why?'

'It's Sunday,' he pointed out. 'They will probably all be home. You want to know how the names of the owners of the flats are listed. Did Meroe put her legal name on her sale notice? What about those two skinny girls with the many-coloured hair? Is that, in fact, where Mr. Nutcase is getting his information?'

'A good notion,' I said. 'I'll go and see Taz as soon as the day is aired, he has all their stuff on his computer. I think they picked Taz to go on the committee because he was the only computer literate person in the building. Rather Taz than Mrs. Pemberthy,' I added. 'You remember her.'

'The lady with the blue-rinse hair and the horrible little dog? And I think she had a husband, somewhere in the background,' he said.

'That's what everyone remembers about poor Mr. Pemberthy. All right, Taz and the cops. Now, what did you want to speak to me about?'

'Something so serious that it needs fresh air. Let's pack a little picnic—I bought a pain au chocolat each—and the rest of the coffee and go up to the garden.'

'All right,' I said. 'You take Horatio and I'll take the food.'

I poured the coffee into the thermos and we went up in the lift to the garden. It was cooler this morning. Trudi was out and about, snipping off dead heads. I left Daniel and Horatio and went over to talk to her. I had forgotten Trudi in my count of possibly unchaste women.

Trudi is Dutch, down to earth and sixty-five. She has never really got the hang of English. She has those crow's feet possessed by people who stare over great distances while fighting a losing battle with nature, like sailors, cricketers, golfers and farmers. I have never seen her dressed in anything other than a pair of stout boots, jeans and a jumper; cotton for summer and wool for winter. To judge by her clothes, her favourite colour is blue. Like her eyes. Her hair is cropped short, probably so that she can get the mud out easily. And she grows really lovely flowers. She lives just under the garden, in 8A, which is Ceres, goddess of fertility and mistress of the corn.

'The roses have been wonderful this year,' I said as an opening gambit.

'Ya,' she said. 'But the lilac is not so good and so dry, the grass withers. Rain soon, perhaps.'

There didn't seem to be a polite way to say this so I just came straight out with it.

'Trudi, several of us have had strange letters lately.'

'Calling you whore?' she asked, head on one side like a bird.

'Among other things, yes,' I admitted.

She pulled a familiar letter out of her pocket. It was considerably marked with honest toil, but it accused Gertrud Maartens of being an unchaste woman.

'He is wrong,' she said. 'We are not whores. Also this is not my name.'

'Not at all?' I asked. This was the first time that Mr. Bible Class had made a mistake. Trudi shrugged and stomped an unwary snail.

'Not for many years. I married once, now not married. My husband went off with his secretary. Now, she was whore. Me, no. You want the letter?'

'I do seem to be collecting them, yes.'

'They paint on my pots. Also they steal my insecticide. Tell the cops,' advised Trudi firmly, deadheading a rose with unusual firmness.

I took the letter back to Daniel and Horatio, put it in my pocket, and ate a pain au chocolat, probably the most luscious sweet bread ever invented. Though I do put in a bid for my date and walnut loaf. Daniel poured me more coffee. I was now as awake as I was going to get. Gusts of rose scent blew over us. Horatio went stalking off into the undergrowth.

'Tell me,' I demanded.

He seemed unwilling to begin. He averted his face, allowing me to notice that he had a five o'clock shadow and very well shaped ears. I took his hand.

'Someone's killing the drug addicts in Melbourne,' he said. 'There are too many for them to be accidents or coincidence. You saw the latest last night.'

'And the police are investigating,' I prompted.

'And they can't find out what's going on,' he said with a flash of anger. 'Because drugs are illegal, the police and the junkies are at odds. Junkies don't tell cops anything. Junkies are, in any case, not reliable people. They'll even leave their lover, their best friend, to die alone rather than stay in a house and have to explain when the ambulance arrives. You saw how they melted away when that death was discovered. Few people take drugs alone. Someone was with that boy when he injected poison into his veins.'

'And you've been asking around,' I said.

'I know most of the homeless who stay in the city,' said Daniel. 'They aren't all junkies. In fact not that many are junkies. They are alcoholics or speed heads or they are victims of circumstance. Runaways who think that living on the street will be cool. Runaways who can't stand their parents anymore. Kids out of foster homes. Abused ones and raped ones and don't cares who are made to care. Some are actually thrown out. Most exist from mate's place to mate's place, never actually sleeping out, because it's so dangerous. As long as you have a cup of coffee you can sit in some of the chain restaurants all night.'

I felt that he was getting off the topic. 'Your point being?'

'That someone knows something,' he said, balling his hand into a fist. 'There aren't that many dealers on the street and everyone knows who they are. They don't belong to any one ethnic group, no race has a monopoly on bastardry. The kids talk about the man in the red Porsche who supplies all the drugs; he's a myth, although some were boasting a week or so ago that they'd stolen his car. There are a lot of fairytales on the street.'

'Why do you think you can solve this mystery?'

'Because they all know me, and they all trust me,' he said. This was patently true. 'And if we don't find out and stop it, then more will die. That boy was only seventeen and now he'll never know what being eighteen feels like. Will you help me?'

'I don't see how I can,' I said honestly. 'But I'll try.'

'And I,' he said, 'will help you find your madman, and then we will have words.'

I felt the strength of his grip and saw the ripple of muscle along his shoulders and cheered up. If Daniel wished to exchange views on whores with our madman, Mr. Nutcase would know that he had been in a robust discussion.

Chapter Nine

Daniel went away on business of his own, promising to be back after five. And just what was Daniel's business? A cop? Probably not. A crook? Perhaps. He would tell me in time. Taz wasn't awake but Gully answered the door when I rang at Hephaestus after noon. He was the neatest of the Lone Gunmen, which wasn't saying much. He waved me in past a huge heap of laundry. Heaps of jocks, socks and t-shirts were topped with aged hole-studded work pants.

'Sorry. Rat's Mum is coming to pick up the washing,' he said. 'What can I do for you, Corinna?'

'I need to check the residents' committee's list of owners,' I said. 'And I need to do it now. Can you help me? There will be Arctic Death in it for you when the liquor shop opens,' I hinted. He brightened right away.

'This way, and we'll just find it. You want a printout?'

I nodded. Gully sat down at a terminal—the apartment was lined with terminals—and found the right disc. Then there was that brief magician's flourish of fingers which marks the really experienced geek, and a printer began to whirr. I grabbed the paper. I was there and so was Trudi, but under her present name, Johanson. Meroe was listed as Meroe and the flat in which Kylie and Goss lived was under Kylie's father's name. Wherever Mr. Fruitcake had got his information, it hadn't been here.

'Thanks, Gully,' I said, and rose to go. Then I had a thought. 'If you wanted to find out what people were called twenty years ago, how would you do it?'

'From publicly available information? No hacking?'

'No hacking. This man is just about able to press "enter." If that.'

'I don't know,' said Gully. 'I'll have to think about it. Ask Taz, perhaps. Can I get back to you?'

'A six-pack for any helpful leads,' I told him, and went out. Although Hephaestus wasn't actually dirty, because the boys had a cleaner in once a week, it smelled too strongly of old pizza, ancient tacos and long worn sneakers for comfort.

When I got out into the street Senior Constable White was just about to buzz my buzzer. I grabbed her arm and she shook me off.

'I have to talk to you,' I said. 'Last night—'

'Can we get off the street?' she said. She had a plastic folder in her arms.

'Yes, of course, come into the lobby. When I came in last night—'

'At what time?' she asked.

'Four a.m.'

'Were you alone?'

'No,' I said. I lost any urge to volunteer further information. Ms. White was not in a merry mood and she was snarling at me as though I had personally offended her. This could go one of two ways, I realised. I could retreat into just answering the question and thus possibly leave out some useful fact which might help find Mr. Nutcase. She, sensing that I was holding back, would become more aggressive. Making me more defensive. And so on. Or I could try to break through this formal dance and make some sense of the situation. I shut the door behind us and sat down on the corner of the impluvium. The fish, I was glad to see, were still alive and the water was clear. Their recent food supplement had not disagreed with them so far.

'Shall we start again?' I asked, making my voice slow and gentle. 'We seem to have got off on the wrong foot. Hello, Senior Constable White, I'm so glad to see you, I'm scared and so is every other woman in this building and we hope that you can help us. We have a madman and he's escalating.'

She stared at me for a full minute. As the seconds ticked past, I wondered if you could be arrested for being too friendly to a police officer. She had tired brown eyes with shadows under them and a disciplined mouth, tucked in firmly at the corners like a hospital bed. Then, at last, when I had begun to think of who I could call for a bail application, Senior Constable White sighed, almost smiled, and took a deep breath.

'Tell me all about it,' she said, sinking down on the edge of the fishpond.

'When I came in last night in company with Daniel Cohen, after going out on the Soup Run and meeting Sister Mary—what a woman!'

'So she is,' agreed Lepidoptera.

'Someone had splashed what I thought was blood all over the lobby. Daniel found that it was actually tomato sauce. There must have been litres of it. Written on the wall in what I thought was blood was "Death to the unchaste." In that same childish hand-writing, I might add. I know you're going to be cross with us but we mopped up the sauce and cleaned off the inscription.'

'I would be cross but I'm too tired and in any case I might have done the same if it was my place,' she said. 'Lucky it was you who found it and not, say, one of those girls.'

'My thought exactly. Or Trudi, who has a bad heart, or Mrs. Pemberthy, who would still be having hysterics. It was obviously meant to be found on Sunday morning when our more respectable tenants go to church. It really did look ghastly.'

'I'm sure it did,' she said soothingly. Senior Constable White would have seen enough real blood to fill the lobby and probably wouldn't have turned a hair.

'Then when I talked to Trudi this morning, she gave me a letter which she'd received. The same as the others. If you'd like to come to my apartment I'll show you the others.'

'Purpose of visit,' she said briskly.

When she was seated at the kitchen table I fetched the folder and added Trudi's letter.

'Sorry about the muddy fingerprints,' I said. 'Trudi's a gardener. But the strange thing is that she says she hasn't been Gertrud Maartens for years. Neither has Meroe been Miriam Kaplan. I checked the list of tenants on the residents' committee records and the two girls aren't listed at all. The apartment belongs to Kylie's father, of course.'

'Strange,' said Senior Constable White. She had accepted my offer of a cup of coffee and a coffee scroll and now she made up her mind to share some information. 'Here's Mistress Dread's letter,' she said, opening her plastic folder. 'I'm not showing you this and I'm sure that you will never refer to it outside this room,' she added firmly.

'Scout's honour,' I agreed. The letter was the usual script and layout. It was addressed to Anthony George Davis. Well, that answered that question.

'How long has Ms. Dread been, well, Ms. Dread?' I asked.

'More than ten years,' said the police officer.

'So what do you make of this?' I asked. 'Has Mr. Nutcase got the info from an old source? Passports, perhaps?'

'Maybe, but I don't think that it's a mistake,' she said, sipping coffee. 'I think this is a mind game. You have to forget everything you ever saw on *Silence of the Lambs* and read in Patricia Cornwell. Serial killers aren't masterminds. They're nasty little mean-minded bastards with dreams of blood. They act out of obsession, not out of deep planning, and they don't leave Agatha Christie clues. I've met several and they're as boring as people who describe the tuppeny Norwegian unfranked blue stamp, except that they're talking about corpses. That's all they think about. Power. Their plots keep them warm at night and their secret obsession makes them think they're better than anyone else. They think they're superman. That's why they fall apart when they're caught. Their whole world is shattered. Their private scenario has been changed. They can't take it. This fruitcake is behaving like a stalker. By coming up with your old identities he's saying "I know all about you, you can't escape me, ha ha." The nasty little shit. Any more coffee in that pot?'

'Plenty.' I poured and she sipped.

'The trouble is that there's not a lot we can do,' she said. 'I'm being frank with you now, Ms. Chapman. So far all we've got is a lot of letters, which would be the basis of a charge of threat to kill, and some property damage by tomato sauce. In a magistrates' court that would get someone with a good solid psych report a bond.'

'That's outrageous!' I exclaimed. She shook her head.

'No one's been harmed,' she said. 'Threats break no bones. I'll put the letters into forensic but I doubt they'll find anything. If you get another, don't handle it, slide it into a plastic sleeve. Then we might be cooking if we can find the owner of the fingerprints, if there are any fingerprints, and even the lone loony these days knows to wear gloves.'

'So, what do you suggest?' I asked. 'We just wait until someone gets murdered?'

She shrugged. 'You need to stay alert but not alarmed, as the prime minister says. So far this nutter hasn't hurt anyone. I'll keep looking,' she said. 'I've put out a call for known nutters. But what with the heroin deaths and the Keep Melbourne Clean people and the press, we haven't got a lot of people to spare. I'm only on this because my sergeant doesn't like me. He doesn't want me on the heroin task force so he's sent me to investigate this to keep me out of his hair.'

'I didn't think there were still bosses like that,' I sympathised.

'Sure are. Well, thanks for the coffee. I'm going to talk to all the other women in this building and make sure everyone knows they're in danger. A bit of a warning goes a long way, I always think.'

She got up to leave. She hadn't said anything about Daniel. I had a question.

'Did the lab find out what was killing the junkies?'

'Yes,' she said, after taking a moment to underline that she was imparting privileged information. 'No rat poison, no speed. Just pure heroin. Far too pure. Something like thirty per cent. Known in the trade as a hot shot. Too rich for our junkies' blood. Our street heroin at the moment is about three per cent. The rest of the mob is out rousting every informer we've got, trying to find out if someone is selling it or whether we've got a revenge murderer or the Lord knows what. One thing at least on this case, the company is better.'

'Thank you,' I said, and saw her out.

So, the police weren't going to be able to do much about our madman. We might have to do it ourselves. Now I was bound by a promise to myself. I had to go and see Holliday, who might even remember me, and at least say hello.

I was not looking forward to this at all.

I searched around for a present, found a really good fruit cake and sliced it. It is made by a friend in Shepparton. She always stuffs it full of the rarer dried fruits, like dried cherries and cantaloupe, as well as the thin connecting fabric of butter and flour which binds it together. I decided to call on the Professor first for some words of wisdom. When I got to Dionysus I found that he already had visitors. I was about to excuse myself when he invited me in in such a marked manner that I went. Never argue with a man carrying a stick.

Oh dear. Mr. and Mrs. Pemberthy and Traddles. They were sitting on the Roman couches as though they were missionaries who had strayed into a cannibal convention. Mrs. P was scraggy, blue-haired and vehement. She wore bright pink lipstick mostly on her mouth and had the terribly white teeth of one who soaks them at night. Traddles was a silky terrier so fat that his feet hardly touched the ground. He had bald patches, a nasty temper and a disapproving manner. Other than that he was a nice little doggy. Mr. P was a dim shadow. He was balding and self effacing. I believe he had once been a lay preacher and something in a bank but had retired long ago. Spiritually, he still wore a grey cardigan with leather patches on the sleeves.

A nice congregation to walk into on a Sunday. I gave the Prof a reproachful glance and he smiled his Juvenalian smile.

I set down my cake plate and said hello to Traddles, who snapped at me and missed.

'Oh, it's you, Corinna,' said Mrs. Pemberthy without any pleasure. 'Did that insolent policewoman visit you as well?'

'Senior Constable White, yes, I spoke to her,' I said. 'Why do you say "insolent"? She seems to know what she's doing and this is a nasty situation.'

Mrs. Pemberthy reached over her shoulder without looking and Mr. Pemberthy put a fresh linen handkerchief into her hand. He never raised his eyes, though occasionally I could see his sad grey moustache whiffling.

'She said that someone was sending letters alleging unchastity to the women in this building,' said Mrs. Pemberthy. 'No one has ever suggested that I was unchaste!'

'I'm not sure that anyone's said that to Trudi either,' I said. 'Or Meroe or the girls or me. It's some madman. We need to be on our guard. That's what Ms. White was doing here.'

'I'm leaving,' she shrilled. 'If it wasn't for Traddles I'd be leaving at once. He so hates being moved to kennels, poor dear. They don't understand him. No one understands him but his mother. Doesn't she, my darling?' There followed some ritual acts of dog worship which even Traddles seemed to find embarrassing. He wriggled out of her perfumed embrace. Mrs. P continued, 'I'm not staying here where someone can say such a thing about me!'

'Now, dear,' soothed Mr. Pemberthy. 'You know you're not well.'

'Peripheral neuritis,' said Mrs. Pemberthy proudly, as though this conferred some credit on her choice of disease. 'My specialist is quite puzzled. He says I'm an interesting case. But I'm leaving this place. No, we shall sell this apartment and find another in a nice new building where such things do not happen. And that's my last word on the matter!' she said, and Mr. Pemberthy said, 'Yes, dear.'

One got the impression that he said that a lot. Mrs. P rose and left. She trailed a cloud of very expensive perfume, in which she must have been bathing. Traddles had a go at my ankle as he left, and missed again—his aim was off. Then Mr. P, refusing to look at either of us. Poor man. He probably liked it here and didn't want to move. It didn't sound like he was going to get a lot of choice in the matter, though. What Mrs. P said clearly went.

'Phew,' said Professor Dion.

'Phew,' I agreed. 'Have some fruit cake. I'm just off to say hello to a man whose daughter ran away and was never found and I was hoping for some pointers.'

'That would be dreadful,' he said, stroking his neat, trimmed beard. 'Death is one thing, it's final, you know the person has gone and is not coming back and therein lies the wound. But just run away, might be alive, might be dead. Uncertainty has nothing going for it.'

'Amen,' I agreed. 'Take some cake. I've got to go and see poor Holliday, and he probably isn't hungry.'

'It's another of the corporeal works of mercy,' he said, sounding a little like Sister Mary. 'How did the Soup Run go?'

'Grand guignol,' I said. 'All it needed was gas lights and it would have been an engraving by Doré. I never thought such things happened in a civilised city.'

'Civilisation is as thin as a cigarette paper,' he told me. 'The Romans knew that, and the Greeks. We have forgotten it.'

'Indeed,' I said, and went off to Holliday's apartment, Daphne. I rang the bell. The door opened.

'Hello,' I said. 'You might remember me—Corinna? My ex-husband James mentioned you when I was dining with him last night.'

He was a fattish man, dark shadows under his eyes, heavy alcoholic breath at two in the afternoon. Clearly after his daughter had run away he had hit the bottle and it was now hitting back. He blinked.

'James' wife? Aren't you called Yvonne?'

'No, that's his present wife. I'm the original. I live here. James said you had moved in and I thought I'd come and say hello.'

'Hello,' he said vaguely.

The door was open so I went in.

The walls were flanked with boxes. I knew how depressing all those boxes were. You stacked and put away and stacked and put away and at the end of a fifteen hour unpacking spree, there were just as many boxes as you had had at the beginning and you still couldn't find (1) the floor or (2) the frying pan. You could always detect the recently unpacked by the way they refused a packing box at the supermarket. The sort of reaction you expect from a shipwreck survivor asked for some helpful comments on tides. It had only taken me three days to unpack when I moved in, because I had an unpacking party and laid on quite a lot of wine. Some of the things were later found in interesting places—I still don't know who put my envelopes in the freezer—but at the end you can do a merry box flattening dance and get rid of the buggers along with all those empty bottles.

Holliday had unpacked as far as finding the scotch, a glass, a packet of cigarettes, an ashtray and the TV. One armchair was set in front of it. I turned another the right way up and sat down on it.

'I don't even know your first name,' I said. Those cigarettes were beckoning. Come to us, they said. You remember us.

I did remember them. My love affair with tobacco had been long and passionate. Holliday stopped standing by the door and slumped back into his armchair. His hand groped for the remote. Then he spoke. 'Andy,' he said, in answer to my question, which had crept its way along his synapses until it found one which still fired.

'Give me a smoke,' I said. Oh, Corinna, called my conscience. You have failed! 'And tell me. Are you happy here just drinking yourself to death, or would you like some food?'

'Food?'

I sat still and smoked that cigarette down to its butt and I felt wonderful. Slightly dizzy, but wonderful. Then I went into the kitchen, which was bare of any comforts but the drinker's friends, Berocca and coffee. Instant coffee. A big box on the floor marked 'kitchen' yielded five shirts, a book on regional wines and a handful of cutlery. One under it gave me a saucepan, a tin of gourmet game soup and a box of matches from The Club. I didn't want to know what sort of club it was. I made the soup according to the label and then rummaged for a cup or bowl. I found three in the parlour in a box marked 'misc.' Andy Holliday hadn't moved a muscle.

When I came back I put the mug in his hand and said, 'Drink the soup,' and he drank the soup. Possibly I was copying my manner from Mrs. Palmer, a strong-minded nurse who definitely had the Prof's *auctoritas*. I made him drink some more soup and then have a cup of coffee with a piece of fruit cake. He was starting to sober up.

His hand crept to his pocket and he showed me a picture of a sharp-featured girl in disco gear. She was very blonde with narrow eyes and strong bones. She was tickling Andy Holliday with a long feather and laughing. Andy looked much younger, almost as I remembered him.

'That's her,' he said. I had never heard a voice so defeated.

'What's her name?' I asked.

'Cherie. She was Daddy's darling,' he said. 'And then she ran away.'

'How old is she here?' I asked.

'Fourteen. That was three years ago. I looked for her. I'm still looking. She went off at night without leaving a note and—and…' He dried up. 'My wife didn't believe her, you see, Tina wouldn't believe what Cherie said about her uncle. And it didn't seem possible, did it, such a nice man, so fond of children? I told her I didn't believe her and she ran away and she never came back.'

He started to cry.

'Was it true?' I asked.

He wiped at his streaming nose. I gave him a tissue. 'Oh yes, it was true all right. He was caught molesting his other nieces—my brother had enough sense to believe what his daughter said and he caught him at it, actually caught him in the act—and now he's in jail and I hope he never comes out because if he does I will kill him. And his sister, my wife, Cherie's mother, for God's sake, she stuck by him, said it was because of their own father. I divorced the stupid bitch. But my innocent daughter, my darling Cherie, she went away and I never saw her again.'

'And how have you tried to find her?'

'I was on *Australia's Most Wanted*,' he said with faint pride. 'I paid a fortune to a private detective but these kids never get onto the records and half of them use false names. He came up empty, said he'd be wasting my money if he went on. Nice guy, ran an agency called "The Open Eye." He said she wasn't dead, at least no body matching hers had been found, she was not an unclaimed body or in hospital under her own name, and hadn't applied for a passport or got a learner's permit. I was going to teach her to drive,' he mourned.

He lit another smoke from the butt of the previous one and I didn't. My conscience faded out, nagging as she went.

I wasn't going back to being an addict. I merely liked the occasional taste.

'So you're just going to sit here and sink into melancholy,' I commented as lightly as I could. I couldn't imagine what this sort of pain was like. I had lost Horatio for two days once, when he got shut in a house which was being renovated, and I had suffered agonies imagining him dead or maimed. That had only lasted two days. This had lasted three years.

'The guy said that she was most probably in or around the city, not in St. Kilda or in a brothel or massage parlour, where they have to keep records. So I'm going to put out posters. When I get a little more organised.' He looked around helplessly at the mountains of boxes.

'I'll see if I can send you some help,' I said. Meroe would be perfect at unpacking, divining what was in each box by touching it. I was sure that I could ask her for some help for this human wreck. The karmic benefits would be huge.

'And when you are ready to issue your poster,' I said, 'I know what you have to say on it.'

'Thanks, Yvonne,' he said sleepily. 'Give my regards to James.'

I let myself out. At least he had coffee and fruit cake for breakfast. I acquitted Andy Holliday of being our nutcase. He was in too much pain and he was far too drunk to compose letters. Also, he had no computer and James had said that Andy had been sacked, therefore no workplace with an iMac and a wobbly laser printer. Just another person to add to the free bread list. But I did know, with absolute certainty, what message would bring Cherie Holliday out of whatever hole she had hidden in. And that was at least one useful deed for the day.

Meroe opens the Sibyl's Cave on Sundays, so the Christians don't have it all their own way. I stopped to stroke Belladonna on the way in. She is so black that if it wasn't for a faint thinning of fur around the eyes and the outlines of the lips, she would look like a cat composed entirely of licorice. She greeted me politely and scooted back inside as rain began to fall. This would please Trudi and might save the grass.

'I thought witches liked thunderstorms,' I commented as Belladonna dived straight under the table which Meroe uses as a counter. The black cat packed herself into the corner, tail to the wall, and sat down on her paws.

'Witches, yes, witches' cats, no. Bella is sensitive to vibrations and storms release a lot of them. Look at the poor little creature's whiskers quivering!'

Meroe dropped a fold of her long woollen shawl over Belladonna. Belladonna didn't object. This meant that she really was scared. Most cats like to see what is going on.

The shop smelt gorgeous, a rich, oriental fragrance new to me. I asked.

'It's frankincense and myrrh,' said Meroe. 'I needed to be supported in my spirits, after such a shock. How went the Soup Run with the tall, dark and handsome one?'

'It was very strange and will need some thought before I can really tell you what it was like. Daniel is lovely and he doesn't talk in the morning.'

'Now there's a match made in heaven,' said Meroe. She has seen me in the morning. And tried to carry on a conversation with me.

We had a lot to talk about. I relayed what Senior Constable White had said about Mr. Fruitloop and told her about the tomato sauce in the lobby.

'Yes, much anger and bitterness and a need for power games. Let us see if we can devise one for him,' she said. 'Think about it, Corinna. We need to go on the offensive.'

'I'll think about it. Meanwhile, we have a case in need of care under our own roof. Poor Andy Holliday, who has lost his daughter, is drinking himself to death in the middle of a pile of boxes approximately the size of Mt. Kosciuszko. This should be a group effort. I don't want him fixating on me as his new career. Can you help?'

'Certainly,' she said. 'I didn't get many presents as a child and I love unpacking. What if he gets his daughter back and it's too late, his liver has finally given up the ghost? He needs some vitamins and maybe a talisman and certainly some incense to cleanse his vibrations. I agree with you that we should do it together. And you are sure that he needs help. We don't want to make the Mr. Pemberthy mistake again.'

I agreed. We had been sorry for the downtrodden Mr. P until he told us he liked being a slave and showed us—erk—his slave collar and frilly apron.

'Good. When?'

'And maybe it would be useful to do the ritual of return,' she said. 'But the ingredients are expensive.'

'When we sober him up a little. Tomorrow, Meroe?'

'After you have cleaned your bakery,' she said. 'Come and get me and I will close early. This sounds like a job for a practising witch.'

I couldn't have agreed more. Since a practising witch is as good as anyone else at finding the frying pan. Better, perhaps.

Chapter Ten

Meroe had reminded me that I was going to get up at four a.m. and make bread so I went back to the Prof, whipped us up an omelette aux fairly fines herbes, since there was no tarragon but plenty of parsley, and sat drinking wine and looking out of his windows at the city as the sun began to go down. It was very peaceful. I told Professor Dion all about poor Andy Holliday and he suggested that I send him down to sit with the Prof while Meroe and I attacked the unpacking.

'There is, at least, a comfortable couch to recline upon while drinking. In fact, that couch was designed by people who truly did like a drink—and perhaps he might like to talk,' he said. 'I can always listen. And I can't help with the unpacking. I have enough trouble finding my glasses. Though my leg is really much better now.'

I thought this was a wonderful idea, kissed his cheek, and went back to my place to feed the cats and assemble the makings of tomorrow's bread. Everything appeared to be in order, though I admit I was listening for footsteps following me on the stairs. No letter under the door and no tomato sauce in the lobby, all to the good. I sat down in my parlour to read a few instructive chapters of Jade Forrester and finish a box of chocolates I had started before Easter. Last year.

I don't eat a lot of chocolates.

The first thing anyone thinks about a fat woman is, disgusting creature, I bet she stuffs herself with Mars Bars before breakfast and eats her own weight in chocolate every day and we don't, generally. My mantra is that I am fat because I am fat and there is not a lot I can do about it. And I have the example of Gossamer and Kylie always before me. I could not get that thin if I starved for ten years, and that is a fact. We are famine survivors, we fat women, and ought to be valued for it. We must have been very useful when everyone else collapsed with starvation. We would have been able to sow the crop, feed the babies and keep the tribe alive until spring came. If you breed us out, what will you do when the bad times come again? At the very least, you could always eat us. I reckon I'd feed a family of six for a month. Properly pickled, salted and cooked, of course.

There was a reason why the oldest depiction of a human is the Venus of Willendorf, a huge fat woman. We were genetically designed to keep your tribe alive so that the thin people could be born. So be nice. Or at least shut up about it. Every time I turn on a TV I see (1) a car ad and then (2) some simpering female telling me how easy it is to lose weight by some new means and how wonderful she feels now she's thinner, just send lots of money. Then I snort and turn on cable. If you want to believe some lies, believe the one about how getting a new car will make you a fantastic driver and instantly attractive to tall willowy women in bikinis. It's probably more true.

I had set my alarm clock and was now trying to convince my weekend self that the carnival was over and that eight o'clock was a good time to go to bed when I saw a man-sized shadow at my window and froze.

Then I unfroze. I am not going to become a prisoner of fear in my own home, I told myself sternly in my Nurse Palmer voice. I seized the breadknife and threw back the curtain. My heart was hammering. My feet were strangely unwilling to move. But I was resolved. If Mr. Fruitcake was on the balcony, he was shortly about to be off the balcony.

Fortunately, it was Daniel. Even more fortunately, I didn't stab him.

He was standing on the balcony and the wind blew his coat open, like wings. Street light and shadow made his face a mask. In the darkness, there was the glint of eyes. For a moment I could hear the rustling of a dark angel's wings. I felt like Glory in *Buffy the Vampire Slayer*—'Did anyone order an apocalypse?'

Ah, oh, but he was attractive. I now knew how iron filings felt when a magnet came past. Drawn. Dragged. But I was presently angry, as an alternative to being terrified.

'What are you doing there?' I yelled. 'You almost scared me to death!'

'Put down the knife,' he said. He sounded surprised at my reaction. 'I am often in the dark. I belong to the night. I didn't want to ring the bell in case you were asleep, and I wondered if your madman could reach your apartment via the balcony. And he could.' He stepped back a pace and half turned, both hands on the rail. 'But I shall leave, if I am not welcome.'

'No,' I said. Vampires can only come in if they are invited, I thought. Well, I was going to invite this one. 'But first show me how you got up.'

I stood next to him and looked down to the lane.

'Easy,' he said. 'There's the downpipe, and then a little traverse across to the balcony with at least two good handholds. Thereafter just up and over.'

'How can I stop him? Barbed wire? Plant cactus?'

He chuckled. 'I don't think you need go as far as barbed wire. Just a good coating of Vaseline on the rail, and the only thing you'll hear is the scream as he falls off. Then you can call the police in perfect safety. Good evening, Corinna.'

'Good evening,' I replied, still a bit bemused. 'Do come in. I was just about to go to bed. I have to get up and bake in the morning.'

'I know. I'm sorry that I startled you.'

'Yeah, me too.'

I was not feeling gracious. Nothing makes one feel sillier than overcoming terror to find that instead of confronting a murderer you are about to stick the breadknife into a future lover. Not that I did this a lot.

'Put it this way,' he said. 'Wouldn't it have been worse if I had been a real murderer? And you were brave. I bet you didn't know you were brave before.'

'I was terrified,' I mumbled, sitting down and drawing Horatio into a hug.

'But you armed yourself and opened the window,' he reminded me.

'That was better than sitting here being terrified,' I said, not thinking that I deserved a lot of credit. Horatio does not like unsolicited hugs and he removed himself pointedly to the other end of the sofa. Daniel sat down and provided a substitute so I hugged him instead. He smelt of the outside, of cold and dark. An unsettling, exciting scent.

He held me for a while and I began to lose my adrenaline-fuelled edginess.

'That was such a silly thing to do,' he said to himself. 'I can't imagine why I did it. How else are you likely to react? I'm a fool,' he said. 'Forgive me?'

'Of course,' I said.

'I have found out something interesting,' he said.

'And so have I,' I told him. 'You remember that friend of James' who moved into the apartment? He's lost a daughter. A runaway. Cherie Holliday. If I get a picture of her, can you show it around?'

'Possibly. What is the situation? I have known fathers desperate to find children for many reasons, and some of them are not good reasons.'

'Because they abused them and want to keep it secret? Yes, I worked that one out. In this case, Cherie tried to tell her father about her uncle abusing her and he didn't believe her. Now he does. And the bastard is in jail. I've interrupted Holliday in the process of drinking himself to death. Finding his daughter might save his life.'

'In that case there is no harm in showing a picture,' said Daniel. He seemed a little distracted. I could hear his heart. It had a very slow, reassuring throb. 'How long has she been away?'

'Three years.'

'Not so good,' he said. 'He might not want her back. The street is very hard on girls.'

'This one looked pretty strong minded,' I said. 'And I got the impression he'd want her back, whatever state she was in. Meroe and I are going to unpack all his belongings tomorrow and then we can get the Lone Gunmen to do a flyer. What have you found out?'

'There are three main contenders for the hot shots,' he said. 'The Triad of Retribution, recently arrived and very unpleasant. The John Smith family. And a strange character called Lestat. The street people have seen him around. Dresses like a Goth. He's been seen speaking to all the victims, a day or so before they died. They're scared of him. The street is very superstitious. They've probably not read Anne Rice's *Interview with a Vampire*, where the name comes from, but they know a baddie when they see one. He dresses entirely in eighteenth century clothes. He has long blond hair.'

'I think I saw him in Meroe's shop,' I said. 'I'll ask her. He might be a regular.'

'Good. If he is killing the junkies I can't imagine why.'

'Fun?' I asked. My adrenaline had drained away and I felt very tired.

'Possibly. We need to find him and have a talk. We have no chance whatever of finding anything out about the Triad. The police know about them and so does the Chinese community. They probably won't last any longer than the other Triad invasions.'

'There have been others?'

'Oh yes, over the years. They swagger in, full of confidence, and then somehow one doesn't hear anything about them until they are picked up, usually at the airport, by an alert customs officer who just thought that they might have a look in their baggage, and lo and behold! They are carrying heroin and will spend the next twenty years in jail. Haven't you ever wondered about that alert customs officer? Does he, in fact, have a mobile phone and an attentive ear for anonymous calls in a Chinese accent?'

'That's clever.'

'And absolutely bloodless. They don't want to attract official attention. But it discourages the Triad. And everyone is happy again until the next one comes barging in, demanding to be cut in on the action. That's happening at present and an arrest is expected shortly, I have no doubt.'

'So if it is them handing out overproof drugs, we can't catch them.'

'No, and we shouldn't try. They have a short way with inter-lopers.'

'What about the John Smith family?'

'They run most of the heroin in Melbourne,' he said. 'They're a criminal family—every one of them is involved in crime. For two generations so far and I hear that their youngest son has just reached the children's court. They are not nice people,' he said. I had a feeling that this was an understatement of titanic proportions, like the claim that the coalition of armies which invaded Iraq was a 'modest force.'

'Do you know any of them?'

'In passing, yes, and I can't say that I want to further the acquaintance. But what I wanted to talk to you about, ketschele, was the victims. We have to find a pattern, if there is a pattern. I have a list of them here, with everything the police know about them.'

'And you got that from…?' I asked, waking myself up enough to sit up and switch on a standing lamp.

'A friend,' he said. 'So far there have been four deaths and three near deaths. The first one was Collins. Nineteen, came from Frankston, away from home for two days. Heavy heroin user. Second, Hughes. Eighteen. From Abbotsford. Overdosed in the Treasury, away from home for two years, worked as a labourer when he could. Heavy user. Had booked himself in for a detox. Survived and is in detox now. Third, Suze, who overdosed in your alley and gave me the pleasure of your acquaintance. Real name MacDonald. Seventeen. From Toorak. Also survived and went straight back out and scored again. She's on her way out, poor Suze. Fourth, Venetti. Found dead at the station—'

'Stop,' I said. 'I need to put all this in a table. Then we ought to be able to see a pattern. If there is a pattern.'

I turned on the computer and called up a spreadsheet and entered the data he had given me. When I had finished it looked like this:

Name	Sex	Age	Origin	Date of OD	Place of OD	Alive?
Collins, J	M	19	Frankston	19th	King St.	no
Hughes, M	M	18	Abbotsford	20th	Spencer St. station	yes
MacDonald, S	F	17	Toorak	22nd	Calico Alley	yes
Venetti, G	M	19	Carlton	23rd	Spencer St.	no
Nguyen, T	M	15	Springvale	25th	Flinders St. station	no
Udall, H	F	18	Footscray	26th	Hardware Lane	yes
Trench, S	M	16	South Yarra	28th	Treasury Gardens	no

Daniel looked at me over the printout. 'You have a gift for organisation,' he said. 'There is one pattern which leaps out instantly.'

'He skips a day,' I said. 'He, she or they skip a day, I mean. I wonder what they were doing on the 21st, 24th and 27th?'

'Indeed. Not much connection between the victims, though. Not on the face of this.'

'Well, it must be something other than where they came from. They are all pretty young. I reckon this creep or creeps might hang around the stations, though.'

'Possibly because the victims do too.'

'We need to talk to the survivors,' I said.

'I will try to find Suze tonight. She might talk to me if I can pay for her time. I must leave you now, ketschele. Keep the window locked and grease that balcony rail, and do you know, I think I'm falling in love with you. How do you feel about that? I mean, hypothetically?'

'Hypothetically? Very positive,' I said.

'Good,' said Daniel. He kissed me on the throat, and left. And I went firmly to bed. But instead of visions of sugarplums, visions of victims danced in my head and it was quite a relief when the alarm clock went berserk and I realised that it was four a.m. and instead of being dead of a heroin overdose at the age of sixteen, I got to eat breakfast, drink coffee, and do the baking. Horatio must have thought the same, for he wolfed down his breakfast with unusual appetite and even accompanied me downstairs for the rat count and breakfast with the Mouse Police.

It was to the happy whoofling of feeding cats that I started my dough hooks and whistled while I worked.

When I opened the door there was Jase. Relatively clear eyed if dirty as to clothes. 'Help you with the baking for a shower?' he asked. He whipped inside very smartly and I wondered if the Blues Brothers man was after him again.

'You aren't getting anywhere near my bread with those fingernails,' I said firmly. 'I'll lend you a gown again. Scrub those hands,' I yelled after him as he retrieved his towel and gown from the dryer where I had left them and dived into the shower. Puffs of steam and the scent of ginger shower gel inspired me to make gingerbread muffins this morning. And a good if fiddly job for those clean hands was called 'cutting up the crystallised ginger,' after which he would need another shower. But we had endless hot water and Jase wouldn't shrink if he had two showers in one day.

By the time he came out I had done the dry muffin mix. Jase put his clothes in the washer and started it. He showed me his hands, front and back. They were scrubbed almost raw. Then he tied his gown around him tightly, rolled back his sleeves to the elbow, and began chopping up crystallised ginger. He was neat and was doing a good job so I went back to my dough.

'That's rye bread,' he observed. 'It smells different from that crumbly stuff.'

'Yes, it's the yeast. This crumbly stuff is health bread and it doesn't have any.'

'Why not?'

'Because the customer wants bread without any salt, sugar, gluten, oil, yeast or taste, and the customer is always right.'

'Yuk,' he commented. 'Must be mad. As if! When they could get the good stuff!'

'They're paying for it, so I'll bake it,' I said. 'You've worked in a kitchen before.'

'What gave me away?' He looked panicked.

'The way you hold the knife. Professional. It's all right, Jase. I'm not prying. It was just a comment.'

He relaxed enough to go back to the chopping. 'I was a kitchen hand, and that's what kitchen hands do, they chop. Vegetables, salad, potatoes, anything. Did food technology at school. Wanted to be a chef. But I like baking better. It's a kind of magic.'

This was the longest speech I had ever heard Jase utter. He realised it too and shut up like a clam. This did not bother me as I have a preference for silence in the morning. Jase finished the ginger, washed his hands again, then helped me unload sacks of flour into the hoppers. The Mouse Police slept on the empty ones but I didn't need cat hair in the full ones.

'Would you like some breakfast?' I offered.

'What y' got?' he asked, having returned to his customary taciturnity.

'I could go so far as a cup of coffee and a gingerbread muffin.'

'Coupla rolls?' he asked. 'With cheese?'

I left him in the bakery while I got the coffee and some cheese. He tore into the rolls as though he was starving. Still had all his top teeth, I saw. The Mouse Police scented cheese and came to his feet and he almost snarled at them. Nature red in tooth and claw, I thought, and I didn't even like that on the Discovery Channel.

I gave Jase more cheese and more rolls and I cut up small bits for the cats. Everyone was full by the time I ran out of cheese and Jase unbent so far as to offer the last crumb to Heckle, who gratefully bit his finger.

I waited to see if he was going to cuff Heckle, in which case he was out of my bakery forever, but he just laughed.

'I should'a given you a bit when you asked nice,' he said to Heckle, who flattened the stubs of his ears in acknowledgment.

'Time to take the stuff into the shop,' I said.

'Wait till me clothes are dry and I'll help,' he offered.

I was a little suspicious of this sudden helpfulness but it was a fair offer and the trays were heavy.

'Is someone waiting for you outside?' I asked.

'Maybe,' he shrugged.

'Then you can stay here and mind the oven while I start loading the bread for the carrier. Don't touch the thermostat. I'll be just through here.'

I began to count loaves into trays destined for various restaurants. Jase was sitting as I had left him when I came back. He didn't know that there was a shiny metal vent in front of me which enabled me to see into the bakery. He had got up, bent to examine the oven, wandered around the room, opened the washer and loaded his clothes into the dryer, fiddled with something in the bathroom, come out again and sat down. I was actually watching to see if he was going to mistreat Heckle for biting him. But Heckle and Jekyll were out in the street, begging Kiko for scraps of fish.

I would have to watch him closely before I could leave him in the bakery unsupervised. I'm not going to have my cats terrorised by the hired help.

What was I thinking of? Leaving a heroin addict in my bakery, where a mere stout door and a few locks stood between him and the looting of all my possessions? I had obviously gone mad. He was going out as soon as his clothes dried.

But meanwhile he was company and he did chop very well. Presently Heckle and Jekyll came back, smelling strongly of endangered marine species of the Southern Ocean, and settled down on their flour sacks.

I poured the milk and water into the muffin mix, belted it around a bit and ladled it into the muffin tins, which Jase had already sprayed with oil. I passed each one on to him to have its bit of crystallised ginger popped onto the top and then he slid them into the oven. We worked smoothly together and when they were all in the oven Jase's clothes were dry.

He changed into his skivvy and jeans and re-assumed his horrible sneakers. If the health inspector saw them in my bakery he'd condemn us on the spot and probably prosecute me under the Strategic Arms Limitation Treaty for having a weapon of mass destruction. I wondered how I could get him another pair without transgressing the 'no work, no pay' guidelines and decided that perhaps it might be easier to wash them next time and see if the dryer could deal with drying them. Then, if they fell to pieces, I could get him another pair in good conscience.

I realised that I was definitely thinking of Jase as one of the staff and shook myself. I couldn't adopt every stray in Melbourne. We loaded up and began carrying bread into the shop.

Jase was stronger than he looked. Goss was already outside as I opened up and she gave him a considering stare. It was the sort of measuring gaze of a young woman who is wondering whether that seconds dress, not quite right about the hem, is worth the sale price or whether it would be too much work to make it wearable. I was glad she wasn't directing it at me, but Jase seemed unaffected.

'Seen you around,' she said to Jase, opening the cash register and ostentatiously counting the float.

'Yeah,' he muttered.

'You were at Blood Lines last night,' she said, never taking her eyes off him. Jase set down the load of bread and turned to go back into the bakery. His ears were burning red. I felt pleased. So he did have some human emotions apart from hunger.

'You were with Suze,' said Goss. My, how broad was the acquaintance of my shop assistants. Where on earth had Goss and Kylie met Suze? Assuming that it was the same Suze. The one that Daniel had said was on the way out.

'Yeah,' muttered Jase, and escaped into the bakery to get some more bread.

'What're you letting him into the bakery for?' demanded Goss hotly.

'Why, what's wrong with him?' I asked.

She was angry. Her nostril ring twinkled as she panted.

'Well, duh, you aren't to know, but he takes drugs,' she told me solemnly.

'Yes, I know. He doesn't take drugs here. He scrubs the floor.'

'Oh,' she said. 'I suppose that's about right. Hey, scrub boy!' she yelled. 'Fucking junkie!'

I was about to suppress Goss, who had never behaved like this in my shop before, when Jase came tumbling back, dropping his tray of bread on the table so that it rang.

'Not!' he yelled right back into Goss' face. 'Not a fucking junkie. Not for a fucking week. Not a junkie. What would you fucking know about it anyway?' he sneered. 'Little Miss Daddy's Girl, going to the clubs, thinks she's a fucking princess.'

'Goss,' I said. 'Jason. Behave. What's it to you anyway, if I employ an assistant baker?'

Jase swelled with pride. Goss slammed a braceleted hand down on the counter with an angry jangle.

'Suze was my friend,' she said. 'We went to the same school. She was a good girl! Then she met that shit of a fucking junkie!' She pointed to Jase, who was backing away.

'I never!' he yelled. 'She was on the fucking stuff before I met her! I tried to fucking help her!'

This was all sounding like a soap opera and I have never had any patience with soap operas. I grabbed Jase and hustled him back into the bakery and told him to stay there until I came back. That should ensure that he would run like a hare.

I grabbed Goss and hugged her. She broke into angry tears immediately. I patted her back. So thin that I could count every vertebra, feel every rib. I longed to feed her. But the best I could do was to murmur the old lie, 'It will be all right, Gossamer, it will be all right.'

'I liked Suze,' she sobbed. 'She was always so cool. And now she sucks old men in the alley behind the club for a hit. And it's all down to that Jase cunt,' she spat.

'What he says might be true,' I said. 'Stranger things have happened. People who are the coolest at school do tend to have peaked early. She might have been taking drugs all along. And if Jase brought Suze here to collapse on my grate then he saved her life. Come along, Goss, stop crying, wipe your face. Go into my bathroom and fix your make-up. Daniel is looking for Suze and he might be able to do something for her. Then come back and tell me about this club. Interesting name.'

Eighteen is, thank the goddess, a distractible age. Gossamer disappeared into the bathroom and I went into the bakery. Jase was, of course, gone. I was a little disappointed about that. I closed and locked the outer doors, patted the Mouse Police and, escorted by Horatio, went into the shop and opened the shutters.

Horatio levitated to his usual place next to the cash register, awaiting worship. The door was open and the buyers of bread began to wander in, seeking gingerbread muffins and French twists to fortify themselves for the coming toil. It was half an hour before Gossamer came back. She was beautifully made-up and composed. She had even stopped swearing, though the two of them had used 'fucking' more like punctuation.

'I'm sorry I yelled at him,' she said. 'I'm sorry I swore like that in the shop. You might be right. Maybe he even cares for Suze. And you'd like Blood Lines. It's a Goth club. You have to wear Goth clothes or the door bitch won't let you in. And I met the coolest guy there. I'm feeling a bit lost because Kylie managed to get off with that Jon guy she's been after. But I met the coolest of them all. I'm seeing him tonight.' She turned her kohled eyes to me and said in an excited whisper, 'His name's Lestat.'

Chapter Eleven

Only extreme control suppressed my yelp. How is it that some women are attracted only to the man who is guaranteed to do them the most harm? If Goss' Lestat was the same person as Daniel's Lestat then I had to say something. But what? Any indication that he was dangerous would just make him more attractive. I stacked the bread for the carrier at the door and tried to think.

Then, of all things, the newspaper rescued me. Goss regulates her whole life by the astrology column in the daily astonisher and she was reading it and frowning.

'Shit,' she said in a low voice.

'What's the matter?' I asked.

'It says this is a bad time to make new friends,' she said, pointing out the advice for Libra. 'So I'll have to see him another time.'

'Can you contact him?' I asked. She gave me that 'what was it like in the fourteenth century, anyway?' look to which I had become accustomed.

'Mobile number,' she said.

Unobtrusively, I watched over her shoulder as she called up the address book in her phone and, while she tapped it in, I wrote the number down on the top of a pile of paper bags. I then folded the bag and put it in my pocket. It is uncool to talk on a mobile phone these days. Uncool travels fast in these days of amazing technological advances. I remember when Sony Walkmen were the epitome of cool. And I rode a stegosaurus to school, as Goss might have said. I remember when video recorders were the coolest thing. Nowadays if you haven't got DVD you are prehistoric.

Goss sent a text message. Her fingers flew. I was impressed. In the old days Goss would have made a wonderful morse code operator.

We settled down to sell bread. For a Monday, we did quite well.

Everything proceeded. I told Goss about Andy Holliday and his missing daughter and she was round-eyed with sympathy. I asked her if she had heard the name Cherie Holliday. She shook her head. Her hair was blue today, and flew around her face.

'But she wouldn't be calling herself that,' she said. 'Not if she went off in such a snit. I mean, her uncle was…doing what she said. Her dad didn't believe her. She must have felt, like, gutted. She just went off into the night and he never saw her again and now he knows that she told the truth and he can't tell her. That's the saddest thing I ever heard.' There were tears in her eyes. They did her credit. This from a girl who had hounded a recovering heroin addict out of the shop. The young have such cheap, hard judgment, as Irene said in Galsworthy long ago.

I decided to press my luck.

'So, when I get the flyers printed, will you help me spread them round?' I asked, expecting the answer 'as if.' But Goss revealed hidden depths of compassion.

'Sure. We can tape them onto lampposts, I always read the stuff on lampposts. If there's a picture. Have we got a picture?'

'Yes. I'll pick it up when Meroe and I go there today to help him put all his stuff away. You know what a terrible job that is.'

She giggled. 'Some of my stuff is still in boxes,' she said. 'I'd come too but I've got an audition. Second call for a soap. Wish me luck?'

I pressed my lips to her cheek and wished her luck.

I added 'buy a large roll of sticky tape' to my mental list of things to do, which was getting alarmingly long.

Then we sold some more bread. By shutting-up time we had done reasonably well. There was still a sack for the soup van but every single gingerbread muffin had been sold, which was nice. I made another mental note that I must tell Jase, if I ever saw him again.

I put up the shutters and went into the bakery to start cleaning. Horatio removed himself to the stairs and sat there with the Mouse Police as I swilled and washed. I opened the door into Calico Alley and there was the said Jase. He looked embarrassed. He hung his head and mumbled.

'Sorry,' he said. 'Can I wash the floor?'

'If you explain,' I said. 'I can't have Goss upset like that.'

He thought about it, lingering in the doorway. I didn't say anything. This one he had to decide for himself. Finally he decided to talk.

'I know Suze,' he said. 'I met her when she'd been six months on the gear. She was lonely and so was I. So we sort of hung together. I swear I never turned her onto it. Some other dude did that, not me. She hangs out with some Goths at Blood Lines, that's why I was there.'

'You're a Goth?' I asked, looking critically at his clothes.

'No, they're all fucking mad. But they like…company. Some of us used to hang outside Blood Lines and…'

I thought of a face-saving formula. 'Make certain deals,' I said. He looked relieved.

'Yeah. And Suze…makes deals. Blood games. Clean,' he said when he saw my face. 'New syringes and all. I don't understand it, really. But they pay her real good.'

'What's a blood game?'

He shifted his eyes uneasily. 'They like to drink blood. Our blood. They don't take much. And they pay well—in heroin. I been working at the club and Suze has been selling blood.'

'All right, I believe you. And you're off drugs?'

'Didn't mean to but I ran out of money. Then I thought, I'm sick of hassling for a living, why not stop? It can't kill you. Fucking near did. Been a week,' he said. 'I was real sick for a couple of days, just hid in a squat. Then I got so hungry I came out.'

'Well, at least I can feed you,' I said. 'Have two leftover ham rolls and get on with the floor,' I instructed, and he ate the ham rolls in three snaps of his jaw and got out the mop. In Jase, my need to feed people might have met its match.

He mopped the floor downstairs while I assembled a picnic supper out of the remaining ham, a good hunk of egg-and-bacon pie and a few slices of fruit cake. He deserved it for his morning's help in the bakery. I put it all in a supermarket bag. If he had to sleep rough he would at least be well fed.

I returned as he finished the floor and rinsed the mop.

I slid onto the wet slates with my feet on a duster and handed him the bag.

'Supper,' I said. 'And here's your ten bucks. Thank you, Jason.'

'See you tomorrow, Miss,' he said, and went. I locked the door behind him.

In view of my agreement with Meroe, I was going to omit the g-and-t and Horatio's walk on the roof. He, however, stood at the door and cried until I gave in and carried him up to the garden. There he disappeared into the undergrowth where he clearly had some appointment. I sat down in the rose bower. No one on the roof but Mr. Pemberthy, exercising Traddles. He didn't even lift his eyes as he stopped near me for Traddles to pee on an innocent bush.

'How is your wife?' I asked.

'She's at the specialist's,' he said. 'They don't seem to know what's wrong with her. She gets into these states. Nothing will please her but to try to sell the apartment. Since those letters came,' he said.

Then he seemed to run out of words. He waited until Traddles had finished christening the bush and went on his way. Poor sad, defeated man. It must have taken Mrs. P years to grind him down to his present status of something lowlier than the average worm. He didn't even bother about his clothes anymore. His tweed coat was frayed at the elbows and there were stains on his tie and on his sleeves. But as he had told Meroe and me, he was into dominance and loved being Mrs. P's slave.

Horatio came back as I finished my drink, chirruped invitingly to me as a signal that he was now ready for an extensive afternoon nap, and we went back to my apartment. There I left him and went to fetch Meroe to tackle the Great Unpacking.

Andy Holliday was a bit more together today. He gave me a picture of his daughter and allowed me to conduct him, and his bottle, down to the Prof's flat. As I closed the door I noticed that he was actually pouring a glass for Professor Dion, which at least cut down the amount he was going to be able to drink.

Meroe and I surveyed the apartment. She set down her basket on the TV and said, 'It's no use relying on the labels. At least Lady Diana's furniture is here and she loved cupboard space. You start in the kitchen and I'll see what I can do with the clothes.'

Boxes, naturally, were mislabelled or unlabelled until you turned them over and found that the labels were on the bottom. We called out discoveries to each other. The moving men appeared to have just dumped everything down where they felt like it and poor Andy had been too miserable to protest. Thus Meroe found the dishes neatly stored in the bathroom, and I found the linen offloaded into the kitchen. We swapped boxes and carried on the kind of long distance conversation only possible between two good female friends.

'I've got the computer,' I cried. 'And the printer.'

'Good, the telephone jack is just behind that polished wood table. I found it when I was looking for a power plug.' There was a ripping noise. 'And I've got the phone and the answering machine.'

'I'll come and get it in a minute. Are you doing shoes? I've got a whole box of shoes here.'

We shoved and sorted. Meroe, who is very neat when she isn't being amazingly messy, hung every shirt and suit in a huge wardrobe which Lady D had had especially built, tall enough to take ball gowns, she said. It was also big enough to take a bag of golf clubs, a very old hockey stick, a huge pile of *Playboy* magazines and a basketball. The bedroom was taking shape. We made his bed with new sheets and his own doona, instead of the sleeping bag in which he had been reposing. In the built-in drawers we placed diaries, coins, a finger ring with a university crest on it, a bunch of keys, spare reading glasses and a pile of cards, including those for a dentist and a doctor, which he might need again.

The kitchen was simple. We just had to put away the cutlery, the crockery and the two pots (a saucepan and a frying pan) and install the microwave. The fridge contained nothing but my fruit cake and some long-life milk and the freezer was full of frozen meals and bottles of Stoli.

I was stacking books in a bookshelf (mostly paperback thrillers) when I heard Meroe say, 'Oh!' in a sad, broken little voice.

In eight cartons Andy had packed all of his daughter's possessions. Her school books, her pink diary with a lock on it, all her clothes. Her seven stuffed toys, including a big white teddy bear with a lot of personality. Her bottle of Charlie perfume had leaked and hung heavy in the air.

'We'll put all of her stuff in the second bedroom,' I said.

'And shut the door,' agreed Meroe. 'But I'd swear she isn't dead,' she added. 'Not from these things.'

'She owned these things before she ran away, and she was alive then,' I reminded her. 'By the way, I met a pretty Goth in your shop the other day. Ruffled shirt. Long blond hair. You don't see long hair often.'

'Lestat,' said Meroe, shutting the door to Cherie's room. 'The "my gift is death" Lestat. Changed his name by deed poll. Lives in a penthouse somewhere. Believes he is a vampire. OD'd on vampire films and may not be entirely sane.'

'No shit. What does he buy from you?' I asked, fascinated.

'Spells,' said Meroe. 'He's looking for a spell for eternal life. He buys all the most abstruse books on ritual. He's on the mailing list of most of the rare and occult booksellers in the world. He's a customer I could do without, to tell you the truth. He gives me the creeps.'

'But you're a witch!' I exclaimed.

'Doesn't mean I can't have the creeps. Vampire films don't do some people any good,' she added, rummaging for more underwear. 'There, that's all the clothes, I think. Do you want to set up the computer while I connect up the wires?'

'Deal,' I said. Meroe crawled on the floor while I read the manual and eventually we had everything up and working; all the essential machines, the phone, the stereo, even the DVD player.

We put his toiletries in the bathroom, including a bit of shaving soap which had hairs in it, and a worn-through soap-not-really-attached-to-the-rope-anymore. His aftershave was Brut. And he had a lot of mouthwash from when he still met people who didn't know that he was a drunk. His towels were, however, new.

And then we could survey Andy Holliday's life. He had a lot of cassette tapes and a fair number of CDs. He didn't read much and when he did he read Michael Crichton, Wilbur Smith and true crime. A lot of true crime. His video collection leant heavily towards the pornographic and the thriller/action hero Schwarzenegger/James Bond/Van Damme sort of thing.

He had eight bottles of scotch and one bottle of wine. And no mixers.

'A man with a little imagination,' said Meroe, stacking paper into the printer.

'Just enough to give him nightmares,' I agreed.

'A drunk,' she said, opening her basket and taking out a flat brass dish. She poured some sort of gum into it and set it alight.

'A man in total despair,' I said. I packed stationery and paper-clips and all the junk an office needs into one desk drawer and laid a huge pile of correspondence on it, as there was no room in the drawers for so much paper. In the mass were unopened envelopes and I sorted them to the top. Tax Department. That was a bad sign. Three of them. I could not resist the impulse. I took the paper knife, a silver one with an inscription, and slit the envelopes, tossing them into a recently discovered wastepaper basket.

My eyes widened. They were cheques. The Tax Department was actually paying Andy Holliday money and he didn't care. They had never been cashed. That's the best description of total despair I could have come up with offhand. This man was in a very bad way.

The smoke was swirling upward from Meroe's burning resin and I sat down to watch her do her cleansing ritual. It seemed simple. She just walked into the middle of the room, gestured with the smoke to the four corners, then chanted something in an unknown tongue and moved into the next room. I followed and she said to me out of the corner of her mouth, 'Open the door onto the balcony,' and I did. Fresh air failed to blow in, but the sweet smoke billowed out. Meroe put the dish down on the balcony floor and said, 'That's the best I can do. The man is a jangle of terrible pain.'

'We can keep him alive for the moment,' I said. 'And maybe we can find his daughter.'

To that end I took the picture to the Lone Gunmen and asked them to do me a hundred flyers. I also took them a six-pack of Arctic Death and a promise of more, plus proper payment for their labours. They were all together for a change. They accepted the bottles and promised the flyers for tomorrow, no probs, Corinna. Collectively, they looked worried, even guilty. None of my concern. Perhaps they had been spammed by all those people who promise to enlarge my penis. Any nerd is going to find that worrying.

Then I went to rescue the Prof from Andy Holliday, who must have had more than a medium adult dose of drunken misery for one day.

But when I got to Dionysus the Prof was ending a funny story with a gesture of his elegant hands, '...but on Thursday it's your turn in the barrel!' and Holliday was laughing. Not hysterically, not a fall-off-the-chair-and-wet-the-pants laugh, but definitely laughing. Also, the level in the bottle had not fallen like the tide.

'M'sieur's apartment is prepared,' I said, and Holliday got up. He thanked the Prof for a very amusing visit and went with me like a lamb. Then he stared as he saw his unboxed rooms. He sniffed the oriental scent of the burning incense. He picked up, and then put down, the remote control for the TV.

'It's a miracle,' he said. 'You can't have done all this in one afternoon.'

'I had help,' I said. 'Allow me to introduce my friend and fellow unpacker, Meroe.'

Andy Holliday took Meroe's hand. I expected to hear violins. His expression resembled a flatfish that had just been dazzled by the physical attractions of another flatfish and belted over the head with an anchor at roughly the same time. I thought it best to leave them together.

Besides, I was grimy and dusty and I wanted my bath. Something with a lot of foam. And, by the look of my hands, unparalleled cleansing power. I was tired of other people's problems and wanted to get back to Jade Forrester. How was she going to get her hero and heroine back together again?

These things concerned me as I took the lift down, too tired to take the stairs. Rats. There was Mrs. Pemberthy in the lobby, looking frail. Traddles didn't look too good either. They were both leaning against the lift door, wheezing.

I don't like Mrs. Pemberthy and she doesn't like me, but what could I do? I took them both into the lift. Mrs. P waved her wrists at me, the hands falling loose.

'My hands won't do as I tell them,' she said. 'And the vet just can't tell what is wrong with poor Traddles.'

I could tell that Traddles was sick. He hadn't tried to bite me in minutes. I got them out of the lift and opened the door for them. Mrs. P looked so limp that I helped her inside. Mr. P wasn't there.

The Pemberthy apartment was overdecorated in the same way as the sea is wet. Every surface that could possibly be decorated was decorated. The furniture was fussy, expensive copies of Sheraton, and every surface was covered with little knick-knacks. Expensive knick-knacks, like Japanese ivory carvings and those little trees made of gold wire and semi precious stones. They must have been hell to dust.

Mrs. Pemberthy fumbled with her shoes and I knelt to take them off. She leaned back in her rose-damask chair and sighed.

'My milk drink,' she said. 'Elias always leaves it in the microwave.'

I had never thought of myself as a lady's maid but what could I do? The woman looked like death. I went into the kitchen and opened the microwave. There was a dainty rose-spattered mug but the milk within smelt off. I was about to pour it out and make another when Mr. P came in and almost grabbed the mug out of my hands.

'That's all right,' he said, and he looked straight into my face. 'I'll do it. She likes me to do it,' he said.

'The milk's off,' I told him.

'I'll do it,' he said again. I was suddenly very uncomfortable. 'Women like to be waited on,' said Mr. Pemberthy. 'I could serve you, too. I would like to serve you.' I noticed that his grey moustache was yellow near his mouth. He was standing way too close to me. It was time for Corinna to be out of this kitchen.

On the way out I asked Mrs. Pemberthy for the name of Traddles' vet. My own Irish charmer was moving to Benalla. Any vet who could put up with Mrs. Pemberthy could put up with me. She gave me his card.

Then, at last, I got to go home, run a sumptuous bath and pour in bath foam. I lay in it for some time, considering various things, like Daniel saying that he was falling in love with me, until I was very clean, my fingers looked like I had been taking in washing since childhood, and the water was lukewarm.

I didn't feel like going out again. I made myself a dish of pasta carbonara with a lot of fresh ground black pepper, drank one glass of wine and went to bed, like the epitaph on a party girl, early, sober and alone. Well, not alone. Horatio, as usual, reposed beside me, purring just above the level of hearing, a very soothing sound…

Unless they are bouncing all over you, climbing the curtains, engaging in an extensive wash with that infuriating 'pick, lick,

lick, pick' noise or drinking deeply from your bedside glass of water, cats are very good bedfellows.

Morning dawned as usual and I went down to the bakery with my second cup of coffee to hear someone knocking on the outer door. It was Jason and he just nodded, dived into the shower and threw his clothes out to be washed. 'I might as well have a son,' I thought, a little nettled. I remembered that I actually had a baker's overall somewhere and resolved to find it. It was, of course, in the broom cupboard. I thrust it into the bathroom, averting my gaze.

When he came out clothed in the white overall, I gestured to the muffin mixture while the dough hooks scythed through the flour.

'Your gingerbread muffins sold out yesterday,' I said. 'Today we're doing apple and spice. Measure out the spices and don't put them in until you show me. I'll read you the recipe while you eat.'

I fetched another cup of coffee and some of the leftover bread which Daniel had not come to collect. I had been too tired last night to wonder where he was.

On cue, there came another knock on the door. Daniel stood there, outlined against the black alley. Lestat could take lessons from him on how to appear on the wings of a thought.

'Bread?' I asked.

'Last shift,' he said. I gave him the sack, Jason snatching another baguette from it as I passed him. Daniel shot the boy a considering look, smiled, took the bread and went.

Thereafter we made bread. Because I was busy and because they are relatively easy to make, I let Jason do the muffins from beginning to end. He was tense with concentration but he managed to combine the mixture without overstirring and glop it into the muffin tins without incident. This takes skill, because it is lumpy. When they came out of the oven he took one, examined it from all angles, then broke it in half and bit into the spicy crumb. Then he smiled.

I had never seen Jason smile before. He seemed to glow.

I wondered how old he was. That was the smile of a happy baby. I gave him a one-armed hug. I had a load of tins in the other arm.

'Very nice,' I said, tasting the bit he held up to my mouth. 'Just right.'

'More coffee?' he asked. 'I can make it.'

'No,' I said, too quickly, and watched him crumple. Dammit! I still wasn't going to let a heroin addict into my own living quarters. On the other hand, this was Jason. I made amends as best I could.

'Tea,' I said. 'You can eat anything you find in the kitchen. Horatio has had his breakfast so do not believe anything he says on the subject of starving cats.'

He beamed again and ran up the stairs in his thongs. Had to get him some shoes. I went back to the bread and worried until he reappeared with a mug of tea for me and a sandwich for himself. It dripped.

'And what is that?' I asked.

'It's a fried egg and chili sauce sandwich,' he said, faintly surprised that I had not immediately recognised it. 'They're well sick.'

'That I can believe.'

'Make one for you?' he offered.

'No, I've had breakfast. Thanks anyway.'

I averted my eyes as he finished the loathsome concoction with every sign of enjoyment and took the dishes up to my kitchen. Well, he had got into my apartment now, and if he had pinched anything, I would know how far to trust him.

I was probably mad to trust him at all. But he made a neat job of learning how to construct French twists and we got the baking done early. It was nice to have an assistant. Even one who, offered a whole cuisine to choose from, elected to eat fried eggs with chili sauce.

Then it was time to open the door to the street, sweep out the spilled flour, and say hello to the day. It didn't say hello back. It was a nasty, cold dawn with a spiteful little wind which blew sharp dust into the eyes. The Mouse Police scooted out for their fish scraps then trotted right back inside and found a convenient flour sack for a nice day-long snooze.

And someone had painted 'whore' in big red letters on my wall.

Chapter Twelve

I wasn't scared because I was so cross. If this was how Mistress Dread had felt then I thought her restraint admirable. If I'd had a whip I would have used it.

Jason cowered as I turned on him.

'Was this there when you came along the alley?' I demanded.

'I dunno,' he quavered. 'It was dark. I don't think so. I didn't smell paint.'

'You wouldn't,' I snarled. 'It's spray paint again.' I grabbed hold of my temper. I was scaring the staff. 'It's all right, Jason, I'm not blaming you,' I said. 'Come on, let's get the bread into the shop and the trays out to the carrier and then I'll ring the cops.'

'I've…er…I've got things to do,' he said.

'I understand,' I told him. 'I'll wait until your clothes are dry. The sign isn't going anywhere. Don't worry.'

'Thanks, Miss,' he muttered. Gone was the Jason who had smiled with delight as his first muffin turned out to be delicious. It was a pity. I wondered why he was so scared of the police. This was such a stupid thing to think that I shook my head and picked up a load of bread. With a heroin lifestyle, almost everything one did was illegal. We loaded the bread into its proper places and Horatio stepped down into the shop. Everything was done and it was only eight o'clock.

Goss hadn't come in and Kylie was not there when I opened the shutters.

'Jason?' I asked. 'Want to serve in the shop?'

'No!' he said in a frightened squeal. 'What, like this?'

I thought he looked very eighteenth century in his overall and he was decently covered down to ankles and wrists.

I said so.

'Someone might see me,' he insisted.

Since this was a function of shops I had to agree. 'All right. You stay here and do the waybills. When the carrier comes, make sure that he signs each one and knows that the health bread has to go first. If he makes any comment about the graffiti, tell him that I've already called the cops. All right? Can I rely on you?'

'Yes,' he said, letting out a sigh of relief. For some reason Jason had attached himself to me like a lost puppy falling in to any stranger's heel, desperate to belong. He wanted to please. But he really couldn't afford to be seen. Interesting.

I locked up my own quarters. Jason might not steal from me but I would have to leave the bakery door open and some of his friends might decide to flatten Jason and loot the place. He had seen me lock my private apartment at this time each day so he wasn't offended. He sat by the door with the sheaf of waybills, looking responsible and important.

While I sold bread, made change and wondered why Jason's apple and spice muffins were better than mine, I thought about our manifold problems. We had three questions to answer. Who was killing the junkies? (Subsidiary question: why?)

Who was terrorising Insula? And where was Cherie Holliday? Quite enough for one day and I didn't have the faintest about any of it.

I was just reflecting that now I had an assistant I could make potato bread without getting up at three to peel the potatoes when Kylie came in. She looked radiant. Her cheeks were flushed and her navel ring was twinkling.

'Got it!' she said. 'Start Monday! And Goss too!'

'Wonderful,' I said.

'At least three months' work,' she continued, entranced with her good fortune. 'The director said we were perfect for the part.'

'What part?' I asked keenly. Oh, for a girl's role where they would have to put on some weight.

'We're anorexics,' she said blithely. 'So is the main character. It's about the fashion industry. It's called "Cat Walk,"' she said to Horatio, tickling his ears. 'Only trouble is we have to smoke and I promised Dad I wouldn't.'

'No problem,' I said. 'Go ask Meroe for some herbal cigarettes. And thank her for that talisman,' I added.

'I will! It worked!' she said and floated off. 'Goss'll be in later,' she added from the door.

I was, of course, pleased for them but that did mean I would have to find another shop assistant. Jason was no use in his present state of extreme shyness. Tuesday was not working out too well, so far.

The morning rush dwindled and I went out the back to find that Jason had talked to the carrier, got a signature on every waybill, and was now eating his way solidly through his leftover baguette. He looked, in his overall, just like every other working boy I had seen.

'Put your sneakers on,' I said. 'Slip out to Cafe Delicious and get some food. I'm going to have a busy day. Get me moussaka if they have some and get some for yourself as well,' I said.

'Thanks.' He took the money. By the time he came back with the moussaka for me, he had already eaten his own portion and was finishing the last crumbs of the baguette.

I suppose he had a lot of starvation to make up for.

'All right,' I said. 'Get changed and come back for the floor as usual. I've got to call Senior Constable White about the graffiti.'

He nodded, changed in the bathroom, and went. Now that my bakery was free of alien influences, I called the number the police officer had given me and she promised to visit. I sold more bread. Customers patted Horatio and the day began to fall into its accustomed pattern. Routine is soothing. I like routine.

Meroe came in about ten, looking shocked. She smelled very strongly of something chemical, which rather clashed with the bread.

'What's the matter?' I asked. 'Sit down, Meroe.'

'Someone poured metho through what they thought was my door last night,' she said. 'Actually it was the gap between the two brick walls. There's a decorative air brick there and it does look like it goes into the shop, if you haven't ever been in it.'

'Shit!' I remarked.

'He tried to light it. There's a bunch of dead matches outside. But he couldn't. Now the whole place stinks of metho. Luckily I smelt it or I would have lit a stick of incense and that would have been it. I've called that cop,' she said. Things were serious if Meroe called the cops.

'Why couldn't he light it?' I asked.

'Because that sort of fire needs a wick,' said Senior Constable White from the door. 'It was a good attempt at arson, though. He meant to burn you out. We've got to lay hands on this shit. You were right, Ms. Chapman, he's escalating. Step by step. Closer and closer to…'

'Murder,' I said. 'Do come in, officer. If you would like to step through into the alley, I'll show you my latest decoration.'

'I'll mind the shop,' said Meroe. She sat down behind the counter. Horatio sniffed and withdrew to the furthest corner of the counter. Meroe smelt of accelerant and he didn't like it. Cats can wound your feelings, sometimes.

'Same writing,' observed Lepidoptera as she gazed at the inscription. She took a digital camera and a folding ruler out of her bag and snapped several pictures. 'Same weak loops, same unformed hand. Now, at least, we know something about him.'

'What?'

'How tall he is,' she said. 'That's the full reach of his arm, that capital W, and there's nothing here to stand on. Reach up beside it. How tall are you?'

'Five six,' I said, miming a spray can user.

'And I'm five eight. He's about the same height as you. Small man's complex as well as the other problems,' she added. 'Great.'

I led the way back inside and locked up the bakery.

'Any idea when it was done?'

'No,' I said. 'Overnight is all I can say. When I opened the door at five, I didn't notice it. When the sun came up at seven, I saw it. It could have been there all night. There's not a lot of lighting in Calico Alley.'

'Oh, well. I'll ask around. The beat cops come through here at three or so, depending on the rota. This metho-based arson attempt is more serious. If he'd used petrol it could have been very bad.'

'But it's all gone amiss for him,' I commented.

'Well, of course it has,' Lepidoptera smiled. 'Your friend the witch put a curse on him.'

'Do you believe in curses?' I asked incredulously, sure she was pulling my leg.

'In the police force you see a lot of strange stuff,' she evaded.

'How about the heroin deaths?' I asked.

'Another one last night,' she said. 'Found on the steps of the station. Nice boy from South Yarra. Only seventeen.'

'That's awful,' I said.

'Pretty awful,' she said. 'But there's no sign that they're being held down and injected by force, you know. They're doing it themselves.'

'And that makes a difference?' I demanded.

'Yes,' she said flatly. 'It does.'

Clearly this was going to be one of those things on which Ms. White and I disagreed. There was nothing much else for me to say so I left Meroe in the shop and went over to Mistress Dread's. I knocked at the door of her salon and she answered in person. Black corset, black fishnets, heels, tumbling red hair today.

'Yes?' she asked from her glorious height.

'I need the name of the firm that cleaned off your graffiti,' I said, daunted as always by her magnificent appearance. And her commanding manner. If I was a masochist I would have been crawling on the ground at that point, begging to kiss her stilettos. She unbent immediately.

'Oh, Corinna, you, too? Same guy?'

'Yes, he's got an extremely limited vocabulary.'

'I've got their card somewhere. They did a very good job, not a trace of red left. Here.' She fished a card out of a tall brass urn by the door.

'Also, he tried to burn down Meroe's shop,' I added. Mistress Dread drew herself up to her full height, an awe-inspiring sight.

'If you can point him out, dear,' she said in her deep growl, 'I'll deal with him. Personally,' she added, cracking her riding crop against her muscular thigh.

'If only I could,' I said. I went back to Earthly Delights where Meroe was selling apple and spice muffins and Ms. White was examining the Bosch picture which gave the shop its name.

'Very interesting,' she said. 'Was the artist on drugs?'

'Don't know,' I said. 'Probably,' I added, when I had thought about it. 'But they must have been herbal ones.'

'Might have been mushrooms,' Meroe commented. 'Or he might have been licking toads.'

Ms. White and I looked at each other.

'I expect you are going to explain that,' I said.

'Certainly. Grab a toad and frighten it and it exudes a poison, called bufotoxin, which deters predators. Cane toads do it. Poisons dogs. But a small dose of it sends humans off on interesting trips. A large dose of it sends them into their eternal rest, and the trouble with bufotoxin is that an effective dose is very close to a fatal dose. Witches were supposed to use it. You know, "eye of newt and tongue of frog." Also, a certain stone was supposed to be found in a toad's head which counteracted all poisons. It was called a bezoar stone and—'

'Enough,' I said. She had started a train of thought.

'And you don't sell anything like that in your shop?' said Senior Constable White.

'Of course not,' snapped Meroe. 'You could eat your way through my shop from end to end and all you'd get would be a bellyache.'

'I'm sure,' said Lepidoptera. She still had reservations about Meroe. I, of course, didn't.

But I drew Ms. White out of the shop and suggested a line of inquiry to her. I even provided the phone number. She looked dubious but said she'd look into it, advised Meroe to flood the metho with water. And not to use any naked flames for the rest of the day.

This meant that Meroe was not going to open, as she relies on incense to create an ambiance. She left my shop to put up her closed sign, drag Belladonna out from under the desk and carry her upstairs into her own apartment, Leucothea. She did not seem too badly scratched when she came back so I assumed that Belladonna had been glad to get out of the metho-scented room.

I left Meroe in the shop while I fetched the flyers from the Lone Gunmen. Gully was seated behind the desk, barely visible over unfiled documents. How they did their GST I could not imagine. When he saw me he jumped and knocked the pile over.

I knelt to gather great swathes of paper into my arms. Gully danced around begging me not to bother. He was reacting very strangely. What did he think I would find? Their weekly porn video order? All I had were invoices, made out in the proper form. Why was Gully behaving like a Mexican jumping bean? Was it a by-product of their unhealthy diet of chili con carne and tacos?

I dumped the papers on a chair and received a nicely pack-aged bundle of flyers. They had done a really good job. I bought a large roll of sticky tape and paid the modest total. Gully was avoiding my gaze. But I had things to think about other than the sins of the Lone Gunmen (in any case, erk!). I had, with any luck, the magnet which would draw Cherie Holliday back to her father.

In the shop I displayed one to Meroe and Goss.

'Do you think that is enough text?' asked Meroe doubtfully. 'It's a bit X-Files.'

But Goss was wholly in favour. 'It just tells her what she wants to know,' she said, holding out her hand for the sticky tape.

The flyer had the picture in the middle, Cherie's name at the top, and under that was the legend 'I believe you' and her father's name and phone number.

'Let's go,' said Goss, and she and Meroe took half the flyers and left the shop to placard both stations. I put one up in my own window and saved the rest for Daniel and the Soup Run. It was an ordinary sort of day thereafter. I called the wall-cleaners and they came, armed with some frightful compound which probably sterilised newts but which got red spray paint off walls at the speed of lightning. Goss and Meroe came back at one p.m., reporting that they had put up a flyer wherever young persons gathered, like picture theatres, fast food restaurants and clubs. They seemed to have had a lovely time. I paid Goss off and she left, still floating on air from a combination of a good deed done and a three-month contract gained.

Then I did the washing. When Jason turned up I marched him to the nearest shoe shop and bought a pair of white cook's shoes in his size, also some new underwear, another overall and a couple of white t-shirts.

'These stay in the bakery, right?' I demanded. 'You can't go running around that slate floor in thongs, it's unhygienic. Plus you'll catch a cold and maybe give it to the Mouse Police.'

Jason, who had begun to look a little hunted—what sort of background did he come from anyway?—laughed and promised not to sneeze on the cats. Then we cleaned up as usual, I gave him his ten dollars and a large bag of food, and went upstairs to bathe. Lily of the valley bath foam and cucumber lotion on my face, a hot washcloth over all and I sank into a trance.

Then, in front of my dreaming eyes, Daniel came in and sat down on the edge of the bath with Horatio. I was so sleepy and comfortable in the warm water that I didn't register his appearance as an intrusion. He smiled gently and caressed my shoulder, sliding his fingers down to cup a wet breast. Then he got up and went into the next room. I would not have sworn that he had really been there, until I got out of the bath, dried and dressed, and found him sitting on my couch.

'Haven't you ever heard of doorbells?' I asked, too comfortable to get very angry.

'I knew you'd be in the bath and I wanted to watch,' he said simply. 'You said that I could, before.'

'Yes, but...' I had, hadn't I? 'And?'

'You're beautiful,' he said. 'I thought you would be. And as for how I got in, I remembered the door code. I have a good memory,' he told me. 'Have you got the flyers?'

'On the table,' I said. No point in arguing with Daniel. He didn't recognise boundaries and he probably turned into a bat during the full moon, but we could work around that. He examined the face in the photo.

'No, I don't recall seeing her before,' he said. 'But it's hard to add years to a young female face. I've only been on the Soup Run for six months. And what is this?' he asked. I looked and saw that he was holding the glossy folder which James had pressed upon me.

'Some sort of prospectus for a company James wants me to sell my flat to invest in,' I said.

'And are you going to do that?'

'Not a hope. I like it here and, besides, I wouldn't invest in anything which relied on a small player joining up with a big player. Under those circumstances someone is going to get loaded with the non-yielding or bankrupt bits of the big company and thence misery and ruin. *Hinc*, as the Professor would say, *illae lachrimae*.'

'Sorry, I only do Hebrew, Greek and Arabic,' he apologised.

'Do you? How very enterprising. It's Latin. "Hence these tears." I don't suppose you've done any economic studies or accounting? No? Then if you do have any money, never put it into a company whose prospectus cost more than the GNP of a central African republic. Look at this one. New acid-free paper, glossy cover, binding not staples, high resolution images. It's like these beautiful share certificates my grandpa had. Silver River Oil. Argentinian copper mines. An engraver's masterpiece, every one of them, and every one not worth a pinch of pelican shit. A *small* pinch of pelican shit.'

'So I should go with the company that prints its prospectus on toilet paper?'

'It's a good principle, and indeed, what most prospectuses deserve. Shit,' I said, staring at the open page.

'What?'

'The aim of this company is to buy up old, still sound buildings and rebuild them,' I said. 'James told me to sell my apartment to invest in this company. The bastard. He always was an utter, utter bastard.'

'Corinna, what are you talking about?' asked Daniel patiently.

'Read this,' I said, thrusting the offending document at him. He scanned it and gave it back.

'I've read it,' he said.

'And?' I demanded.

'And, nothing.' Daniel spread his hands.

'What was the address of the first building they were going to demolish and rebuild?'

'156 Little…' There was a pause while two was added to two. 'Oh, Lord,' said Daniel.

'Exactly. James wants me to invest in a company that intends to sell the place where I live—in order to invest in the demolition of the place where I live. That's this building. That is Insula.'

I was so angry that I leapt to my feet, almost tripping over Horatio. 'And I tell you who's trying to scare us into selling. It's James, that's who it is.'

'Have you ever invited him into this apartment?' asked Daniel, holding me by the shoulders as I paced by him.

'No,' I said. 'I split with him a year before I bought this place.'

'Does he know anyone here?'

'Only poor Holliday. And all this started before Holliday got here. In any case the man is in no position to hold a paint can. Or even identify one.'

'That's true. But, Corinna, calm down, listen. Even if it is James, it won't help if you just storm up and confront him. His hands won't have a speck of paint on them. He must have an accomplice. Someone who knows how to get in and out. James doesn't.'

'True,' I admitted. 'All right. You can let go of me. I have to apologise to Horatio anyway.'

'I'm going to grease your balcony rail,' said Daniel. 'Strange twisted sexual thoughts about women are two a penny. But money, that's a serious motive.'

I managed to coax Horatio out from under the sofa, assuaged his hurt feelings with kitty treats, and tried to get control of myself. James! The cheek of him! And to expect me to just agree without argument! Had I done that a lot when I was married to him?

I thought about it as I got out the gin. Probably, I decided. His habit of having robust discussions in the morning had ground me down and I generally agreed, first because I wanted to please him and later because I didn't care what he did. He might have got the idea that I was perfectly malleable, a yes-sir, no-sir girl. His shock when I declared that I was leaving and here were the keys must have been profound. He had reacted badly. One of the reasons I hadn't really been looking for a new lover was the intimate ugliness of that break-up. We sort of forgave each other eventually, but we were never going to be close friends again.

And certainly not now. I would have to ask all the other tenants if they had received any little feelers from the Renew company. And chop them off at the socks if they had.

There was nothing good to be said about James. So I didn't bother not saying it but read the rest of the prospectus carefully. To an accountant's eye it was full of gaps. Some were little ones (What about council permits? Height restrictions? Heritage concerns?) and some were gaping great big ones into which one could fit Port Phillip Bay. Funding? Assets? Capital?

Capital being the main problem. I could not tell what the source of the company's capital was, apart from the public float, of course. I wondered if it had anything to do with this Singapore bank. The figures had not exactly been fudged. They were projections, written more in hope than confidence and, when Daniel came back from greasing the balcony rail, I said so.

'Will they get their investors, then?' he asked. 'Perhaps the venture will fail if it's this vague.'

'We can hope,' I told him. 'But weirder things than this have sold a lot of shares. The share market works on what the Americans call sandbox politics. If one child declares that red lollies are the absolute best, every child wants one. It's a sort of "me, too!" thing. Red lollies will then boom. If it is then found that red lollies stain the lips or green lollies make you a better skateboard rider, then red will crash out of favour and green will boom. The market has all the subtle psychology of a kindergarten playground.'

Daniel looked a little shocked, as most non-money people are when they realise how basic the emotions which rule the money world are. I continued with my lecture. Daniel seemed amenable to being lectured, which was nice.

'However, he has to make us all sell. We are owners, not ordinary tenants. He would have to convince each and every person to sell.'

'So far he's been relying on scaring women,' Daniel observed.

'Perhaps that's just in the nature of a good start,' I said sourly.

We went up to the roof in no pleasant good frame of mind. I really love this place, I thought. I'm not going to have James' friends push me out of this garden, this view. We sat down in the rose bower and poured a drink. Horatio vanished into the bushes again. I wondered idly what he was doing.

Then Trudi cried out and we ran to her side. She was pointing down at the turf which she was so proud of. It had strange beige marks in it. I realised that the marks were stripes of dead grass, and they spelt out 'Whore.' Trudi was crying.

I had never seen her cry before.

'How has he done it?'

'Things going missing,' sobbed Trudi. 'My pesticide. Then my weedkiller. This is done with weedkiller. He just pours it on the grass. When I catch him—' She stopped sobbing and put her hands together. Strong gardener's hands. 'When I catch, I kill.'

'Let's call the poor policewoman again,' I said. 'Come on, Trudi. This isn't aimed at you. Have a sip of my gin and tonic and wipe your eyes.'

She had already stopped crying. She didn't bother with the glass but grabbed the bottle. She took a deep gulp of the gin and shook her head.

'Was shock,' she said briskly. 'But I still kill him.'

Chapter Thirteen

I'm sure that poor Lepidoptera White was sick of us but she came anyway, inspected the burned turf, and pointed out one thing we had missed. There was the mark of a toecap in one of the down strokes.

'Whoever he is, he's probably got a sore foot, and certainly got a ruined shoe,' she said. 'The only other thing we know about him is that he is clumsy. Though maybe that's the curse.'

Meroe, who had retired to the roof garden for some peaceful contemplation since she could not open her shop, unbent enough to smile. That was a first! Meroe, smiling at a cop! When Ms. White had taken her pictures we comforted Trudi some more and soon it had turned into an impromptu party. The Prof, making his first outing without his stick, was enthroned in the rose bower. Andy Holliday (and the bottle which was his inseparable companion) was enticed out of his apartment into the afternoon light.

The workers were all at work, of course, and no one expected a nerd to voluntarily leave home by daylight in case they turned into a video game monster or dissolved into dust. I went down to my apartment for some more glasses and some leftover muffins.

Senior Constable White accepted a muffin and a seat and was soon discussing azalea culture with Trudi. I had no idea that there was so much to be said about azaleas. Daniel and the Prof settled down to a comfortable chat about the state of the world (parlous) and the possibilities of peace (minuscule). Meroe and I found a place to sit and absorb some sunshine. Holliday blinked at the light and sighted upon Daniel.

'Seen you before,' he blurted.

'Very likely,' said Daniel, without missing a beat. Andy seemed content to just sit there on a white wicker chair and not talk so I began to ask if anyone had received an offer to sell their apartment recently.

'Just last week,' said Meroe. 'Man on the phone. Told him to go away,' she added.

The Professor swallowed his mouthful of muffin. 'Yes, I think it was Wednesday, perhaps? I was still incapacitated so I was answering the phone just for amusement. It wasn't very amusing. Apart from a few old friends and an invitation to the University Club's Moorish evening, there was a man asking me to sell. I didn't take much notice. I dislike unsolicited phone calls and I treat them all the same. I just tell them that I am not interested and hang up.'

'Young man? Old man?' I asked. The Prof shrugged.

'I didn't really notice. it was a man's voice, I am sure of that.'

'Yes,' said Meroe. 'And I thought it was a middle-aged man, so that's halfway between young and old.'

'Rang me,' said Trudi. 'I said "go away." Like it here. Or did,' she said, looking sad. I could tell she was thinking of her ruined turf.

'When this is all over,' said Daniel, 'I'll come and dig up your lawn and we will re-lay it.'

Trudi leaned over and prodded Daniel in the bicep. Her forefinger bounced off the hard muscle. She nodded her cropped head. 'Good,' she said. 'We do fast if you do digging.'

'No one rang me,' I said.

'Nor me,' said Holliday. 'But I might have been out of it,' he added. 'I'm mostly out of it, these days.'

I decided to share my suspicions about my ex-husband James with Senior Constable White and decoyed her into my apartment as we came down from the garden. Other people had work to do. Meroe was going to do a ritual of return for Andy Holliday which needed his active cooperation. Trudi was deadheading roses. I needed to do some accounts for the end of the month. It was time for Professor Dion's afternoon nap. And I had a request to make of Daniel. Fair was, after all, fair, and the sauce for the goose was also the sauce for the gander. Or so I had always been told.

I gave Ms. White the prospectus and James' address and saw her to the door. Then I shut it and leaned against it. My breath was catching in my throat.

'You came in to see me naked in my bath,' I said.

'Yes,' he agreed, lounging on my couch with Horatio.

'I would like to see you naked,' I said.

'So you shall,' he said agreeably, and bent to unlatch his boots.

One of the most erotic experiences of my life was unfolding in front of me. Without making a vulgar display but with an air of rather shy pride, Daniel took off his boots, shucked the leather jacket and undid the white shirt. He was so beautiful that I had to blink to stay conscious. The lines of his shoulders and back were perfect. Sculptural. Michelangelo would have been groping for his chisel, or other things. He didn't have that heavy bodybuilder's Schwarzenegger bulk. He was a climber and a runner. The muscles were all long and smooth. I watched as his shirt fell away from his torso and dropped to the floor.

I saw that a star-shaped scar marred the beauty of his hip as his jeans slid down his thighs. He took them off and then the prosaic black briefs and there was Daniel. He allowed me to stare at his front, then turned slowly to exhibit his back. He was a mannerist Saint Stephen without the arrows.

I don't remember crossing the floor but I found myself standing behind him. My hands slid down those rounded buttocks and found the exit wound, another star-shaped scar on his back. His skin was as hot as fire. I wrapped my arms around him from behind and laid my face between his shoulderblades. His skin tasted salty.

'Yes?' he asked, not moving. I felt him shiver.

'Not yet,' I forced myself to say. I couldn't, not yet. I just couldn't. I sank down on the couch and watched as he resumed his garments, again without any hurry.

'But soon,' he said. I nodded. Certainly, soon. Otherwise I was likely to self-combust. I laid a hand on the scar as his jeans slid up his admirable thighs.

'That's a bullet wound?'

'Shrapnel, from a grenade,' he said. 'It was curved so it left a big scar. The boy who inflicted it died. So much evil,' he said. Then he gathered me close to his chest in a massive hug. 'And now, so much good,' he said.

'The boy died?' I asked, sensing that I was about to find the key to Daniel. A key, anyway.

'Of course,' he said, face muffled in my hair. 'I shot him. Killed him instantly. He was fourteen.'

I held him close. He did not cry. I expect that he had already wept all the tears he had for futility and horror and nightmare. He unbuttoned my shirt and laid his face against my breast. We did not speak.

The light began to wane. I watched the sunbeams travel from one side of the window to the other before Daniel sat up and kissed me, hard, on the mouth.

'Corinna,' he said, looking deep into my eyes.

'Daniel,' I replied.

'I must go. Now, you can ask me. Ask me anything you want to know.'

I couldn't think of anything to ask but, 'Where do you live? How can I find you?'

He let go of me to write down an address and a phone number on the memo pad. Then he said, 'Ask,' and I asked the question which I really couldn't phrase properly.

'Why do you find me beautiful?'

'Because you are,' he said simply. 'Think of where I have been, what I have seen. In Palestine, thin means hungry, starving, sick. In Melbourne, thin means a child, a heroin addict or an anorexic. I love your flesh, your curves.' He caressed my thigh and hip. 'May they never grow less,' he added. 'I am going,' he said, and kissed me again, and went. He remembered the bread and the flyers for Cherie Holliday and closed the door gently behind himself.

I simply didn't know what to think, or feel, and I sat on the couch until the sky was dark and it was time to feed cats and myself and go to bed. So I did those things, and dreamed fiercely erotic dreams which woke me at four flooded with heat, sweating freely, and in need of a nice cold shower.

The morning began ordinary and continued so until nine. I rose, I baked, I taught Jason more useful facts about yeast, I fed him and the cats and myself and sold most of the morning's bread. I made some phone calls. Meroe came in. She seemed pleased. She was wearing a red silk wrap with sacred ibis embroidered on it.

'How did the ritual go?' I asked, handing over blueberry muffins and knot rolls.

'Very well. Should bring her within three days. I gave Andy some herbal tea. I think he might have slept. Alcoholics don't sleep properly. Cheer up, Corinna! So far today our own little mental health casualty hasn't done anything unusual.'

'The day is young,' I said gloomily. I had half expected to see Daniel. But it was too early for those who fly by night.

Meroe asked, 'Who are you going to get to help you in the shop now that those girls have an honest job?'

'I really don't know.' I sighed. 'As for the other problems, I have set up a meeting with James and I intend to skin him alive.'

'What if it isn't him?' she asked.

'Then on general principle. Do him good. Why? Do you suspect someone else?'

She made a fluid gesture with the red silk wrap.

'It is an illogical universe until you discover the underlying sense,' she told me.

'I understood everything you said until the bit about "under-lying sense,"' I said.

Meroe went out. Goss came in.

'I can help out until Friday,' she said. 'And if you could give me the wages up to then I could get my dress early.'

'Carol will keep it for you,' I said soothingly. I do not pay wages in advance. Carol Holland, though she is a Goth whose features are hard to discern through that thick white pancake they wear, is a reliable young woman and she and Goss were quite close. I told Goss so. She grimaced.

'Don't do that too often, the wind might change,' I warned her.

She got behind the counter to complain to Horatio, who never minds complaints as long as they are accompanied by skilled ear-tickling and fur-caressing.

'So, you've been to Blood Lines before?' I asked. 'How did you come to go there? Just a whim?'

Silence. Goss wasn't talking to me yet.

'Have you actually read *Interview with a Vampire*?' I continued. 'It's quite a remarkable book. Started a whole fashion. If it hadn't been for Anne Rice, Buffy would never have existed. Or Angel. No one has tried to make vampires sexy since the Hammer horror movies. I was there for the revivals. Christopher Lee. They used to film them in Highgate Cemetery near where I lived in London. He was a very suave, very cool vampire. "I vont to drink your blode."'

I managed the accent with the effortless ease of someone who had seen every Hammer horror movie, even *The Revenge of Dr. Phibes*. Actually, I had seen them in secret. Grandma would not have approved of vampire movies. So they had a sweet, secret charm. My adolescent rebellion. That, and cigarettes of course. Of the two, Hammer was only slightly less addictive.

'I saw the film,' mumbled Goss.

'*Interview with…*?'

'*A Vampire*. Yes. It was cool. Way cool. I saw it six times and bought the DVD. It's got extra scenes,' she announced proudly. Goss was talking to me again, which was good.

'If you liked the film so much, you must have been drawn to Blood Lines. Is it a Goth club?'

'Goths, some S&M. There's back rooms, but you have to be a member to go in there. Lestat told me they had a torture chamber in the crypt.'

'Well, of course,' I began and bit my tongue. Sarcasm is fatal to conversations with anyone under twenty-five. Either they don't get it and you have to explain, which is embarrassing, or they are much better at it than you and you get withered. Neither assists communication. Goss gave me that look which said 'are we having a conversation or is this one of those attempted mother–daughter things which is going to be so uncool that I will have to have a ritual bath to wash off the uncoolness?' and I shook my head.

'I'm just curious,' I said. 'Who was it who invited you and Kylie to a weekend Slayerfest before Daddy got you cable? And who still has my tape of the Buffy musical which I would like back sometime, if you please?'

'Sorry,' she said. 'I thought you might be about to tell me to stay away from bad company,' she said, laughing to show that it was a joke.

'I would,' I said. 'But I don't consider Goths bad company. No one who takes that much trouble over their costumes is trouble, usually. Besides, we have the best-dressed Goths in the southern hemisphere, which is why they filmed the triumph scene of *Queen of the Damned* here,' I said knowledgeably.

I knew about that film. I had supplied the bread for their sandwiches.

'Oh yeah, that's right. Well, let's see. You go up the steps and convince the door bitch to let you in, then you go into a sort of lobby, then there's the big room, they call it the Théâtre des Vampires, all hung with red velvet. Big screen. There's lights in the curtains too. But it's pretty dark.'

'What sort of music?'

'Techno,' she said. 'Eversun. SPF 1000. You know.'

I winced privately. Ever since I had set my face against disco, things had got worse. Now there weren't even the sugary tunes and we were rapidly running out of Bee Gees. Now there was a repeated phrase, perhaps, an uncomfortably inorganic beat, and a few thousand k's of unrelated pictures.

'They play all the old vampire movies,' Goss told me, clasping her little hands in what looked suspiciously like girlish delight. She could have been a Victorian maiden describing her favourite bouquet, except for the hair. It was green today. 'All the Hammer horror, and that real old one, black and white.'

'Oh yes, that one. *Nosferatu.*'

'Scary,' confessed Goss.

'Scared me and Horatio both so much we spent the rest of the night under the doona,' I confessed in turn.

'I think it was those teeth,' said Goss. 'Like a snake.' She shook her green head. 'Anyway, there's dancing, and you can only buy red drinks—wine or red cordial. Sometimes they have competitions. One of the people is given a little bottle of water, and you have to chase your favourite vamp and splash him or her, and there's a prize for the best death scene. It's so cool,' she enthused.

It sounded harmless enough to someone who had spent her schooldays playing murder in the dark. A lot of revenge can get taken in a girls' school in the dark. Chasing a costumed person with a bottle of holy water seemed tame by comparison. Though of course it would allow for a lot of incidental collisions and embracing and so on, which ought to ensure its popularity. While hormones remained hormones.

'I've seen Mistress Dread there,' said Goss. 'Well, Kylie said she saw her. Carol says that Mistress Dread runs the dungeon.'

'She was born to run a dungeon,' I said. Goss giggled. 'And I bet she runs a very well-conducted crypt too, with only the best of resurrected corpses,' I said.

'No, the crypt master is Lestat,' said Goss. 'He's a bit scary. Even though he asked me to, I don't think I want to go down there,' she added reflectively.

I didn't dare say a word. Goss was acquiring common sense, that rarest of commodities. Any word from me would produce an adverse reaction. I didn't quite hold my breath.

I waited for her to go on. She seemed reluctant.

'The kids say…that things happen in there. But they're just bullshitting, I suppose.'

'Bad things? Like poor Suze?' I ventured.

'Suze doesn't go in to the club,' said Goss. 'She doesn't have the clothes and they know she's a junkie. She just goes round the back, in the lane. It's not just the vamps from Blood Lines with Suze. Daniel says she won't last much longer.'

'Yes, it's very sad.'

'And it's not fair!' she burst out, with one of those young-person changes of mood which keep all people over thirty on their toes. And sometimes drive them out of their minds. I was groping for a response when a familiar voice said, 'Where does it say it has to be fair? You show me where it's written that it's a fair universe.'

'It still isn't, Daniel,' mumbled Goss.

'The only answer that God is likely to make to "Why me?", Gossamer, is "Why not you?" And it's not a useful answer, and not a useful question either. Why so sad on such a nice day, ladies?' he asked.

I was suddenly short of breath. Just seeing Daniel without warning had the same effect on me as a punch in the solar plexus I had long ago received in a minor altercation in an Irish pub.

'Suze,' said Goss. Daniel gave her a big grin.

'I am pleased to tell you that Suze got knocked down by a car last night,' said Daniel. 'No, wait, that isn't quite what I meant. I mean, poor Suze, pelvis broken in two places, but lucky Suze, because—'

'She'll have to stay in hospital for weeks and weeks,' said Goss, cheering up right away.

'And I have already called her mother to tell her that Suze will need rehabilitation and a place to live and that from about Wednesday she will be off drugs. I have also told the hospital that she will need special care as she detoxes. God knows how they are going to manage a broken bone without opiates. Mama's happy to have Suze back if she's off the stuff,' said Daniel.

'It's just what she would have wanted,' said Goss, clasping her hands again. Goss had given me such a lot of useful information that I relented on the dress. I opened the till and counted out three days' wages.

'Go and get your dress,' I said. 'You deserve it.'

Goss counted the notes. 'You forgot to tell me to go to the movies,' she said cheekily from the door. 'That's what my sister always did when her boyfriend—'

'Or I could just take the money back,' I said, and she squeaked and fled. Daniel watched her go.

'You know, I don't think I was ever that young,' he sighed.

'Me either. Oh well. I'm so pleased about Suze. Best thing that could have happened. Daniel, you weren't driving that car, were you?'

'No, ketschele, but I admit that if I had been and she had happened to totter across the road in those broken heels, I might have been tempted. Luckily, some other public-spirited citizen did. Pity he didn't leave his name,' said Daniel grimly. 'When they found her, she looked just like a broken doll, flung into the gutter by a bad-tempered child.'

'Do you think it's connected to the heroin deaths?'

'I don't know.' He sat down heavily in the shop chair. 'The police have taken paint scrapings from her clothes. There were bits of glass on the road. He may have broken a headlight. And she would have left a dent in his bumper. The accident investigation guy said that the driver was doing about thirty k's. If it had been just five k's faster she would be dead. In other news, I haven't heard even a whisper about Cherie Holliday. No one knew the face or the name. She might have moved on. Would you mind if I just sat here for a while, Corinna? I like your shop. I like the way it smells. You don't need to take any notice of me.'

As Kylie would say, as if. But people came in demanding bread and I sold loaves and cheese rolls and more muffins. That Jason had a perfect light hand with muffins. They were definitely better than mine. I was so used to bread that I tended to overmix them.

I gave Daniel a muffin, before they all got sold, and a cup of strong coffee. He looked very decorative against the wall of trays. They were silver and caught the light. With his dark, clean outline, he looked like a fallen angel repenting his error, sitting down at the gates of heaven until God changed his mind.

Of course, a fallen angel would probably not be eating blueberry muffins and drinking coffee. Then again, if they don't have coffee in heaven, and bread, I'm not going. So there.

I was just handing over the last muffin to a customer who had always refused to eat them 'because they were soggy' and who was now an enthusiastic convert, when I heard 'Psst!' from the bakery.

'Yes, Jason?'

'Is Daniel there?'

'Yes, but he's resting. Just give him time to finish his coffee, eh?'

'Oh. Yeah. Right,' said Jason.

'The muffins have sold out again,' I told him. 'You've got just the right touch for muffins. We'll have to make more tomorrow.'

'Thanks,' he said, sounding a bit stunned. I toned down the enthusiasm. The young find enthusiasm uncool. The whisper came again, more urgently.

'Did Daniel say something about Suze? Is she all right?'

The shop was otherwise empty, apart from a contemplating angel. I went to the bakery door. Jason grabbed my hand. He was really worried.

'Sort of all right. The bad news is that she was knocked down by a car. The good news is that she's alive with a broken pelvis and she'll have to stay in hospital for ages. Also, her mum is willing to have her back if she's off drugs.'

'Hey,' he said, blooming into that happy smile. 'Sweet as!'

'Daniel thought so,' I told him. 'So do I. So did Goss. Who is out, by the way, if you want to come into the shop.'

He shook his head for no. Still very street-shy, our Jason.

'Can I go and see Suze?' he asked.

'Maybe,' I said. 'You'll have to get some better clothes and perhaps if you go with Goss or Kylie or me they might let you in. They know she's an addict. They won't let anyone in who might be…sorry, Jason…'

'Smuggling in stuff,' he completed the sentence. Instead of going off the planet, as I expected, about anyone questioning the purity of his motives just because he was as thin as a wraith and had needle scars on both arms, he thought about it. Goss was not the only one who was exhibiting signs of growing up today.

'I better leave it a week,' he said soberly. 'She's gonna be real bad for a week. Suze was up to five hundred a day.'

'Five hundred what?'

He gave me the identical Goss/Kylie 'what's the weather like on your planet?' look. He rubbed finger and thumb together in a very universal gesture.

'Dollars,' he said.

I boggled. When I thought of what Suze would have had to do to how many people in order to earn five hundred dollars every day I was profoundly glad that she had broken her pelvis in two places. Apart from anything else, she needed a rest.

'What was your habit worth?' I asked, as if it was an idle question.

'Not much. Couple of caps. Just to dull it out, you know?'

'So that it didn't hurt so much?'

'Yeah,' he hung his head. I wasn't going to push him.

'Do you feel better now?'

'A bit. Everything hurts, though, you know? Like I just burned my finger. It's not bad, see?' He showed me a small red patch. It would not even blister. 'But it hurt like I'd put my arm in the gas flame.'

'That's bad,' I commented. I would have to ask Daniel about this. I knew precisely as much as the ordinary person knew about heroin, which was nothing at all.

Jason shrugged. 'Why don't we make doughnuts?' he asked.

'Because I'd need to buy a fryer,' I said.

'You could do that,' he said.

'Yes, but I would also need to learn how to make them, have a hot tray to keep them warm, and enter into direct competition with the doughnut shop just near the station,' I replied.

He looked a little crestfallen. 'But if you'd like to invent some new muffins, I'll be happy to let you try them,'

I said.

'New muffins?'

'Yes, why not? Try some combinations, maybe put nuts in them. There's a shelf of books over there. Why not have a look?'

He looked evasive. 'I…lost my glasses,' he said.

'I've never seen you wear glasses,' I said, surprised.

'I don't read that good,' he mumbled as the moment stretched out. 'I'm stupid. Didn't you know that?' he demanded savagely. I had to think of something fast.

'That's because you've never wanted to read,' I said. 'They never gave you cookbooks to read, did they?'

'No,' he admitted.

'Well, then. Take down that little one—yes, that one—open it at the first page, and read it to me. I'm not going to watch. I have to get back into the shop.'

Very reluctantly, Jason dragged himself across the bakery, found the book *Muffins and Tea Cakes* and I heard him begin to read as I went back into the shop.

'Tea is a meal wh…whi…Shit. Must be which is taken in the…after…afternoon,' he said. 'Tea cakes or muffins are usu… usua…whatever, served at tea.'

We had limped and stammered through two pages when Daniel stirred. Goss had come into the shop, almost dragging a Goth girl by the hand.

'Hello, Carol,' I said, peering at her as I always did. There must be a face under all that make-up.

'She isn't Carol,' said Goss, bubbling over with excitement. 'She's Cherie. This is Cherie Holliday.'

Chapter Fourteen

'Hello, Cherie,' I said. I couldn't think of anything else to say. Not for the life of me. Apart from 'would you like a ham roll?' which didn't seem appropriate. Daniel rescued me. He took the girl's hand in both his own and she thawed a little.

'No wonder no one knew you on the street,' he said easily. 'You weren't on the street.'

'Never was,' snapped Cherie. 'I had some money. I stayed at a hostel. I got a job. At the boutique. Did you do the posters?' she demanded of me.

'Yes,' I admitted. She looked ready to fly at me with those black nails.

'Is it true?' she said in that tight, hard voice. For a moment I didn't know what she was asking. Then I caught on.

'Yes, it's true,' I said. 'The man was caught, he's in jail, and your father believes you. He knows it was all true.'

'He called me a liar,' she said. I felt helpless. This was not the return of the prodigal daughter for which I had been hoping.

'Hey,' said Daniel gently. 'The man's been suffering to the max.'

'So have I,' she returned tartly.

'He made a mistake,' Daniel said relentlessly. 'Have you never made any mistakes? Call the Guinness Book of Records,' he said to Goss. 'A girl who's never made a mistake.'

'Carol,' Goss urged, embarrassed. 'Don't be such a bitch! You should see the poor man. He's sorry. I never saw anyone that sorry before.'

'I don't care,' snarled Cherie.

'You don't have to see him,' said Daniel. 'You can go back and hug your pain and humiliation to your breast and sour your life with it. We can't stop you. We'll tell him you're still alive and you still hate him,' he said.

There was a long pause. Then Cherie drew herself up.

'I'll tell him myself,' she replied haughtily.

'Good,' said Daniel. 'Goss, go get Meroe. Tell her it's an emergency,' he added. 'Tell her that you can mind her shop.'

'Cool!' Goss raced out. I pictured the scene. Goss selling the wrong kind of newt eyes. Goss telling fortunes with the wrong kind of cards. Goss telling the customers that magic was so cool. In spite of the seriousness of the situation, I smiled.

Daniel caught the smile. He was thinking the same thing.

'She can't go far wrong with "you will cross water and meet a tall dark handsome stranger who is like totally cool like Tom Cruise,"' he suggested.

Carol/Cherie had felt our attention turning away from her and didn't like it.

'Who's Meroe? What's happened to Mum?' she demanded.

'Divorced,' said Daniel. 'She stuck with your assailant. Your father divorced her for it. This woman is Meroe the witch, and I'd moderate my tone, if I were you.'

'A witch?' Cherie was impressed. 'Not the Sibyl's Cave witch? Everyone says she's mega cool. And powerful. I've got one of her talismans.'

'The very same. She's been looking after your father. I'd be polite,' Daniel advised.

He didn't need to warn her. By the time Meroe, hair flying and trailing a sky-blue silken wrap, sailed into the shop, Cherie was very biddable.

Goss had already explained the situation. Meroe inspected Cherie. Cherie allowed the inspection.

'We must clean your face,' said Meroe firmly. 'He will need to see you as you are, not as you choose to face the world. And you shall see him as he is. Come with me. You too, Corinna,' she ordered, and I fell in at heel as well as Cherie. *Auctoritas*, as the Prof said. Meroe definitely had it.

Daniel sat down behind the counter and patted Horatio.

Meroe took Cherie into her own bathroom and they emerged, ten minutes later, heavily scented with some aromatic oil. Cherie now looked like her picture. She had a strong, determined chin, a pale complexion, a high forehead and sharp, intelligent eyes. I could not read her expression. All her emotions were tightly corked. And were likely to go off with a bang.

'Oil of…?' I asked, sniffing.

'Sage,' said Meroe. 'For clarity. Come,' she ordered, and we followed her into the lift. Meroe had her usual basket. Cherie clutched her leather handbag closer to her bosom. I was hoping that she wasn't armed. She might have spent three years contemplating revenge on a father who had betrayed her. Or she might just be intending to tell him that he was a bastard and walk out. In which case, she would about finish off poor pathetic Andy Holliday. He would dive into a bottle and in due course they could just pour him into his grave.

Meroe calmly entered the door code and we went in unannounced. Andy was lying in his T-chair, almost watching some football. He turned his head as we came in. He wasn't drunk, but he had definitely been drinking. Cherie stopped dead and stared at him.

Meroe left them there and went across the room to open the door of the second bedroom. I had no idea what she was doing. I felt like I should incant something because this meeting had every chance of going horribly wrong.

'I saw the poster,' said Cherie in that tight voice.

'Baby?' asked Andy Holliday, trying to get to his feet and wallowing in the chair.

'Is it true?' she demanded.

He wrenched himself upright and stopped just out of touching distance while he stared avidly at her, from head to feet and back again.

'It's you,' he said. 'I looked for you everywhere and I couldn't find you.'

Cherie nailed him with her hard eyes. 'Is it true? Do you believe me now?'

'I believe you,' he said. 'I think I always believed you, but your mother…but I got rid of her. I believe you,' said Andy Holliday, sagging down to the carpet. 'I believe you.'

'Daddy?' she said in a high, child's voice. They stayed just where they were, frozen, Andy on his knees on the floor, Cherie poised to run. Something had to happen to break the impasse and I could not imagine what it would be.

Then Meroe brought the large white teddy bear out of the second bedroom and thrust it into Cherie's arms. She was shocked out of her bitter concentration and her face crumpled immediately. She dropped down to join her father and buried her face in the teddy bear's fur. Andy Holliday embraced her and began to cry.

'You brought Pumpkin Bear,' she wailed. 'Daddy, you brought Pumpkin back.'

Meroe joined me at a distance. She lit a small dish of gums and set it down on the marble table. I stole a cigarette from the packet and lit it. Ah, sweet goddess Nicotine, how I still miss your worship. I inhaled deeply.

'I put a few drops of that Charlie perfume on the bear,' she said. 'Scent is more evocative than sight, sometimes. The frankincense will cleanse some of their bitterness and fear. They'll be all right. I'll come up and see them tonight.'

'You're amazing,' I told her. She grinned her witchly grin and draped the azure silk around her shoulders. 'Come along,' she said. 'I have to get back to my shop. I've left Goss in charge, and though she is mostly a sweet girl…'

'With you all the way,' I said, stubbing out the smoke.

The pair on the floor had forgotten that we were there and I'm sure they never noticed that we had gone.

Meroe ran back to the Sibyl's Cave before Goss could sell someone the wrong ingredient for a magic potion and I went back into the bakery and evicted Daniel from the chair. My need was greater than his. I had interrupted Jason's reading practice in mid-recipe and I gestured for him to go on.

'Mix lig…liggly?'

'Lightly,' suggested Daniel.

'Spoon into greased muffin pans and bake at three-fifty for ten minutes,' Jason concluded triumphantly. 'What happened upstairs?' he asked.

'It's all right,' I said to Daniel and Jason. 'They had a reunion and are presently sitting on the floor, hugging each other and crying. Not that it wasn't tense. Meroe was wonderful.'

'Well, duh! She's a witch,' said Jason. 'That's nice. Suze is in hospital and Cherie Holliday is home. That's a nice day,' he said.

And so it was. So far.

I did not know why Daniel was staying with me, but it did allow me to leave the cleaning to Jason. He looked very nice in his overall and white shoes, very much the baker. Probably more than I was, at least from the tracksuit. I went to see if the Prof was home and interested in some good news. He was, both.

'Send to slay the fatted calf, for this my son was lost and is come home again,' he quoted. 'How nice, how very, very nice.'

'It was touch and go for a while there,' I told him.

'Well, naturally, it would be. Happy endings require preparation. They don't just spontaneously arise, like mushrooms. Good of you to come to tell me, Corinna.'

He was dressed in a very nice suit. He looked dapper.

'Going out?' I asked.

'Lunch at the University Club,' he said. 'Likely to be sadly boring but the food is always good. Nice to be able to walk without that wretched stick too.'

'Where is it?' I looked around. 'I meant to have a look at that Anubis head handle.'

'Oh, sorry. Mr. Pemberthy borrowed it this morning. He's twisted his ankle or something, poor man. May I escort you to the elevator, Madame Boulangère?'

'Delighted,' I said, accepting his arm.

When I got back Jason was well into the scrubbing and Daniel was sitting with Horatio, Heckle and Jekyll on the stairs. They looked very comfortable together. I ducked across to the Cafe Delicious and bought lasagne for three. Then I thought about it and doubled the order. I still had a recovering drug addict to feed. And he was also a teenage boy. Put that together and you have an appetite which could dine at Olympic gold-medal level. You have a boy who could eat whole cities into subjection.

The scrubbing lasted another hour. The lasagne lasted six minutes. Jason wiped his mouth, ate a casual baguette, polished off the last of the Coca Cola he had bought to refresh his labours and sighed. He was, I believe, actually sated at last. For, oh, I don't know, minutes, before he would be hungry again. I gave him the bag of food and he changed clothes and left with a 'bye.' That was another innovation. Usually he just vanished.

'He's improving,' said Daniel from the other side of the clean floor.

'I wish I knew where he slept,' I said.

'Flagstaff,' said Daniel. 'He's there every night. He gets fresh rations from each circuit and even Sister Mary has limited him to three sandwiches and two cups of soup each time. Though she did say that God loves a willing eater. Which he is. Can you lend me your couch for a few hours? I'm going to need some sleep. Also a shower? I had to carry an OD to where the ambulance could get to him. I'm feeling grubby and I've got to go out on the van again tonight. Then we might have some dinner?'

'My ablutions are your ablutions. My couch is your couch,' I said formally. 'But I'll be using the desk in the parlour, so why not have my bed? You will have Horatio as company but he's very civilised. If you don't want him, shut the door. I'll just do a few chores here and I'll be right up.'

He kissed me gently. He seemed very sleepy and I let him go. My mystery man. Perhaps he really was a vampire. Then I pottered around a little, washing Jason's clothes and sticking them in the dryer for the morrow. I was still not relying on Jason. It was nice to have him but Daniel had warned me that at any moment Jason might revert to Jase and vanish. I could still do the whole baking on my own. I was just wondering where I was going to find another shop assistant after Friday when I was aware that someone was standing in Calico Alley. Leaning on my doorpost. A big man in a Blues Brothers suit. Last seen beating my assistant baker and knocking out one of his teeth.

'Yes?' I asked in my best middle-class voice. 'Can I help you?'

'That boy,' he said in a gravelly tone probably borrowed from the Godfather. Or maybe the Sopranos. I don't watch Mafia films much. Unless there's really nothing else on.

Or Animal Planet has reset to crocodiles. Or sharks. Or crocodiles and sharks. Both of which were closely related to the man in the doorway.

'Which boy?' I elevated an eyebrow.

'Jase,' he snarled. I decided not to be too clever.

'He's my assistant,' I said. 'Jason.'

'He been working for you long?'

'A couple of weeks,' I said. At the time it really seemed like that, though in fact it was only a week.

'He always here early in the morning?' he asked. I did not like this at all. The man was big, strong and unpleasant.

I edged my hand towards the mobile phone into which I have programmed the police emergency number. I switched the phone on. It beeped. His eyes flicked to it.

'I start at four,' I told him. 'When the ovens come on.'

'And he's here?' he demanded, with menaces.

'Yes. What are you asking all these questions for? I've told you, he wants to be a baker and he has to start at four. Who are you, anyway?'

He made a very fast movement. It could have been the death of Heckle, but alley cat reflexes never fade. As a hard heel came down, viciously, towards Heckle's exposed white belly, he did a lightning wriggle which would have broken an eel's back and wasn't there when the heel cracked into the flour sack. I yelped and pressed the speed dialler on the phone.

'I've just called the cops,' I said. 'Do stay and wait until they come.'

'You want to be careful with them vermin,' he said, and grinned at me. A sadist. Great. Just when it had seemed like such a nice day. I felt sick to the pit of my stomach. I also felt that if I could reach the breadknife I would have cut this man's throat. In a church. But I knew about bullies. Some will be placated if you do just as they wish. Some can be confounded if you do something unexpected, like not reacting to the attempted murder of your cat. I decided to try this. I wanted him out of my bakery, out of my life, as soon as possible. The only way to win this cat-and-mouse game, as the Cat said in *Red Dwarf*, was not to be the mouse.

'What do you want with Jason?' I demanded. I wasn't confident of the way this interview was going but I could get Daniel to warn Jason to stay away if his hunters had grown this bold.

'If you ain't lying,' he said, 'we don't want nothing to do with the little cunt. You can have him. You better not be lying,' he told me.

'You can check,' I pointed out. 'Everyone knows what time I start work. Now, if there's nothing else…?'

'Nah,' he said. He stepped back from the doorway and I shut the door in his face. I locked both locks and heard the steel wards snick home. I threw the bolt. I cancelled the emergency call. Then I burst into tears. I found Heckle and hugged him while he growled and told me what he would have done to the bastard if he hadn't been twenty times his size and had such hard hoofs. I spread kitty treats recklessly to apologise for belonging to approximately the same species as that creature.

Then I went up to my own apartment. I found Daniel neatly asleep in my bed. I slid in behind him, embraced him as though he was a large, breathing teddy bear, and fell instantly and heavily asleep.

We woke at six, when the light moves across the window and falls on the pillow. Daniel turned over, exclaimed, 'What?', felt over my face and grunted, 'Oh.' Having thus explained to his own satisfaction where he was and who was lying next to him, he opened his eyes and said, 'Hello, Corinna.'

'Hello, Daniel.' I snuggled closer to him, then forced myself away. 'Let's go and get some dinner.'

'We could just stay here,' he said dreamily. 'Very nice bed. Nice cat. Nice company.'

'No, I'm getting up, I need to talk to you.'

'Talk here,' he offered, but released me when I sat up.

I had gone to bed in my clothes and I felt frowsty. I shed them and went into the bathroom and had a short, scalding shower and put on clean clothes, which always makes me feel better. When I returned Daniel was sitting at the kitchen table with a cup of coffee. I don't know how he makes it so fast. Some sort of magic, perhaps. Meroe would know.

'So, what's wrong?' he asked.

I told him about the Blues Brother and his attempt to kill Heckle. My voice shook.

'I wonder what our Jase has been doing?' said Daniel into his cup. 'As I said, he really should be too minor a player to attract heavy duty attention from the John Smiths. Tell me exactly what he said. Tell me slowly and don't leave anything out.'

I complied. It was not a pleasant retelling. Daniel tugged at where his beard would have been if he'd had a beard.

'You did well, ketschele. Got out of an interview with Big John unbruised. Not many can say that. You must have reminded him of his parole officer. Well, whatever it is they are investigating, it must have happened after four in the morning and you have given Jason an alibi. Inadvertent and, as you say, false, but it might distract them. I don't see any major harm in Jason but the mind boggles at what he might have done, or been on the edges of.'

'Do you know anything about Jason? Such as why he left home?'

Daniel delivered a report like a police officer, in a monotone. 'He was the third child in a big multi-father family and they all picked on him. Dysfunctional families quite often have a scapegoat. The psychs used to think that it had something to do with relationship by blood—the cuckoo in the nest theory—but it doesn't. They can elect any one kid and make his life hell. Jason managed okay until the latest stepfather decided that he really couldn't stand having Jason around and threw him out.'

'Just like that?'

'Just like that.'

'How can his mother allow it?' I protested. What a romantic thing for me to say. My own mother had left me ploughing barefoot through icy mud because she didn't believe in shoes. They cut off a child's natural contact with the earth, she thought. I had the chilblains for months. And the pneumonia for weeks. If Grandma Chapman hadn't rescued me I would have died, because Father didn't believe in antibiotics. Mothers, forsooth. Families, forsooth! Daniel took my hand.

'Imagine this. You are born into a dysfunctional family yourself, where no one cares about you. Even worse, you are alternately hugged and slapped, neither for any good reason. You know that no one loves you. You are starving for affection. You lie down for the first boy who asks and you get pregnant. Then the boy leaves and you only have the baby and you know that the baby will love you alone, except that's not what babies do, and you are miserable and trapped and even lonelier. Then another boy comes along and the same thing happens again. After three or four children you don't have your looks anymore and you have to accept older and possibly violent men, and they still leave you, partly because you now have a brood of underfed, insecure children with no manners.'

'That's awful,' I said.

'Yes,' agreed Daniel. 'Jason's mother might have really wanted to love him but she had to choose between Jason, who was difficult and aggressive and actually believed it when they told him he was stupid, and the latest boyfriend who, this time, might stay with her.'

'How old is Jason?'

'Fifteen.'

'Shit,' I said.

'Quite.'

I drank coffee. Daniel drank coffee. Horatio sat on the windowsill and tried to outstare the setting sun. He does this sometimes. I've never kept count but the score is probably about fifty-fifty sun/cat.

'Where shall we get some dinner?' I asked.

'How about asking Meroe and the Prof and sending out for some gourmet takeaway?' he suggested. 'And Trudi and maybe Cherie and Andy. Assuming that they've actually bonded again.'

'Too early for that,' I predicted. 'She is still so angry with him.'

'You'd be amazed,' said Daniel, smiling at me affectionately. 'She'll have shed a lot of it by now. She's been carrying it for so long. It'll be such a relief to put it down. But you were right about her, Corinna. What a strong-hearted girl! Out at fourteen and an abuse survivor and she finds a job, finds a place to live, finds a passion.'

'What passion?' I asked.

'The Goths,' he said. 'Just the right philosophy—world weary, sophisticated, a little edgy. Very detached from the world of abusive uncles and nice middle-class fathers and betrayals.'

'You like them,' I said.

'They're like the Society for Creative Anachronism,' he said. 'Or the war-game people. Or the science fiction fans. They have created an elaborate fantasy to comfort them for the shortcomings of the modern world. They put a huge amount of effort into it. For example, learning languages and courtesy, making perfect period costumes, memorising every move that Napoleon made at Austerlitz. Even sitting through seven hundred episodes of "Star Trek." This means that, unlike most people, they have a mission. They have things to think about apart from the mundane.'

'So there aren't any bad Trekkies?' I asked sarcastically. 'Ones that die young and fester instead of live long and prosper?'

See previous comments about the dangers of sarcasm. He just answered me as if it was a serious argument.

'Oh yes, of course there are bad Goths and nasty SCA people and evil dungeon masters. But they are in a society that really wants to maintain its fantasy. So they get thrown out if they make too much trouble for the others. I don't think it matters what fantasy it is. As long as it is a courteous, creative, intelligent fantasy, then it rejects someone who, for example, wants to discover how fourteenth century soldiers handled rape in armour or wants to re-enact the fall of Calais with real blood. The fantasy people self-select for intelligence and good manners. There are way worse people to learn your social interaction from. As I get older I begin to believe that good manners are much more important than most social skills,' said Daniel.

'This must not be taken to apply to Nerds Inc.,' I commented.

'They don't get out much,' he agreed.

'And bikie gangs,' I added.

'You'd be surprised,' said Daniel ambiguously. 'Now, what about some dinner?'

I started telephoning and found all in favour of gourmet pizzas from the Pizzeria De Luxe, which were always superb. Also they deliver. Cherie answered Andy's phone and said she'd be glad to come but they couldn't stay because she and her father were going to pick up her stuff from the room she shared with four girls in a hostel in Carlton. She asked if she could bring Pumpkin and I said yes, a little bemused. Most seventeen-year-olds didn't bring their teddy bear to dinner.

'She's really only fourteen,' said Daniel. 'That's when her old life stopped. And she's been abused. That puts bookmarks in someone's life: Before and After. So she's oscillating, at the moment, between about seven and about fifty. She'll settle down. Shall we pack the chateaux collapseaux and a few glasses? And does Horatio attend these gatherings?'

'Of course,' I said. 'He might like to keep Pumpkin company.'

Chapter Fifteen

We had a very agreeable little party. The Prof had brought a bottle of bubbly (superior bubbly, of course, if not actually French) and we all drank to Cherie's return. She divided her time between urging her father to eat and scolding him for not talking. Horatio greeted Pumpkin politely and ambled off to keep his rendezvous in the lilac bushes. I did wonder who he was meeting. Were we going to be introduced?

Trudi had recovered from her shock and was describing the spring plantings she intended to make, urging us to dig deep and pay for some very superior lilliums which she said were perfumed like heaven. She obviously had decided to stay. Kylie, a little downcast, joined us and ate three olives and an anchovy. That was binge eating for Kylie.

'Jon's gone to Namibia,' she said. 'Just when it was all cool.'

'Never mind,' soothed the Prof. 'He'll be back. Have some champagne.'

Kylie had heard about Cherie's reappearance. 'So, you weren't a junkie proz on the street like they thought,' she said. Daniel, placing a suppressing hand on her thin shoulder, said, 'Kylie, you really ought to eat something,' which always guaranteed a rave on the subject of fat and its avoidance by the latest 'famine' diet. Gossamer nudged her into silence. The sojourn in the magic shop had changed Goss' life, she said. Now, she wanted to be a Wiccan witch. Meroe uttered a brief invocation to the mother goddess which I assumed was devout. Goss and Kylie dragged her away to be cross-examined.

The pizzas were interesting. Teppanyaki. Sushi. Barbecued chicken. Tomato and goat's cheese. One with every possible kind of salami. If Jason was here he would be asking me why we didn't make pizza. How could anyone have thought that he was stupid? He was bright as a button and full of interesting ideas, though I was intending to confine him to muffins for the time being. Families, I decided, were strange. It was not a new thought and I was bored with it long before it reached its conclusion that there was nothing to be done about them.

Daniel, Horatio and I left early, dead-heating Andy and Cherie for the lift. She was scolding him for drinking too much and he was leaning against her, one arm draped around her shoulders. On his face was a blissful smile.

'That's a happy sign,' said Daniel as we went into my apartment.

'It is?'

'You don't scold someone unless you care about them,' he answered. 'Now, you need to go to bed and I need to check all these rosters before I go out later.'

I ceded him my desk and took myself off to bed. I fell asleep wondering why sex had gone off the agenda. Then realised that I had taken it off. I tried to remember what sex with James had been like and shuddered myself off to sleep. Oh yes. Like that. No wonder I had given up on it.

I woke at four when the alarm shrilled. Daniel was not there. I had only known him for a short time but his absence left a gap in my life. I fed everyone and met Jason at the door. He slipped inside for his shower and donned his baker's clothes.

'Miss?' he asked me, eyes wide.

'Corinna,' I said. 'I'm not a teacher.'

'I heard…the kids told me that Big John came here looking for me and you told him I'd been here for weeks,' he said, very fast.

'And if he's a friend of yours I've got some advice about choosing them,' I said. 'He tried to stomp Heckle. I near as dammit called the cops.'

'He thinks I did something but I didn't,' explained Jason, hardly at all.

'Yes,' I said. I have commented previously on how I hate talking in the morning.

'So now he knows it wasn't me so he's not chasing me and I can serve in the shop if you like,' he said.

'Good,' I told him. 'What sort of muffins are you going to make for the customers today?'

But I was missing an emotional nuance, which I often do at four a.m., not a good hour for emotional nuances unless one has been smoking dope. Jason shifted from foot to foot.

'I mean, thanks,' he blurted out. 'Thanks for saying that. Saved my life,' he added, and leaned across and kissed me.

I hugged him heartily. He had definitely put on weight. I couldn't count every rib anymore.

'That's the last lie I tell for you, Jason, so don't press your luck.'

'I won't,' he said. Meaning that he would. 'I got this idea for a sort of plum pudding muffin. It would have spices and sultanas.'

'Not very plum puddingy,' I commented, setting dough hooks in motion.

'No, but it also has candied peel and brandy. Or maybe rum. What do you think?'

'What's in the store cupboard?' I asked.

'Got the peel and the sultanas,' he said. 'And the spices. I checked yesterday. No rum. But we've got brandy.' He produced the bottle. From that very bottle had Daniel Cohen poured a tot to recover a shocked baker when Suze had nearly died on my grate. I regarded it sentimentally.

'So we have. You do know that the alcohol gets cooked off? You aren't going to put anyone over point o-five with your muffins. All right. I leave it up to you.'

'Great!' He seemed genuinely pleased. And if it didn't work, we would know soon enough, and we could make a batch of raspberry replacements fast. I could afford to lose a few muffins in a failed experiment.

'Keep in mind that muffin crumb isn't very strong, it's not going to be able to carry anything like as much fruit as a pudding, which is a load of dried fruit glued together with suet. And it's boiled.'

'And it's supposed to be heavy,' he agreed. 'I reckon the same proportion as the apple muffins, what do you think?'

'Sultanas are dried, they take up moisture. You'll need a bit more wet. But the proportions sound right. I'll leave you to get on with them, and I'll do the health bread.'

I mixed the crumbly stuff and got it into the oven. Then I busied myself with a second cup of coffee while all around me the yeast was working its alchemy. Heckle and Jekyll were bouncing up and down at the alley door so I opened it, even though it was still dark. The rodent count was down again. Either the cats were spending more time asleep, had reached an accommodation with the mice, or the rodents had moved to somewhere less well defended. The Mouse Police sniffed the night, approved, and wandered out to spend more time with it.

I didn't want to disturb Jason's concentration so I didn't try to talk. Time passed. The Mouse Police came back, looking smug. The first batch of rye bread went into the oven. Jason rattled his muffin tins into the hot depths and closed the door gently.

'Ten minutes,' he said, wiping his forehead. 'Then we'll know.'

He leaned on a mixing tub and watched that oven as I have seen Jekyll watch a mouse hole, willing the muffins to rise. When he crept forward to take a peek I warned, 'Don't do it,' and he snatched his hand back as though he had burned it. Opening the oven to see if a cake is rising is like pulling up the radishes to see if they are growing.

The tension was getting to me. I went upstairs to get more coffee. Now that we had two bakers I ought to get a coffee machine for downstairs too, I thought. When I came back he had taken the trays out of the oven and was levering one free, desperate to find out if his idea had worked. I watched him from the stairs. He tore the muffin apart and stuffed a piece in his mouth.

And then he smiled. I let out the breath I had been holding.

'Want to try one, Corinna?' he asked, with really a very good approximation of cool.

I bit. It tasted wonderful. It did taste like a plum pudding too. A light, easy-to-eat plum pudding. Spicy. The texture was perfect. I said so. Jason glowed.

Then he made another batch and we got on with the pasta douro, baguettes and twists and rolls. Our bread—forgive me—and butter. I had a proposition for Jason.

'Jason, how would you feel if I asked you to be my apprentice? It's four years and you have to go to school as well. I think you could be a very good baker.'

He stopped dead as though I had shot him. All the joyous colour drained out of his face.

'I...dunno,' he said. 'I don't know if I could stick to it. I...haven't ever had a real job.'

'Tell you what. Work for me for six months. If you still like baking, then we'll talk about it again, all right?' Clearly I had rushed him and the poor boy was panicking.

'All right,' he said, relieved.

I really shouldn't try to do anything but bake early in the morning. I always get things wrong.

Jason cheered up a little after his next batch of plum pudding muffins also came out superb. He offered one to Daniel, who wafted in about six, looking beautiful and tired. Like an angel who has been given humanity to care for, is sick of the entire species and who is about to petition God to abolish them and try again with the Neanderthals this time.

'This is a wonderful muffin,' he said. 'You are a great baker,' he said to me.

'Not me,' I said, pointing to Jason. Daniel slapped Jason on the shoulder.

'You have hidden depths, Jase,' he said. 'That's the best muffin I ever tasted. Can I have another one and a cup of coffee to accompany it if I ask really nice?'

He sat down and the Mouse Police planted themselves on him. Heckle on his feet, Jekyll on his lap. He looked like he belonged. When Jason brought him coffee and another muffin he ate and drank as though he was very hungry and thirsty. He didn't seem to want to talk so Jason and I completed the baking. I still didn't know anything about him. But did I care? Probably not. My mind had decided that he was a good guy. I didn't know what he had been doing to get so tired, and I didn't care about that either. I had it bad.

'What about trying a caraway seed muffin?' asked Jason. 'In that book it said that they used to make caraway toffee in the old days.'

'How would you reproduce the toffee flavour?' I asked.

'Dunno. Maybe burn some sugar, and use that to flavour the milk and water?' he suggested.

'Interesting. Or you could make some toffee and cool it in threads. There's a confectionery slab over there. The marble one. Then you could put some on top of every muffin. Nice thought. Try it later today with a small batch. I'll give you some money to buy more caraway seeds.'

'All right,' he said.

'Now, can I leave you to take the rye bread out when the bell rings while I lead Daniel up to a convenient couch? I don't want him to fall asleep on that chair. I've done that and it takes days to iron out the kinks.'

He nodded. I de-catted Daniel and led him up the stairs, arranged him on the couch and draped my mink blanket over him. I don't think he was actually awake during any part of the journey and he was certainly asleep as I laid him down and took off his boots.

He had a hole in the toe of his left sock and I had to fight down the urge to peel it off and darn it. Whatever I had, it was acute.

I did a few household things, listening to Daniel breathe. When I went down again, the sun was up, the baking was complete, and Jason was making calculations on a piece of paper and wondering aloud if we had a sugar thermometer.

We had, as it happened. I've no idea why. I have a theory that kitchens, once they reach a certain level of complexity, attract new gadgets into their orbit, like planets. Only this can account for the fact that I own two melon ballers.

We checked off the waybills and stacked the loaves, stocked the shop, and opened the shutters. I left Jason to deal with the carrier and occupied myself supplying the early-to-the-office with breakfast. The poor bastards. They were already sniffing at the Christmassy scent of the plum pudding muffins and they went leaping joyously off the trays.

Jason reported the carrier had come and gone. Then he appeared in his premiere role as baker's boy. I watched him carefully but he gave correct change, didn't offend the customers and even smiled at some of them. When Goss wandered in at nine, full of her Wicca lore, she sniffed at him but didn't say anything.

She took his place at the counter and he surrendered it without comment. He went back into the bakery to start cleaning and I, for the first time in years, didn't have anything to do. It was an odd feeling.

My first impulse was to go upstairs and spend the morning watching Daniel sleep, always a rewarding occupation. But perhaps I shouldn't leave my staff without supervision. I'd never had a staff before. I was new at this.

What did I really hate about supervisors? The way they walked around and poked their noses into things. There wasn't a lot of room in Earthly Delights to do any major pacing so I thought I would take a plum pudding muffin to Meroe and ask how she had gone with her newest recruit. I checked. Jason washing out the mixers in the bakery. Goss behind the counter in the shop. Horatio in his usual place. All present and accounted for. It was probably safe to leave them for a while.

Meroe had a headache. I knew because she was drinking her headache tea, which smells like new mown grass. Her shop smelt of incense, not of metho. Belladonna reposed in the window, batting idly at a Celtic talisman for courage.

'I've brought you a muffin made by my new apprentice,' I said.

She lifted her head as though the light hurt her eyes. 'May you have good fortune with him,' she said. 'Better, perhaps, than I will have with mine. My only consolation is that she will get bored very fast and take up something else. Buddhism, say. They are supposed to be terribly patient.'

'Anyone who makes sand gardens has to be patient,' I agreed. 'Goss gave you a hard time?'

'They both did,' said Meroe, smiling bravely. 'And if, when my head feels better, I hop on a plane to America in order to assassinate the scriptwriters of "Charmed," I must ask you not to be surprised.'

I promised a complete lack of astonishment. I could imagine what those two had put Meroe through. 'When do I get to do love spells?' would be the beginning, and 'How do I summon a demon, they're really cool,' would be next.

I comforted her with the hope that they would definitely get bored when they worked out that Wicca didn't travel on the left-hand path, and went back to Earthly Delights.

I heard no raised voices. Nothing appeared to be broken. Jason and Goss must be staying out of each other's way. There was a rush of business then which kept Goss and me busy for the next four hours. She wasn't talking much and had a prim, self-righteous air which I associated with her recent foray into the occult.

So it wasn't until lunchtime that I went into the bakery and found Jason lying on the floor. I ran and knelt beside him and then I found that he was not dead, he was not overdosed, he had not been beaten. He was drunk. The empty brandy bottle had rolled away from his limp hand. He had wiped himself out completely.

I manoeuvred him onto a couple of flour sacks and had a look at the room. They say Sherlock Holmes invented deduction. Ridiculous. Women invented it. Who else needs to know what, for example, a child has eaten when the child herself will swear blind, between retches, that she hasn't eaten anything at all? And one decides from the green stains on the knees of the trousers and the fact that there is an apricot tree heavy with unripe fruit (which the child has been forbidden to climb) just next door. No one gets lied to as much as mothers. Necessity is the mother of deduction.

The bakery was shining clean, even the floor, and it was dry. It takes half an hour to dry. Jason had started his caraway experiment. The toffee had reached soft ball stage and had been left to solidify in the saucepan. The flour, sugar and caraway seeds were weighed out. The muffin tins were oiled. He had been interrupted after he had finished the cleaning and while he was making toffee by—what?

Or whom?

I went back into the shop with the strong intention of strangling Goss. But I did not yell. I asked her very quietly, 'What did you say to Jason?'

She didn't bother to deny it. 'He said he was going to be your apprentice,' she said. 'He must have been lying.'

'Go on,' I prompted. She was beginning to look a little uncomfortable. She toyed with one of the five rings in her ear.

'I said he wasn't, he was just a worthless junkie,' she said.

'And?'

Now she was really worried. Even Goss has enough sense of self preservation to know when she had gone too far. She was conscious of this, but not as conscious as she would be in a moment.

'And you were just being nice to him because of Daniel. That's all I said!' she yelped as I advanced on her.

'I'm not going to sack you,' I said through clenched teeth, 'because you are leaving anyway. But tomorrow, if you ever wish to be saved, you are going to apologise to Jason. I did ask him to be my apprentice. He has a lot of talent. You didn't notice that. Have I made myself clear, Gossamer?'

'Talent? Him?' she almost screeched.

'Talent, him. Now behave yourself, I've got things to do. If you flounce out,' I added, turning my back on her, 'don't return.'

I went into the bakery. I didn't hear the door slam so I assumed that she was staying. Don't ever tell me that men are more violent than women. They just use different methods. At school I had often thought that a nice, simple, straightforward punch in the nose would be preferable to female methods of torture.

I made Jason more comfortable on a pile of empty flour sacks. The Mouse Police surveyed him dubiously, wondering if he would make a good perch and deciding against it.

It would be hours before he woke. There hadn't been enough brandy left in the bottle to kill him. And he hadn't drunk the vanilla essence, so he probably wasn't an alcoholic. I could have kicked that little bitch Goss. I hoped that Meroe had explained karmic debt, because unless she mended her manners, Goss was going to come back as a slug. And in Trudi's garden, slugs got salted.

Kylie had taken Goss' place when I came back into the shop.

'Goss called and asked me to take over,' she said breathlessly. 'She said she was shaking too hard to message. She's really lost it.'

'She never had it,' I muttered. 'What do you think of Jason?'

'If he made those muffins, he's cool,' she said. 'I just had a little tiny piece. But they smelt so nice. Like Christmas.'

She seemed surprised when I hugged her.

'Goss is jealous,' she explained. 'She thinks you like Jason more than her. I told her she was being an airhead. But she didn't listen. She never does,' said Kylie. 'She just called me a ditz. I hope she likes this new job, or it's gonna be real gross living with her. When she doesn't like things she throws up a lot.'

I refused to be sorry for Goss. But I was. Sort of.

When we closed I sent Kylie to buy me food for three and took it upstairs to see if Daniel was awake. He was still sleeping like a large, unbelievably gorgeous baby so I lunched alone and got on with my GST return, always a constant source of pleasure for an ex-accountant. I wouldn't go back to doing figures full time but it's fun when it's your own business. I am aware that my view is not widely shared.

The computer has taken most of the difficulty out of keeping books anyway. I checked all my receipts and invoices and waybills against the figures on my spreadsheets, and once I was sure that I had everything included, all I had to do was press a button and ask for the balance. And a very nice balance it was, which meant a nice cheque to be paid to the Tax Office. I was doing that when arms came around me and someone nuzzled my neck, sending harmonics down my spine which grounded with a thud.

'Mmm,' he growled. 'I love a woman who's good with figures. Tell me, oh accounting woman, how goes your bakery?'

'It goes very well,' I said. 'Nice cash flow, no debts and a pretty set of numbers. In fact everything is in excellent condition. Except for the drunk.'

'What drunk?'

I explained about Jason. Daniel leaned his chin on my shoulder.

'What are you going to do?'

'Dock his wages for the brandy and tell him not to do it again. Also, he has to clean the toffee saucepan. That ought to be punishment enough.'

'That, and the hangover. He's probably done this before, you know. It's a self-defeating pattern. He goes along well, almost gets accepted, then something happens and he blows it. And he hates himself even more because he has blown it.'

'He hasn't blown it,' I said. 'He's got real talent. I can handle a few hiccups on the way.'

'But you're unique,' said Daniel, and kissed the back of my neck in that same disturbing way. Why wasn't I dragging this man into bed? What was wrong with me?

I didn't know. Now that I was convinced that the painter of signs with the one-track vocabulary was some minion of James', everyone had relaxed. The level of tension in the building had gone down. I was sleeping better. I had just weathered a relapse and I still had Jason, though how he would react when he woke I couldn't guess. I knew what he would say, if he could speak. It would be some variant on 'just let me die.'

But we still had a mission, Daniel and I. Who was killing the junkies? I didn't have the faintest idea. The only pattern I had been able to find had been the missed days, which argued that the killer either wasn't allowed out every night or had a job which kept him away from his victims. There must be hundreds of people in that position.

'We have to find out who's killing the children,' I told Daniel. Trout pool eyes looked into mine, infinitely sad.

'That's what I have been trying to do,' he said. 'Come and hug me. I need a hug, Corinna.'

I supplied the hug. His voice rose from somewhere under my collarbone. He was pillowing his face on my breast with as much familiarity as if he had been nursed there. It felt very good. So good that I missed the first couple of sentences in the glow.

'…and then I went to the John Smith family. It was a little risky because they don't approve of me, though they do approve of the Soup Run. So I took a bodyguard.'

'Who? Ma'ani? He ought to have been proof against anything but a direct hit with a nuclear missile.'

'Worse. I took Sister Mary.' He chuckled.

'Did you tell her who she was going to see?' I remonstrated.

'Oh yes, she knows them. All the Smiths are Catholics. She stings them for huge sums every Easter. And you know Sister Mary. No nonsense. She just said, "If you are doing this then God have mercy on you, John Smith, for I won't have any at all," and he crumpled up immediately. This from a woman who barely clears the height of a parking meter to a man who had three men chainsawed in half and buried in concrete for not speaking respectfully enough of his wife. That sort of thing stays with you,' said Daniel.

'But John Smith swore up, down and sideways that it wasn't him or any of his relatives, and asked who would waste good heroin killing junkies when you could just knock them on the head? Which I have to admit is unanswerable. Then Sister Mary admonished him to mend his wicked ways—some hope—and we left. The heir apparent, Cain, told me that the family was getting out of drugs anyway, and into abalone smuggling. Apparently there's more money in it.'

'It's a strange world,' I commented, stroking his forehead.

'I've covered every dealer, every junkie, every source I could think of,' he said flatly. 'I have it on good authority that it isn't a Triad revenge kick. They are due to be arrested today. I talked to some bikies I know about someone trying to do a Murder Inc. and they laughed a lot and didn't hit me, which is bikie for "good joke, mate." No one knows a thing. Two of the dead kids were friends of Jason's, when he was Jase. He's my last hope.'

'And he isn't in any state to answer questions,' I said. 'So let's just have a nap, and we'll think of something when we wake up.'

Chapter Sixteen

And I did. When I had disentangled myself from Daniel, dislodging Horatio, I did think that maybe Jason might feel like telling us about his dead friends in exchange for a reasonable hangover cure. Meroe made one and I had a packet of the herbs somewhere. They worked too. I had mentioned the merchandising opportunities in a land where a lot of people drank unwisely and too well, but she had sniffed. Some of those herbs were rare. Some of them had yet to be cultivated. Start selling a sure-fire hangover remedy and the plants would be highly priced, packaged mulch in moments and so would the surrounding landscape.

I had to agree with her. Anyway, before it went on general release, something would have to be done about the smell. It had an odd, metallic odour a bit like lemon juice boiled in a brass pot. Getting it down Jason might be the hardest part of the interview. I made the tea, added a dollop of honey, collected the litre of lightly sugared water which went with the cure, and Daniel and I descended to the depths.

A crapulous human wreck was vomiting noisily in the bathroom. When he crawled out he was, I swear, green in the face. He saw us, dived back and threw up again.

'Not used to alcohol,' said Daniel judiciously. 'Notice the slightly amazed look under all that crippling pain and nausea. He didn't know what being drunk does to the body. Apart from the constipation, heroin is a clean drug.'

This came under the heading of things I didn't need to know.

'Get those clothes off him and into the washer,' I ordered. 'He can have James' old gown until he stops throwing up.'

'And why me?'

'Because you're male,' I told him.

Daniel muttered something about 'nice of you to notice' and went off to minister to the fallen. When he brought Jason back he had been forcibly rinsed and dressed in the old gown. He said his first sentence.

'I'm going to die, aren't I?' he asked pathetically.

'No, you only wish that you could,' I told him. 'Now you are going to talk to us and we are going to cure your hangover.'

'Why?' He squinted up at me. 'You're just going to sack me. I stuffed up. I always stuff up. I'm stupid. I'm useless. Don't bother with me.'

I was in no mood for a dose of adolescent self-pity. 'Yes, you stuffed up. Everyone does, sometimes. I am not going to sack you. But if you do it again, I may. You owe me twenty for the brandy.'

'I'll work it off,' he said, with as much dawning of hope as could be expected under the circumstances. 'Thanks. I was going good. Then she said…'

'I know what she said. And what makes the opinion of a jealous eighteen-year-old airhead more important than mine?'

Jason had not thought of this before. He thought of it now with his few remaining brain cells. Then he said, 'Oh.'

'And you will scrub the toffee saucepan. Clean. Now, Daniel has a question and I want you to answer it.'

Jason nodded and instantly winced.

'What did you and those others do that made Big John knock out your tooth?' asked Daniel, in a clear voice calculated to pierce an alcoholic fog. Jason had lost all his defences. He just answered.

'He thought that Vic stole some drugs. Early in the morning, in King Street. From a car.'

'And did Vic do that?'

'I dunno. I suppose. But then he died and Will died and I dunno anymore. I hid away and detoxed. I didn't see them again.'

'Are you being straight with me, Jason?' asked Daniel severely.

'True's death,' said Jason. He accepted the cup of hangover cure. 'What's this stuff? It smells like cat's piss.'

'Yes, and it probably tastes like it, but it will make you feel better, trust me. Have a few sips and then some of this water and then a few sips more and I promise, in half an hour you won't feel like dying anymore,' I told him.

'Where'd it come from?' he asked suspiciously.

'Meroe.'

This satisfied his thirst for knowledge and he sipped immediately. Then he sipped some water. Then he sipped more tea. This was going to go on for some time.

'The John Smiths didn't get their drugs back, then,' said Daniel, 'if they had to attack Heckle and Corinna. Now they don't think that you have them. Who does have them?'

Jason shrugged. 'Who says that they haven't been used up by now?' he asked. 'This stuff doesn't taste so bad now. Can I have some more?'

I supplied more herbal tea. Jason was looking better. Some of his assurance was returning. He had stuffed up as he always did. He had betrayed my trust and expected to be thrown out. I was punishing him for his misjudgment and letting him stay. Obviously this had never happened before. I had, with any luck, begun to break the pattern. An overdose of brandy was a good deal easier to tolerate than an overdose of heroin. Not that I wanted him to make a habit of it. But I do suspect that you get more chances to get off alcohol. Not that it won't wreck your liver and break your family's heart and finally rob you of everything you own, starting with self respect. It just seems to take longer.

Daniel had made coffee for all of us. Jason drank the rest of the litre of water, excused himself, and came back to flood his system with more fluids. The sugar makes it stay in the body longer and be absorbed. It was now half an hour since his ingestion of the first mouthful of Meroe's Mixture. Any moment now Jason was going to say—

'I'm hungry,' he said, right on cue. Daniel rolled his eyes.

'Oh, to be fifteen again. Have some dry bread,' he advised. 'To start with.'

Jason ate his way busily through a whole baguette. Then we went upstairs and they ate lunch, a very tasty pumpkin and pine nut lasagne. I had already eaten. Dessert was a chocolate mud cake which for some reason hadn't sold. If Jason could digest a meal like that I assumed he had recovered.

'Now, what about those caraway muffins?' I asked Jason. 'You game?'

He took a deep breath. 'I'm game,' he said.

I gave him the money for some more caraway seeds and went back to the shop. Daniel stayed to talk to Jason. Goss had come to collect Kylie. She gave me a departing flounce which would have registered about five on the Richter scale. Not as good as usual, that flounce. She must be feeling guilty. Kylie gave me a secretive wave as she left, wages in hand. We would see what Goss would do on Thursday. What did Kylie mean, jealous of Jason? Goss never wanted to be a baker.

We closed the shutters, locked the shop, loaded the sack with bread for the soup van and went into the apartment again. Jason didn't need any helpful advice about his muffins. He was using the two cups of flour I had allowed him and if they worked, they worked. And if they didn't, he could try again.

'It all comes back to Blood Lines,' said Daniel abruptly. 'Suze used to work behind it, Jase and his two mates used to hang there. I doubt very much if anyone is selling drugs inside the venue but it's a part of the city that isn't very savoury.'

'Then we'd better go there,' I said.

'We'll have to go in,' he said. 'And that means we'll need costumes.'

'When do you want to go?' I asked.

'Tonight. No time like the present.'

'That means an improvised costume,' I said, wondering what in my wardrobe could possibly be considered Gothic. By an educated audience who scrutinised each other's clothes. What did Goths wear anyway? The only costumes for hire in

a costume shop for a woman of my size are sad black tents. Or
very large bright tents. No one over size twenty is assumed to
have a sex life or any taste.

'No, it means Mistress Dread,' Daniel told me. He was grinning. He was also plotting something, but I didn't know what.

'Listen, Corinna, we need to make an entrance,' he said. 'So
we need something special. We need to get into that crypt and
we aren't going to be invited unless we look right to start.'

'Yes,' I agreed, dubiously.

'So, trust me,' he said, and took my hand. I agreed, with
reservations, to trust him. This did look like our last resort, so
we might as well put our best foot forward.

Mine, it appeared, were going to be wearing boots. High
heeled boots.

An hour later, Mistress Dread knelt on the floor and shoved
mercilessly. By the sacrifice of a couple of unimportant toes, I too
could have the feet of a sex goddess. Actually, when I wriggled
them, my toes all seemed to be there. The boots had buttons on
them and looked remarkably like the ones which Great-Grandma
had worn. They proved comfortable enough when I stood up
and tried a few paces across the room.

'Good. Now, it's a pity about your dress size, dear,' said
Mistress Dread. I felt resigned. Et tu, Mistress Dread? But that
was not what she meant.

'You're not big enough. My best spare is a twenty-two at
least,' she said. 'Still, perhaps we are going to corset you. Ditch
the jumper and let's have a look.'

Daniel was lounging on a yellow damask love-seat. He smiled
encouragingly at me. I took off the jumper. And the bra. Mistress
Dread turned me around, patted a breast, and pulled at the
waistband of my track pants.

'Out you go, dear,' she said to Daniel. He left through the inner
door with alacrity. What was he up to? Was he enjoying this?

The Queen of the Dungeon came back with a full armload
of red taffeta. She flung it over my head with a practised hand
and it settled on me. I got my arms through the sleeves. The

dress was a full-skirted number with built-in black petticoats, slashed sleeves and a neckline which could be mistaken for a waist it was so deep. It was a gorgeous shade between venous and arterial blood and as I moved I rustled in the most entrancing fashion. Then she slipped a black leather corset over the dress and began lacing it at the front. I watched in amazement as my breasts rose into those perfect 'moon-like, blue vein'd globes' last seen in John Donne's wet dreams.

'Tuck in the nipple, dear, we want an M rating, not an R rating, at least at the beginning of the night,' chided Mistress Dread. 'Not too tight?'

'Am I supposed to be able to breathe?'

'Yes,' she said. 'You're supposed to be able to dance.'

'Then it's too tight,' I squeaked.

The Leather Queen released the laces a little and my breasts stayed where they were. Then she took a handful of my hair, twisted it around and pinned it to my scalp with a long, dangerous hairpin. Spiked bands went round my neck and wrists and she gave me a light black leather whip to hold. She turned me to the wall of mirrors. Then she clasped her hands like a proud mother at the bridal fitting of her only daughter.

Oh my. I was gorgeous. Even without the make-up and the black fingernails. I took a step and the dress rustled. I took up the dress in both hands and inspected my boots. I had a waist! I had the sort of breasts that plastic surgeons weep over because they are so perfect. And I was standing up straight, every inch the Mistress. I slapped the whip against my taffeta-clad thigh. Mistress Dread chuckled. I embraced her.

'It's wonderful!' I said. 'I love it!'

'You'll love it even more with the make-up and the nails. Ask Carol to do them. I mean Cherie. Her poor father could probably do with a couple of hours off.'

'What's Daniel wearing?' I couldn't take my eyes off myself in that mirror.

Mistress Dread giggled. This was not something she did a lot.

'I promise,' she said, and giggled again. 'I swear that you'll approve. Now off with the tat and get back into those unsightly track clothes. See if you can take care of the dress. That's real silk. I'll take you with me tonight, get you past the door vamp, though in those clothes you'd get in on your own. The crypt password tonight is Faust.'

I had to be helped out of the corset. The dress came off next and I decided to wear the boots home. Daniel emerged from the inner room with a large shopping bag, which he refused to explain. Then we went back to my bakery to see how Jason was getting on with the muffins.

His face told us all. We bit. We tasted. While a perfectly good muffin, the taste just wasn't right. The seeds were too strong and the toffee taste didn't come through.

'Try again with honey instead of sugar,' I suggested.

'Nah, gone off the idea,' he said. 'What about a savoury one? An herb muffin?'

'Worth a try. Get over to Meroe and buy all the kitchen herbs she has left—Jason, repeat after me, "kitchen herbs."'

He grinned. 'Sure, okay. Don't want to turn the customers into toads. Toads don't have pockets. Death Lady fix you up all right?'

'I'm gorgeous,' I said, 'and I've got a whip.'

He grinned again. 'So the next time I get drunk…'

'You're in for a good thrashing,' I threatened.

He ran off, laughing. 'He seems happy!' I exclaimed, dropping the rest of my uneaten caraway muffin into the recycling bin.

'Of course he is,' said Daniel. 'Redemption is more intoxicating than alcohol. Now, I must go and tell the Soup Run to find another heavy for tonight and various other things. Watch for me, you, at midnight,' he said softly into my hair.

'Wait for me at midnight,' I breathed. 'I'll come to you at midnight, though hell should bar the way.'

Then my own personal highwayman was gone and I felt like I imagined the other girls at school must have felt when they'd been asked out by the football captain. Tingly.

I found the toffee saucepan, thinking that a good bout of scrubbing would relieve that tinkling of fairy bells in my head, but Jason had cleaned it religiously. If birds suddenly appeared the next time I saw Daniel, I would know that I was in love. Of course, at that hour they would be owls. Or possibly bats.

I put the saucepan down and went upstairs. I rang Cherie and arranged for her to come and do my make-up at eleven. Then I had nothing to do for the moment and I felt like doing it. I laid my dress and corset on my bed, collected Horatio, and was just about to leave when the phone rang. I was fully loaded with cat and basket so I let the machine pick it up and ascended for a drink and a reverie. In, as it happened, the rose garden. I was dreaming through my gin and tonic when I had a horrible thought.

Who, of my fellow tenants, was James' revolting associate? Who was painting the signs and stealing the weedkiller? I knew it wasn't me and I was sure it wasn't Meroe. And Trudi had cried when she'd seen her violated turf. Professor Dion Monk?

A sardonic man with a taste for Juvenal. He might consider it as an interesting social experiment. But he was basically a kind man and in any case, he had a bruised leg during some of it and couldn't walk at all. No cultivated man who could walk would have watched Oprah for so long.

Horatio was away in the shrubbery, doing whatever he usually did. Jon? He wasn't here enough. He'd just come back from Cambodia and now he was in Namibia, he'd had some sort of affair with Kylie, he didn't have time. Mrs. Pemberthy? Too old, too short, and too sick. Nerds Inc?

Now there was a thought. Taz was the same height as me. I could look straight into his eyes, when he would allow me to, which wasn't often. Would the Lone Gunmen paint rude words on walls for money?

Was the sea damp?

The little deadshits! I would personally staple their genitalia to a moving tram when I proved this! I gulped down the rest of the drink. This was no time for sitting in rose bowers. I passed

Mr. Pemberthy as Horatio and I left the roof. He was sitting on the edge of the wall. I greeted him civilly.

'She's in hospital,' he said sadly. 'It's all gone wrong.'

I told him I was sorry and went on. Horatio was wriggling, which he usually doesn't. By the time I had placed him on his sofa I was beginning to simmer down because I had spotted a large fault in my reasoning. What did I know about the Lone Gunmen? Nerds. Definitive nerds. They were to nerdness what the Holy Mother is to virginity. There was nothing in the task of painting rude words on walls—apart from the fact that they would have to go out into the open—which would preclude them from being our Mr. Fruitloop. Though they would probably have had to read the instructions on the paint can. Then again, they may have been ardent graffitists in their youth. No. One could see Rat, Gully and Taz getting a certain forbidden pleasure out of painting 'Whore of Babylon' on Mistress Dread's shop. And they might, if sufficiently paid, have poured weedkiller on the lawn and metho in through the air brick of Meroe's shop. No one said that the Lone Gunmen were more virtuous than other nerds.

But would any power on earth have been able to make them produce a layout as amateurish as the scarlet woman letters? It is difficult for a person who knows a craft to look as if they don't, like it is hard not to swim if you fall into the sea. Even if the swimmer does an impression of drowning, it's not going to have the desperate gulp, bubble, help! authenticity of the non-swimmer. The scorn on Taz's face came back to my mind's eye. I could have sworn that that was a genuine reaction.

Rats. Just when I had a good solid solution, I had to go and talk myself out of it. Idly, I pressed the play key on the answering machine. I knew the voice. It was James.

'I can meet you outside your shop at five if you must see me, though I can't imagine why you want to,' he said all in one sentence. 'Got to go, that's the video phone.'

I looked at the clock. Half past five. I broke the land speed record to the street and met James as he turned the corner of

Degraves Street. Always late, that man. I grabbed him by the sleeve and drew him into the alcove of a record shop.

'James, I have read your prospectus,' I said icily.

'Good! Good!' he said with that well-remembered false heartiness that had edged him so close to being hospitalised with skillet-related injuries. 'You're going to invest?'

'You bastard, James, that's the place where I live!'

'At present,' he said cautiously. 'You would have an apartment in the new block, of course. When it was built.'

'I like the apartment I have,' I said firmly. 'Now I want you to call off your dog, James. No one is going to sell.'

'I don't know what you're talking about,' he snarled. 'You're plotting against me! You always did!'

He was red in the face and sweating in a very unattractive way. I was close enough to see his scalp through his thinning hair. He had always been proud of his hair.

'Well no, actually, James, I never did plot,' I told him. 'But I'm willing to start.'

'You needn't bother! I don't know why I married you. Pity, I suppose,' he snapped. 'You wouldn't have found anyone else to marry such a fat bitch. You needn't worry about the Renew proposal. It's been turned down. No one would invest. No one would sell. It's dead. Finished. I blame you,' he said, with a wild look in his eye which made me exit from the alcove into the nice safe street.

'Sorry about that, James,' I said, keeping out of grabbing distance. 'Now call off your tame painter and we can forget about it, eh? Who was it? Which of us was helping you?'

'I don't know what you're talking about! I never did!' screamed James, and rushed off into Flinders Street, clutching his briefcase to his expensive tailoring.

Well, there went James. I felt better as I strolled back to Insula. It was a pity that he wouldn't tell me who his accomplice was but James was such a liar that it wouldn't have helped if he had. The late afternoon sun winked off the blue-green tiles. Kylie was sitting out on her balcony wearing a bikini which, rolled out, would barely have covered a couple of teacups and a saucer. I rephrase. A couple of egg cups and a wineglass. I waved at her. She waved at me.

'Are you going to Blood Lines tonight?' I yelled up to her.

'Yes!' she called down.

'See you there!' I said, and watched her mouth drop open.

I talked to Jason in the bakery. He had finished his next muffin experiment and it was really good. Just salty enough.

I asked him what was in it. He counted on his fingers.

'Parsley, mint, thyme, some sage and a leaf or two of coriander.'

'I can taste that now. Just the right degree of spice, not overwhelming. Very good, Muffin Man.'

'They would be perfect with soup,' he said wistfully.

'But we don't sell soup,' I said automatically. Still, soup and one of these savoury muffins was a possibility and I could always donate the leftovers of both to the soup van. 'It's a good idea for the depths of winter,' I said. 'Do some research. Find us some good soup recipes. There's a shelf of cookbooks in my kitchen. Jason, you need to find somewhere to live. The nights are getting colder. While you're probably not going to die of exposure, you're too thin to sleep on the ground and the company isn't very choice.'

'The city's pretty dear,' he said. 'But I could get a room in a backpackers' if you start paying me.'

'True. Would you like to do that?'

'What, me own bed? A place to keep my stuff? Maybe some clothes? And not to have to listen out. Yeah,' he breathed. 'Sleeping rough you always have to sleep light. Or someone'll steal your stuff or...you could be in trouble, or the cops'll arrest you. I been sleeping too deep these days to be safe.'

'Right. Let's gather you a change of clothes and you can get a room. I'll pay you the basic apprentice's wage for the time being. You can think about what you want to do later. Where's your stuff?'

'Stashed in the park. I'll go and get it before the blokes come back,' he said. 'You mean it, Corinna?'

'Yes, I mean it,' I said.

He didn't say anything. I gave him a shrunk skivvy and a pair of too-small track pants. I packed up his dinner in the usual supermarket bag. I handed over *Savoury Soups* for his bedtime reading and I counted out his first week's wages and paid them into his hand.

He stared at the money. Then he took half and thrust the remainder at me. 'Keep it for me?' he asked.

I put the money in an envelope and wrote *Jason* on the front. 'Tomorrow you get a bank account,' I said.

'I can't,' he replied. 'I got no ID.'

'We'll deal with it next week,' I said. 'I'll put this envelope under the tray in the till. Tomorrow I might be late. I have to go out to Blood Lines tonight.'

'You still looking for the killer?' he said. I nodded.

Then Jason grabbed me in a hard, unexpected, throttling embrace.

'You be careful,' he said. 'You make that dude Daniel look out for you.'

'I will,' I gasped.

He released me as suddenly as he had grabbed me. 'I'll come at four,' he said. 'If you're not here, I'll wait. Thanks, Corinna.'

He ran off as though he was afraid that I might change my mind. People were running away from me a lot today.

They must be detecting my inner dominatrix. I locked up and went upstairs to get some sleep. Both Horatio and the Mouse Police, unusually, joined me.

Chapter Seventeen

I had dozed the uneasy doze of a woman pinned down by three solid cats at different points on her doona and I was glad to get up, shower and let Cherie in. She looked different, somehow; perhaps older. Or maybe younger. She was carrying a case and when she opened it I saw that it was full of make-up. She took out a large bottle.

'We need to put this all over any exposed skin and sit still till it dries,' she instructed. 'If you move it looks like you're a hundred and five. Good if you're going for that "returned from the grave" look, though. While you're sitting I'll do your nails. Have you got a name yet?'

'You know my name,' I said weakly as she smeared the white foundation all over my face, neck and breast.

'Your Goth name,' she said patiently, smoothing more foundation on my neck.

'I hadn't thought. What sort of names do female Goths have?'

'Depends on who you're being. If you're an Edgar Allan Poe freak, you pick a name like Carmilla. If you're into Angel or Buffy, you pick a Latin name. Or use Demona. Victoria. An Anne Rice name—we got a lot of Anne Rice names. Lilith. What would you like to be?'

'The costume is from Mistress Dread,' I said.

'Oh, then you're a dominatrix. Lady someone. I'll just wash my hands. Through here?'

While she was away I thought about it. There would be Morticias and Incubas and Succubas by the score. Who was the goddess that I felt truly expressed my personality as I wanted it to be? I had listened to Meroe tell me stories about the Celtic gods and the Prof about the Greek ones. Diana/Artemis, the hunter? Would need a more athletic figure than mine. Hecate, the Hag, lady of the three ways, goddess of exits and entrances, Lady of Witches? I wasn't old enough. Rhiannon, Bloddfluedd, Ceridwen? Rhiannon, Lady of Sleep, Bloddfluedd, Maiden Made of Flowers and Ceridwen and her cauldron of renewal. No. Clotho, Lachesis, Atropos? The Fates. The Spinners. Clotho who spun the thread of life, Lachesis who measured it, and Atropos who cut it. None of them really matched me. Astoreth? Astarte? Ishtar? Perhaps I was a muse? I didn't think so. Then I had it. When Cherie came back I said, trying not to move my lips, 'Lady Medusa.'

'Cool,' she said. 'Who was she?'

'A beautiful monster in Ancient Greece. Her glance could turn men to stone.'

'That'll work. Lestat "My gift is death" will be pleased. He likes clever names. He thinks most Goths are unimaginative. You're drying nicely,' she said. She took my hand and began painting my nails bright red. Horatio removed himself. He hates the smell of nail polish. One reason why I never wear the stuff. It had improved since I last used it. It dried much faster.

'Do you know Lestat well?' I asked.

Cherie shrugged. 'I don't think anyone does. He's very respected. But he plays blood games and I never do. If they let you into the crypt you'll see. Gross.' She obviously felt uncomfortable and changed the subject abruptly. 'You ought to come up and see how my room looks now. Dad kept all my stuff. I never thought I'd see it again. Lots of it's just junk but it's my junk, you know?'

'Your history,' I said. 'And your teddy bear,' I added.

'You know, I almost went back for Pumpkin Bear,' said Cherie. 'I just knew that Mum would throw him away. But Dad rescued him. And he looked for me everywhere. But I wasn't on the street so he didn't find me there. He did try very hard. Poor Dad.'

'Are you going to keep working at the dress shop?'

'For a week,' she replied. 'Donna gave me a job when I turned up and said I couldn't go on the books. I owe her. But Dad says he'll spot me to do a catch-up school course next year and then I want to get into RMIT. Do fashion design. Donna's been letting me design Goth stuff for her. From next Thursday, Dad and I are going to have a holiday.'

'A good idea,' I said. 'Where are you going?'

'Here,' said Cherie. 'He's going to take me to the zoo and the movies and teach me to cook. He's a good cook. You wouldn't know it from his fridge, though. We're going to do all the stuff we would have done if…it hadn't all gone wrong. I'm going to help him get off the bottle. We've got a lot of catching up to do. And I never dared take any time off, because I never had enough money and I didn't know if Donna could hold the job for me. I haven't had a day off since I left home, except that one time when I caught the flu. I need a rest.'

It struck me that Donna had got rather a good deal.

I suspected that Cherie might be just the person to design clothes for today's well-dressed Goth. Then again, I had just extorted a week's free work out of an ex-junkie who slept in Flagstaff Gardens.

While she was talking, Cherie had been making up my face with effortless efficiency. She piled my hair up on top of my head and pinned it there with two black lacquered chopsticks and a few invisible hairpins. She buckled the spiked collar around my throat. The spiked armlets closed around my wrists.

I looked into the mirror. My face was bleached white. My lips were red as blood. Dark shadows rimmed my eyes, which looked much brighter in contrast.

I stood up, shedding my dressing gown, and Cherie dropped the red dress over my head without stirring a hair.

I put on the corset and laced it as tightly as I could while retaining any lung function at all.

And there was the transformation. I was stunning. I rustled lusciously as I moved. My breasts rose as though I was floating in water. Cherie picked up my handbag.

'What are you going to need? You shouldn't carry anything in your hands but your whip,' she instructed. 'There're pockets in the dress.'

So there were. Deep ones. I dropped my wallet, lipstick, keys, a handkerchief and a mobile phone into the left one and they vanished without a trace into the depths of the dress. I felt for them and they were all there, hanging at about knee level.

'Make sure the phone is off,' warned Cherie. 'If it rings you are history.'

'It's hardly ever on,' I said. 'Anything else I need to know?'

'Keep your head up and take no shit from anyone,' said Cherie. 'Have a good time. I gotta go. I'm watching *The Princess Bride* with Dad. He bought the video.'

I thanked her and saw her out and indulged myself in a few twirls. I had never worn anything like that red dress. I loved it. I practised walking in it, like a lady, with the front held up in both hands. Then I practised stalking like a dominatrix and found that it swished agreeably as I strode.

Then the door buzzer went and I gathered my black cloak, threw it around me, and went down, almost hoping to meet Mrs. Pemberthy in the lift.

A black stretch limo with darkened windows was waiting. A uniformed chauffeur opened the door. I got in. There was Daniel, swathed in black like myself. He leaned forward and kissed me. Mistress Dread was in the opposite seat. The car pulled silently away from the kerb.

'Have a drink, dear,' said the Lady of Phantoms, opening a drinks cabinet and taking out a cocktail shaker. It was a White Lady, very strong.

'Nothing but red wine in the club,' she said. 'I always have one drink to soothe my nerves.'

'I don't believe you have any nerves,' I said admiringly.

'I have a little drink to soothe the nerves which I'd have if I was another sort of person,' she elaborated.

That made sense to me and we all drank. The limo pulled up outside a large warehouse at the top of the city. A small brass plate, like the ones on a doctor's office, intimated to anyone close enough to read it that this was the home of Blood Lines, members only.

Mistress Dread stalked up the steps as though she was coming to accept the surrender of a small city, and the doors opened before her advance. She did not slow at all as she passed a person of indeterminate sex who was lurking inside the door. The person was wearing peasant clothes circa 1500, including a hood and liripipe. Its face was covered in stitches. I had seen the film. Films. This was the one who was always sent out for fresh brains at three a.m. I had read Terry Pratchett.

'May I drink your blood?' it asked me hopefully.

'No,' I said.

'Then may I take your cloak?'

'Thank you, Igor.'

'Lucky guess about the name, Mistress,' said Igor.

I shed the black cloak and shook myself into order. Daniel did the same.

And there he was. He was naked to the waist. The rest of him was clad in leather trousers and boots. A design had been painted on his chest. There was a studded dog collar around his neck and he dropped to his knees and offered me the loop of his leash.

My hormones did that thud at the base of the spine thing. I was about to protest when his shook his head very slightly and said, 'Please, Lady Medusa?'

'Very well.' I took the leash and tightened it so that I drew him almost to my hem. 'If you are good.'

'I'll be good,' he said, with an undercurrent which went straight through the corset into the breast underneath.

'If you will sign in, Mistress Dread,' said Igor, cringing. 'And you, Mistress,' he added to me. He did not address Daniel.

Clearly pets did not have to register. I signed 'Lady Medusa' and paid over my fee. Igor led the way to the curtained door.

'You are very decorative,' I whispered to Daniel as we went towards the inner door, covered by a heavy red velvet curtain.

'Celtic design. Meroe drew it. It's your mark. It means that I am yours and anyone who wants to borrow me has to ask you first.'

'I have no intention of lending you,' I said. I meant it.

I wondered what Meroe had felt, so close to this admirable body, this smooth skin, this scent of spices, using his skin as her canvas. I hoped she had also given us a spell for success.

I joined Mistress Dread at the curtain, which was drawn back to reveal someone in the last stages of decomposition, dripping with what I hoped was very good fake green slime. Huge screens showed the Hammer horror movie *Brides of Dracula*. Christopher Lee's mouth, fanged and three metres high, approached a vulnerable, proffered neck. I had no need to speak. I would not have been heard if I had. The loudness of the music was almost beyond bearing. Not techno, however. Not Eversun. This was death thrash metal and they were singing about...

'Andre Norton?' I asked.

'It's Blöödhag,' yelled Mistress Dread. 'They combine education with heavy metal. In concert they throw cheap editions of the books at the audience. Their motto is "the faster you go deaf, the more time you have to read." Good, aren't they?'

'Terrific,' I yelled back as the three nerds on the big screen segued into 'HP Lovecraft.' I followed Mistress Dread to the bar. Funnily enough, on the approach of a six-foot woman in a black corset and carrying a whip, the crowd melted away. The bar person was a wolf. I delved for my wallet and the wolf man pointed to a sign. It read 'Blood type O, two gold. Type Rh negative, four gold.' I produced four gold and Daniel leaned up against my thigh, begging. 'Lady?'

The wolf seemed to understand. He gave me some Rh negative in a plastic wineglass and poured more into a bowl marked 'Dog.' I placed it on the floor. I knew I shouldn't be enjoying this. But I was. Oh, I *was*.

Mistress Dread put one stilettoed foot on the brass rail and we surveyed the crowd. The elaborately framed mirror behind the bar produced no reflection. Clever. The room pulsed to the thrash metal beat. There were a lot of vampires, I noticed. Dead white complexions, discreet fangs parting blood-red lips, ruffled shirts for the men, artfully draped shrouds for the ladies. One girl danced past me wearing Ophelia's shroud from the Millais painting, long draperies speckled with flowers from her last bouquet: pansies, rue, rosemary. No violets. 'For they wither'd all when my father died.' Her hair was long and somehow pre-lanked, looking wet and clinging to her pale, greenish, drowned face.

Then three leather Goths strutted past; a knee-length dress made of leather with studs on every available surface and two boys dressed mostly in an assortment of straps. High boots were universal except for the girls in filmy white damsel in distress costumes, who had pale bare feet. I had never seen such a fascinating crowd in my life. Costume parties, yes, I had been to them. People wearing hired clothes and looking uncomfortable, mostly. Whoever had painted the henna designs on that almost entirely naked girl had spent hours worshipping her body. The same went for the guy who had spent a whole weekend armouring himself in a shell of studded leather. There was real conviction in these dancers. They lived their dream.

Admittedly it was a dream of darkness and death. Their only chance of immortal life was to be bitten by someone with the right sort of teeth. But it was a dream and, as Daniel said, they had a mission. I drank the wine, which was surprisingly good. Daniel nudged my knee.

'Will the Lady dance?' he asked.

'Can I dance with you?' I whispered back. He read my lips. It was silly to whisper in a place where Blöödhag was belting out some comments on the literary skill of Frank Herbert with a backing track that sounded like a 747 landing.

'Order me to stand. Flick the whip. Then we can dance,' he mouthed.

I put down the empty glass and tugged at his chain. 'Up!' I ordered. I gave the whip a twiddle and it flicked his shoulder. I stopped myself from saying sorry. We were doing this for a purpose. Daniel stood up, head hanging submissively. I put the handle of the whip under his chin and forced his head up.

'Dance!' I ordered.

At once I was whirled into the centre of the crowd and Daniel was holding me tight to keep us in one place. My previous kiss had reddened his lips. I kissed him again. Something had happened to me which wasn't entirely a product of the costume and the company. I felt powerful. I saw Mistress Dread drinking another glass of Rh negative and smiling at me. I could not feel Daniel's body through the corset and the taffeta but I could slide my hands down his bare skin, relish the muscles, the ordered propriety which was his back. He was mine.

The music faltered. The dancers stopped. Werewolf, hag and leather boy began to bow or curtsy according to taste. Someone was parting the dancers like Moses parted the Red Sea.

He came towards me and I gave at the knees in a proper curtsy, learned in a very respectable school dancing class a very long time ago. Daniel dropped to his knees and grovelled. Mistress Dread stalked to our side and put a hand on my shoulder and she bowed. Just a little. Mistress Dread was not the subservient kind. But everyone bowed to Lestat.

A slight figure, dressed in an eighteenth century suit with embroidered waistcoat, ruffled shirt and stock, carrying a long black cane with gold decorations. His golden hair was clubbed and tied with a black ribbon. He walked slowly, returning the courtesies with the occasional nod. Behind him, stooping, came a figure in peasant clothes. Lestat had his own Igor. When the Master of Vampires came to Mistress Dread he stopped and bowed, a little, in turn. Two monarchs saluting each other.

'Mistress,' he said.

'Master,' said Mistress Dread. 'May I present the Lady Medusa?'

Oh, those strange eyes. I could not see any pupils or any white. The whole eye was velvety black. He was looking at me and I could not guess what he was thinking. The eyes are the window of the soul and this person, quite possibly, didn't have one. He extended a white hand loaded with rings. I sank and rose. He raised my hand and kissed it. His mouth was as dry as a lizard's.

'I am Lestat. My gift is death,' he said. 'Will you honour me with your company? You and your enchanting…pet?'

I pulled the leash and Daniel grovelled forwards. Lestat pushed him aside with the gleaming toe of his boot. Then I laid the tips of my fingers on Lestat's arm and we went through the dancers. A door opened at Lestat's approach. He said 'Faust.' A Woman in White straight out of Wilkie Collins let us through. Blöödhag started up again as the door closed. It must have been padded because the noise level immediately fell to almost nothing.

We came into a chamber hung with red plush like an old cinema. There were lots of chairs and sofas set around the walls and, I suspected, alcoves behind the drapes for more private meetings. There was a large cleared space in the middle where twenty couples had formed up to dance. All vampires, here, except for two Masters with female slaves and one other Mistress, also with a female slave. Daniel was prettier than all of them. Lestat gestured to his Igor to take Daniel's leash and led me into the dance.

This was going to be ugly. Not only had I solely learned boring dances, I had two left feet. I was about to be humiliated but I couldn't see a way out.

Music began to play. Not death thrash metal but chamber music. In fact, I knew it. It was 'Bella, qui tiens ma vie.' With any luck, we were going to dance a pavane, and anyone—I repeat, anyone—can dance a pavane. One could teach a moderately dim orang-utan to dance a pavane. I breathed a sigh of relief.

Originally, pavanes were danced to allow everyone in the room to see what everyone else was wearing and who they were dancing with. This was still their function in this room. We moved. One, two, three paces forward. One, two three paces back. Forward again. Gentleman down on one knee as lady circles him. Lady stands as gentleman circles her. Then forward again. When the whole room has had ample time to look and gossip, it finishes with a curtsy. Very nice. An ideal dance, which allows one to observe and converse.

I observed as Lestat did not wish to converse. From the exaggerated veneration paid the Vampire Master, I assumed that one did not offer any comment unasked. Strong Buffy influence. Two Spikes with bleached hair. A Harmony.

A Glory in a red dress patterned with anatomically correct hearts. An assortment of Scoobies: two Willows, a Tara in a long green gown. Several people in demon masks and a very good werecat; a woman in tight fur with a very convincing tail.

Not a lot of differences from a science fiction convention except there were fewer Klingons. No aliens. No blue-skinned maidens. No lycra. I liked it already.

We paced on through the pavane. I could see the Igor holding Daniel's chain tight, so that he had to sit up on his heels. So far, this gathering might be a little eccentric as to dress and speech but its behaviour would not have been out of place at a Baptist convention. Mistress Dread had not joined us. I assumed that her domain was underground, in the dungeon.

'An interesting pet, Lady,' Lestat said to me. 'Have you had him long?'

'A few weeks,' I answered, and added, 'Lord. A fascinating club, Master. Have you ruled it long?'

'A few centuries,' he replied. 'The city grew up around it, of course. When the ship with my coffin in the hold went off course, driven by the trade winds, there was nothing here at all except marsh and river.'

'You must have been hungry, Master,' I said, carrying on the fantasy.

'I fed,' he said, licking his lips. 'Things have improved lately, of course. But I shall be here when the city is gone again,' he said. 'When the towers fall and the river creeps out of its bed and makes all this marsh again.'

'Eternal Master,' I murmured. Lestat looked at me, possibly with favour. Where was Anita Blake, Vampire Killer, when I needed her?

'It is time for communion,' he said. 'You will join us?'

'Honoured,' I said. I had to talk to Daniel. What sort of communion was he talking about? Lestat led me back to a sofa and reclaimed his Igor. I dragged the leash so that Daniel's ear was close to my mouth.

'Communion?' I whispered. He shrugged.

'I don't know,' he mouthed. 'I've never got this far before. But there's an inner chamber. This is just the public face. You have to convince him to let you closer. Stick with it, Lady,' he said, and slipped down off the sofa to bury his face in my skirts. Igor was bowing. He was so heavily made up and masked that I couldn't tell if he was young or old. The voice sounded like a boy's. I wondered how many Igors there were. This was the third I had seen tonight. A good disguise for an interchangeable servant. I suspected the Igors might be staff.

'Lady Succuba is wondering if the new Mistress would care to share wine with her,' he said, omitting the customary lisp. 'Your pets may like to play together, my lady says.'

I stood and tugged Daniel to follow. He was keeping behind me, I noticed. Surely no one was going to recognise Daniel as a partly naked slave on a leash?

Lady Succuba was wearing a half-mask. Lady Succuba was also wearing a full leather bodysuit, knife point stilettos fully eight inches high and more spikes than a cactus. Embracing her would be like an hour in the Iron Maiden. Which was her point (sorry), perhaps. Her slave was dressed in part of a bikini and a few bandages. Her whole body was painted or tattooed in Celtic designs. She was lovely. But her hair hung down like a curtain and she would not show her face.

Daniel went into an immediate huddle with the tattooed girl. I curtsied to Lady Succuba and she bowed to me.

'First time here?' she asked.

'As my lady says,' I agreed.

'My lady will not find better,' she said, slipping into third person formal. 'The Master keeps perfect order, even in the more...arcane rituals. If it would please the lady, I'm sure that we could show her...things which she has not seen before. If the lady is a true Domina.'

'Indeed?' This called for one raised eyebrow and was a cue to behave like a true Domina. I flicked my whip. 'Dog!' I said severely. 'Behave!'

Daniel whined and let go of the slave girl, curling up with his back to me.

'You have marked him,' Succuba approved. I hadn't. Daniel must have done it to himself. There were two long red weals across his back. I fought down an urge to kiss them. I was sicker than I thought. But now was no time to remember my strict C of E upbringing. Now was the time to remember as many horror stories as I could and to call on my dark side.

Like Meroe, I might easily prove to be better at the dark than the light.

The lights dimmed. An Igor lit candles. Not many candles, either. In the darkness Daniel crawled up beside me, back to the curtains, and leaned his elbows on a convenient thigh. A large table was set up in the middle of the room. Eerie music began to play—Erik Satie, I think. With a flash of light, Lestat appeared and poured red fluid into a huge silver bowl from a silver ewer. It looked like wine. We all got up and moved towards the centre of the room. Somewhere, chanting had begun. A sound like a wind on cold mountains filled the room. Daniel got up to a crouch and stayed close to me. Beside me, Lady Succuba wet her lips.

'Drink,' said Lestat. The quiet, dry voice had great authority. Igors handed out little silver cups. The devil's punchbowl. We dipped and held the silver cups aloft.

'To death,' he said.

And we drank to death.

There was another taste in the wine. A rusty, salty, foody taste. I realised that it was blood and managed not to retch. We circled the table, mistress and slave and demon and vampire, and dipped and drank again. 'To life!' Daniel chuckled very softly by my skirts and I suppressed him firmly. Then a third time, and we drank 'to blood!'

Lestat took my hand. 'Come,' he said, and led me into the inner chamber.

Chapter Eighteen

Here it was wholly dark. I stood still, gripping my whip, conscious that Daniel had come in with me, mostly hidden under my dress. His hand was on my knee. Lestat waited until the small bead of a candle bloomed and I could see the room.

It was all couches, thick mattresses as soft as beds, all covered and draped in deepest black. On an altar at the end of the room, near a small, closed, iron door, lay a languid, naked girl. Her arms were scarred. Her eyes were closed.

'Blood,' said Lestat. 'Blood is life. Let your pet play with you, Mistress, and at your crisis, you will taste blood in your mouth, and that will give you pleasure such as you have never known.'

Blood games. So this was what Suze had been doing. How should I react? I felt Daniel's hand on my knee, urging me towards the couch. I went and lay down, my head near the dirty bare feet of the sacrifice. She was still breathing. As Daniel pushed aside my skirts to kiss my boots, she cracked a wary eyelid. 'Don't sweat it,' she whispered. 'This is a good gig for me.'

Daniel's kisses were moving up my legs. I parted them, and the clever hands slid higher. Lestat watched. He had unwrapped a syringe and was applying a tourniquet to the girl's arm to draw her blood. I couldn't watch because my eyes were dimming. The mouth which was moving closer and closer to my centre was hot, the kisses burned, I felt myself twitch. He was between my legs now, my inside thighs were getting wet, my knees slid over his bare shoulders. I clutched at him as the lips touched, touched and clung, and then I swallowed blood that Lestat shot into my mouth as I bloomed into an orgasm so intense that for a moment I thought I must have died. I screamed with pleasure.

Daniel lay where he was, his head on my breast, panting. I was shaking and dizzy. Lestat reloaded the syringe with a clear fluid, gave it to the girl and opened the little iron door. She went out into the back lane. Cold air rushed in. Daniel stood up and pulled me to a sitting position.

'Igor,' said Lestat.

'Master?' asked an Igor.

'You may now stop the tape and show the lady. She will surely contribute to our crypt when she considers who else might see it. Five hundred dollars, Lady, to begin with.'

'Jason,' said Daniel. 'Shut the inner door. Don't let anyone open it.'

'Okay, Daniel,' said the Igor. Jason? My Jason? There were some small details in his life history which he had forgotten to tell me about. This was one of them. I was a little behind events. Tape? What tape? And how had I just been blackmailed?

'It is no use threatening me,' said Lestat. 'I am already dead.'

'You can get deader,' said Daniel. 'I have some names for you. Listen carefully, dead man. Suze MacDonald. James Collins. Mick Hughes. Gianni Venetti. Tan Nguyen. Hally Udall. Sam Trench. Know them? Recognise them, Lestat?'

Lestat backed away as Daniel came forward. The slave's mouth was wet. His hands clenched at shoulder height. He was magnificent. His voice burned with ferocious contempt.

'You gave them the heroin you confiscated from your slave Vic,' he said. 'One of the poor little bastards who robbed the man in the red Porsche. You used it to pay the whores who participate in your blackmail racket! Lestat!' Daniel hissed, straight into Lestat's black eyes. 'Didn't you wonder why they all died?'

The dapper gentleman faced the half-naked savage and did not flinch. He said calmly, 'But I told you my name. My name is Lestat. And my gift is death.'

Daniel hit him as hard as he could in the face. There was a soggy crack. Lestat flew out the door and into the lane.

I jumped down to follow. An Igor was before me.

'Catch him!' I screamed and a composed, official voice said, 'That's all right, Ms. Chapman. I've got him.'

Of all the people I had expected to encounter in a damp lane behind a Goth club at three in the morning, Lepidoptera White was probably second last, behind Pope John Paul II. She had Lestat in a hurtful and efficient armlock. Several uniformed officers were approaching but she didn't let go of our murderer until he was securely handcuffed. His face was a mask of blood. Daniel sucked his knuckles and spat.

'You bastard,' he snarled. 'I hope you die in jail.'

'I can't die,' Lestat told him through the blood. He was licking it with every sign of enjoyment as it ran down to his mouth. I felt sick.

'He fell against the wall,' Ms. White told Daniel. 'They're clumsy, these murderers. I've known them to leap face first down whole flights of stairs. Thanks, Daniel. We've got the junkie and the syringe. You want to stay out of it?'

'God, yes,' said Daniel. 'Me and Corinna and this Igor. We weren't here. Here's the blackmail tape,' he said, handing over a videotape which a silent Igor had given him. 'There's no harm in the outer circle of the club,' he said. 'Just the inner. No need to scare innocent Goths into another incarnation, is there?'

'Quiet as mice,' she promised. 'I already warned Mistress Dread to bar her doors. Now, you're going home.' She widened her eyes a little as she got a good look at us. 'In a police car. An unmarked one. You wouldn't want to worry the neighbours,' she said, and giggled.

I suddenly felt so relieved that my knees were weak.

I sagged and leaned on Daniel. We got into a car driven by a police officer so taciturn that she didn't utter one word as she drove Jason to his hostel and us to Insula and watched as we went in.

There was no one in the lift. We threw ourselves inside my apartment and locked the door. Then, slowly, carefully, we stripped the clothes off each other and fell into bed. And before the alarm went off I had occasion to scream again.

We hadn't slept. I had lain down in Goth make-up. I was filthy. But I was also terribly happy. I went into the bathroom. There in the mirror was a real Medusa, corpse-white skin, melted mascara circling panda-like around her eyes, mouth red and swollen from kissing and, a final touch, a red bite mark on her throat.

I grabbed a handful of cotton balls and some cold cream and wiped it all off. Only the beestung lips, the teeth-marks and the smile of complete satisfaction remained. I blew Medusa a kiss and washed thoroughly, releasing my mistreated hair and rubbing suds through it. Standing under the hot falling water and remembering Daniel. Then I put on my trackies and padded off to make coffee.

He was asleep and beautiful and although I still had a hundred questions, they could wait. I had bread to make, for one thing. The ovens had come on and hot air was rising. Horatio accepted breakfast even though he had been affronted by another person in his bed. He had been sleeping in the small of a prone Daniel's back. They both looked very decorative. Daniel woke. I set down his coffee and kissed him.

'Corinna,' he said. 'I love you.'

'Daniel,' I answered. 'I love you. Got to start the baking,' I said, and went down the stairs with a refreshed mug of coffee. I was going to need some sort of intravenous arrangement if I was to survive today.

A tap at the door announced a de-Igored Jason.

'You all right?' he demanded, holding me by the shoulders and staring into my eyes. He looked as bright as ninepence. There is no justice.

'Yes, you?'

'Hostel desk dude got a bit of a shock when I came in,' he said. 'I'll give the costume back tonight. What're we making?'

'Just the usual,' I said. 'Switch on the mixer, will you? Rye bread, pasta douro, and blueberry muffins.'

'*Bor*ing,' he replied. I was in no mood for impertinence.

'First rule of the bakery. The baker is always right. You can make the muffins. Any sort you like. Just do it fast. I'm very tired.'

'Sweet as!' he said, flying around the room collecting ingredients, pouring flour, sloshing yeast mixture. In no time at all it was done and we had to wait for everything to rise. I had fed and rewarded the Mouse Police for their measly single rat. But I was in a generous mood. And I needed answers from Jason.

'When did you tell Daniel about your two mates and the pure heroin they got from robbing the man in the red Porsche?' I asked.

'Yesterday arvo,' said Jason. 'When you sent me out for herbs. Vic really believed that he was Lestat's slave. So when he stole the stuff and Lestat saw him, he just gave it to his master. Then Lestat must have given them some and they died and I got scared and ran away. It was easy money, being an Igor.

'I liked it. I never played the blood game but Suze did and she told me what happened. I couldn't tell the cops,' he said, really wanting me to understand. 'I can't be a baker if I'm in jail for ten years. And Daniel told me not to tell you. You understand?'

I did. I gave him a casual hug. He was really clean, smelling strongly of one of those robust soaps—Rexona? Norsca? Pine-scented. He smelled like he had spent the night lying in a spruce forest. Very much a contrast from the way he had smelled when I first met him. I was still trying to make sense of events.

'So someone needed to get into the inner chamber,' I reasoned it out. 'And Daniel couldn't do that on his own, so…'

'So I used you,' said a voice from the stairs. Daniel and Horatio sat there. 'I put you in a position to be blackmailed.'

I thought about it. He was right. Was I angry? Jason had lied to me. Daniel hadn't told me what he was planning.

By rights I ought to have been furious with both of them.

I delved for some fury. I was too tired to be angry. And also, where was the damage to me? Had I been injured or hurt?

No. Had I been betrayed? No. Had I just spent the most erotic hours of my life? Yes. Had I acquired a new apprentice who made muffins which angels would queue to order in a heavenly canteen? Yes. So where was the emotion? I just felt tired and fuzzy.

'I volunteered,' I said. 'I knew you were not what you seemed. You're some sort of detective, aren't you?'

He spread his hands.

'Private. Mostly I look for lost children and erring husbands…'

'The Open Eye,' I said, enlightened. 'That's why Andy Holliday recognised you.'

'I failed to find Cherie,' he admitted. 'Aren't you angry?'

'Because?'

'Take a walk, Jason. Sniff the cool morning air along with the Mouse Police,' ordered Daniel. Jason bounced out into the alley. The Mouse Police went along, tails in the air, hoping that he might do something useful, like turn into a smoked trout. Daniel lowered his voice and came all the way down the stairs.

'Because I participated in a sex act with you while Lestat was watching and taping it. The police now have that tape. I needed to have him on tape, giving the girl the heroin and demanding money from you.'

'Gosh, and I didn't even qualify for Big Brother,' I said absently. 'They should be so lucky. Are you saying that it was all an act; you don't love me?' I demanded with sudden terror. So, I did have some real emotions. He put his arms around me.

'No! Of course I do. I didn't think that this assignment was going to include me falling in love, but it did.'

'And I love you, so that's all right, stop fussing. I don't think Ms. White is going to show the jury the whole tape. If she does, what will they have? An unrecognisable woman reaching orgasm. The place is soggy with happy endings,' I told him. 'James' deal has fallen through so that gets rid of Mr. Fruitloop and now no one is killing the junkies. As far as I can see, we're laughing.'

He kissed me hard on the mouth, stopped in order to chuckle helplessly, and kissed me again. We might have gone on doing this for some time but Jason skidded in from the alley, looking scared.

'You better come look,' he told Daniel. We both went.

On the wall, in the same wearily familiar red paint, was 'Die, whore!!!'

'Oh, shit,' I said, which about summed it up for all of us.

The only useful thing to do was to make bread, so we did that. Daniel went up to sleep on the sofa upstairs for a few hours. I knew that once I fell asleep I might assassinate the person who woke me so I stayed awake, drinking more coffee and a bottle of some venomous green liquid which Jason swore would wake me up. And it did. God knows what was in it. Jason ate breakfast at the Pandamuses' cafe, scoffing down their 'truckie's special,' which usually took two strong men to eat. Del Pandamus told me that he cleared the plate in seven minutes—a Cafe Delicious record. Del was pleased. Apparently wagers had been laid and money changed hands.

I feared that Jason was going to spend most of his wages on food.

I ate a Jason sour cherry muffin, which was excellent. When I went to open the shop Goss was there.

'My last day,' she said.

'Hello, Goss, come in,' I said wearily.

She fingered her navel ring nervously.

'Do I still have to...you know...'

For a moment I could not imagine what she was talking about. Oh yes.

'You still have to,' I said.

Goss stuck her head into the bakery and said, 'Jason? I'm sorry,' and when Jason said, 'Okay,' she said triumphantly, 'Well?'

'Good,' I said. 'This act of propriety will make you a better person. The muffins are sour cherry today. It's your last day. Have one.'

Goss picked up a muffin warm from the oven as though it was an unexploded grenade, broke it, and put a small bit in her mouth. She chewed thoughtfully. She ate the rest. Then she went back to the bakery door and yelled, 'Hey, scrub boy! You make cool muffins!' and I heard Jason laugh.

Ah, reconciliation. This was fortunate because, although I was awake thanks to Jason's potion, I wasn't in a merry mood.

Who was this graffitist maniac? Mr. Detective hadn't worked out who he was. It looked like it was up to me.

About nine a.m.—scandalously early—Gully edged into the bakery as though he was being targeted by a SWAT team. Goss offered him bread and muffins but he refused all food.

'Corinna! I've got something to tell you,' he said.

'So I see. Spit it out, I'm busy.' This wasn't going to be one of my patient days.

'You know when you asked us how you would research the old names of people and I said I'd get back to you?'

'Yes?'

'I know how to do it.'

'Good. Tell me tomorrow.'

'No, you have to listen.' Gully's hands were shaking. 'We didn't tell you that the reason why we know how to find all those names is that we already found them before.'

'You already found them?' I asked stupidly.

'It was just a job,' said Gully.

'He wanted to do all this research. We do research. We found out for him. He paid us. End of story.'

'Except it isn't the end of the story, is it?' I asked menacingly. 'You knew who it was all along. You can't do that "Me nerd. Me no speak Civilization" act with me, you deadshit.'

'Yes!' squealed Gully. 'We talked about it and we said that you ought to be told and I…'

'Drew the short straw?'

He looked at the floor. 'Yeah. What're you going to do to us?'

I didn't answer him directly. Instead I yelled into the bakery, 'Jason! Heat that oil! I want it boiling!'

'Yes, ma'am,' said Jason, who had clearly been listening.

'Get on the phone,' I told Goss. 'Call Ms. White and ask her to drop in. You can stay, or you can go,' I said to Gully. 'But if you warn the man, if you ring him or email him or even sema-phore with your jocks, I will rip off your arm and beat you to death with the wet end!'

Gully fled. Goss said, 'Cool, Corinna! You're all, like, Girl Power!'

'Yeah,' I said. 'I think I've a natural talent as a dominatrix.'

'Yeah, right,' said Jason, in what sounded like hearty agreement.

'And you can mind the bakery while I go and see Meroe,' I told him. 'Don't forget. Every waybill—'

'Must be signed. Right,' he replied. 'Go,' he said.

I went. Meroe saw my face and picked up the dish of charcoal. She censed me with the smoke and muttered a charm. I didn't immediately feel full of sweetness and light but I did feel much more perfumed. She is the queen of intriguing scents. This smelt oriental and almost bitter. Very bracing. I said so.

'It's Chinese. What's happened?'

'The man you put your grandma's curse on. I know who he is. I've asked that lady cop to come. Do you want to see it too?'

'Yes,' she said. 'Kylie and Belladonna can manage for a while. Remember, Kylie, if you don't know what the herb is, don't sell it. I'll be back soon. Been a run on Celtic charms today,' she said, flinging her wrap around her black-clad shoulders. It was a rich, lustrous purple. Belladonna, in the window, waved a relaxed paw.

By the time I got back to Earthly Delights, Jason had woken Daniel, and the Prof, dropping in for a roll, had also been included. Ms. White was there. So were Trudi and the Hollidays.

'All right,' Ms. White said. 'I owe you one. What is it?'

'The tests came back?' I asked.

'Yes. The blood sample was loaded with an organo-chloride poison. The forensic chemist said it was called Buggy Death.'

'Is the patient alive?'

'Yes. They can mop the stuff up with some clever chemical thingy. So who did it?'

'This way,' I said, and led the multitude into the building, into the lift, and in stages up to the correct floor. There I knocked politely and the inhabitant answered. He blinked at so many people in the morning. Ms. White produced her badge.

'Can we come in?'

Mr. Pemberthy shuffled away and allowed us inside the over decorated apartment. He shuffled to a chair and sat down.

'It's all gone amiss, hasn't it?' I said sympathetically. 'Ever since Meroe put a curse on you.'

'Witches!' he snarled with surprising strength. 'Women! All whores! I had you scared, though. I had you widdling your drawers.'

'You did indeed,' I told him. 'Drawers were being widdled all over the building. You know where it went wrong, don't you?'

'It was her!' He shot an accusing finger at Meroe, who smiled sweetly. I suppose it was nice to know that Mamma's curses still worked. 'The daughter of Belial!'

I remembered that he had once been a lay preacher. The vocabulary had lingered. I went on.

'No, it was you. You meant this as a cover for the murder of your wife, a prime candidate for murder, we all agree about that. The Buggy Death was a good touch. But you forgot that she always shared her food with that rotten little mongrel, Traddles. No one was going to test Mrs. P for pesticide poisoning. But vets always test for it because dogs have a habit of eating snail bait. Then, you were hoping to inherit this apartment. You like it here. It would be paradise without your wife. But as a result of your activities, she was going to sell up and leave. It didn't work out, did it?'

'It was just the letters at first,' he said into his yellowing moustache. 'Just to give you all a scare. I used to see you in the garden. Drinking. Laughing! Why should you laugh? I'd show you. I got those boys to find things out for me. Just a joke,' he said lamely.

'Then you stole the pesticide,' I prompted.

'It was just sitting there. She never stores her things properly. It was like a gift. I do all the cooking. I just added it to things with a strong taste. Garlic bread. Curry. She ate it all up like a good girl. Once she even asked for more!' He began to laugh.

'You'll find red paint on his cuffs and pesticide on one of his shoes,' I told Ms. White. 'A Buggy Death burn on his foot.

The Lone Gunmen have tattled. We don't need to stay here any longer,' I said.

'Elias Pemberthy, I am arresting you on a charge of attempted murder,' began Senior Constable White calmly. 'Threatening words. Threat to kill. Attempted arson. Anything else I can think of. You shithead. You are not required to answer questions, but if you do, it will be taken down and can later be produced in court. You are entitled to attempt to contact a lawyer—'

'You're another of the witches! There are witches everywhere!' screamed Mr. Pemberthy.

Ms. White walked him out of the room. She locked the door of the apartment as she left and was gone.

Then we all looked at each other. Such hatred had stung. We must never underestimate, said Germaine Greer, how much men hate us. Pemberthy hated his wife, but he hated all women as well; mysterious, tormenting, dangerous, sinful creatures.

I shivered. So did Meroe. She made a complicated gesture in the air and some of the oppression, I swear, dissipated. I just felt very tired.

'Gross,' commented Cherie Holliday.

'Goddess, did we get *him* wrong,' sighed Meroe. 'This will teach me to believe what any man says about himself!'

'He was very convincing,' I said. He had been, too.

'You work in mysterious ways,' said Professor Monk to me. 'This has all been very instructive. What are you going to do now, Corinna?'

'I'll meet you on the roof at six,' I said. 'Right now,' I grabbed Daniel's hand, 'I am going to bed.'

He came quietly.

Chapter Nineteen

We fell asleep as if poleaxed and surfaced to make love sleepily and sweetly and go back to sleep again. I woke heavy and sated in every limb. The sun was crossing the window. I blinked. Daniel blinked. I could not believe that he was really sharing my bed. But there he was. Smooth, sleek, beautiful Lord-I-am-not-worthy Daniel Cohen.

He read my mind.

'You're still wondering why I love you rather than all those thin girls?' he asked. I nodded, blushing.

'Well, my accountant,' he said. 'Look at it this way. I like long term investments. When all those thin girls are fifty they will be wattled, haggard and wrinkled, mourning the loss of their beauty. You will be plump and rosy and there won't be a line on your face. Or other parts,' he said, running an assessing hand down my shoulder to my breast, then resting it comfortably on my belly.

'I'll sign off on that company account,' I said, and kissed him again. 'Why did you do that to yourself?' I asked, smoothing the two weals from a whip.

'Because I knew you wouldn't hit me hard enough to leave a mark,' he said. 'Why are we getting up?' he asked.

'For the Agatha Christie finish,' I said. 'Have a shower, slave. You're still covered with floor dust and henna. I'll watch.'

He sluiced off dust and grime and scrubbed off some lipstick but the henna stayed. It was my mark, he had said.

I was aware that it was an uncertain world and I was also aware that the last woman Daniel had been close to had only lived for three months after the marriage. In any case I didn't want to live with him, not yet. My life was neat and routine and ruled by yeast and cats and I wasn't ready to change it yet, if ever.

But a demon lover who belonged to the night and appeared suddenly on balconies, who made me feel like fizz and spring and joy, that was worth having. More than enough for me. Much more than I deserved. Something had changed in me once I had put on Mistress Dread's red dominatrix gown. When Daniel was dry and dressed I picked up Horatio and ordered, 'Bring the champagne.'

'Yes, Mistress,' he responded. And there was a tingle. Not a hot flush of mastery, but a tingle.

The whole tenancy of Insula was gathered on the roof and the Prof, I noticed, had already distributed the first round of champagne. Jason was there, in his baker's whites, sipping gingerly. I suspected that he wouldn't be getting stuck into any real alcohol any time soon. Trudi was drinking gin. She did not care for champagne. The Hollidays were sitting on a wicker seat with Pumpkin Bear. He was the only one without a glass. Wonder of wonders, there were the Lone Gunmen, in sunlight yet, sitting together on a picnic rug and looking as uncomfortable as three young men in possession of six bottles of Arctic Death can look.

Mistress Dread, in her Country Road clothes, was sitting with them, talking about a video game, and they were actually talking to her. Strange.

Horatio went off into the undergrowth again. What did he do there? Senior Constable White was lounging on a love-seat and sharing the gin with Trudi. She looked quite different out of uniform; taller and much less tired. Kylie was sitting with Meroe, who was not only drinking but lighting a cigarette.

I went over and borrowed one immediately. A Gitane! Bliss. Everyone I was fond of on the one roof. Daniel opened another bottle. Jason brought around a big tray of muffins. I took one and bit it.

'These are new! Scrumptious! What are they?'

'Apricots. They keep their flavour because they start off dried,' he explained. 'After Goss and me shut up shop I just tried out a few ideas. I cooked the apricots in the microwave in brandy and water,' he explained. 'Try one of these.'

They had a different texture to the ordinary muffin; more crumbly but very light. I gave them their due: 'Equally yum. And they are…?'

'It's the cinnamon and sugar tea-cake recipe,' he explained, beaming. 'They're little tea cakes. I reckon we'll sell as many as we can make.'

'Louis, this could be the beginning of a beautiful friendship,' quoted Daniel.

'Do you like *Casablanca* too?' I demanded.

'One of my favourites,' said Daniel. 'Along with *Blade Runner*.'

'You two are a match made in heaven,' said the Professor. He was pottering about, refilling glasses. Then he stopped and sat down next to Pumpkin Bear, whom he patted absent-mindedly.

'Tell us all,' he decreed. 'Not one more bite or sup do you get until we are thoroughly enlightened.'

'Where do I start?' I asked. 'The junkies, or the Mr. Pemberthy poisoning his wife thing?'

'Both,' said the Professor severely. 'The addicts are probably first in time. Explain, young woman! Expound!' He waved a professorial finger and I began with Suze, Daniel, Jason, the bakery, the soup van and the Goths.

'Lestat was at the club two days on and one day off, when he went to visit his Alzheimer's mother in a nursing home,' I said. 'That accounted for the pattern. The different places of death depended on how far the junkie travelled before they took their hit. He gave them the full syringe. He didn't think it was odd that they died because he's insane and thinks his gift is death. But he was handing out full-strength heroin that Vic stole from the dealer's car. A terrible thing. Of course, if my friend Jason, who worked in the club, had been more forthcoming, we might have solved it earlier, but he makes superlative muffins so we forgive him. Anyway, he told Daniel all about it as soon as he could.'

Jason blushed. Goss was sitting close to him, so I went further.

'And he prevented Lestat from escaping back into the club, which was very brave.'

Goss smiled at Jason. He took her hand. She scowled and snatched it back. Oh, well. I had tried. I went on with my story.

'I did wonder where Lestat got the money to run those three big rooms, a crypt and a dungeon, when the entrance fees were so low. He had a nasty blackmail game going which ensured that once a person had been suckered into the inner chamber, he had a tape which would ensure that they helped him with the upkeep of his kingdom. Mistress Dread?'

She smoothed her beautifully coiffed short brown hair.

'Call me Pat when I'm out of uniform, dear,' she said.

'I never had anything to do with his rooms,' she said. 'But I thought there was something unpleasant going on there. But he was a vampire, what did the Goths expect? Vampires are not nice people.'

That was true. I went on.

'Mr. P always intended to kill his wife, but he wanted it to look like the work of the phantom wall painter. So he sent the scarlet woman letters, made up on his own computer which his wife made him learn so he could do her bridge club minutes and email them to all the other crones.'

'I still feel sorry for him,' said Kylie.

'Feel sorry for his victim,' said Senior Constable White flatly. 'He could have gone away, divorced her, gone on the pension. He didn't need to kill her.'

'True. Though it is hard to feel sorry for Traddles, he gave me the clue. He tried to nip me and missed. Twice. And a nice fat leg within easy munching distance. Something was wrong with him. I knew the vet's name and I asked Ms. White—Ms. White, what is your first name? We must be on first name terms by now.'

'Laetitia,' she said. 'Known as Letty.'

'I asked Letty to check with the vet if he was being poisoned. I knew Mrs. P always gave the little mongrel titbits from her plate. Ergo, if he was being poisoned, so was she, and then I thought, who would want to kill her?'

'Wide field,' said Professor Monk.

'Everyone here,' said Goss.

'Yes, but I mean really actually kill her definitely dead? And it had to be Mr. P. Also, he was a lay preacher and the language was biblical. But it all went wrong for him. She was so scared that she was going to sell up and go, thus taking away what he was poisoning her to get.'

'So it worked,' said Meroe with deep, guilty satisfaction. 'But we didn't guess about him. He said he was happy as a slave. I suppose even happy slaves get fed-up eventually.'

'Yes,' I said. 'Now, give me a drink. That's all I know.'

The Professor obliged. It was very good champagne.

'Not to cast a blight on this gathering,' he commented, 'but this does mean that we get Mrs. P—and Traddles—back, you know.'

'Oh, well,' said Andy Holliday. 'Maybe she'll be nicer. Weirder things have happened,' he said, glancing at his daughter.

'Letty, what's going to happen to Lestat and Mr. Pemberthy?' asked Kylie.

'I don't know,' said Letty White. 'We've got Mr. P absolutely. He confessed to you, confessed to me, confessed to the desk sergeant, confessed to Legal Aid. Clothes had red paint and metho, fingerprints on the wall near that air brick where he poured the metho in. Remains of the Buggy Death in the kitchen cupboard. They'll lock him up for life. Lestat? The forensic psych says he's sane enough to plead.

'We might not get him on the murders but he's got a great video library. It sort of argues against him being insane that he could keep such meticulous blackmail records. He might end up at the Governor's Pleasure in a loony-bin. Where, by the way, they'll take away those contact lenses that make his eyes black. Mental custody's much harder to get out of than a jail. And my sergeant,' she added with a rather nasty smile, 'will not leave me out of any new investigations, because, like your yeast, I always rise. Here's to crime!' she said, and we drank.

'To bread!' chorused Jason and Goss. We drank again.

I felt obscurely worried. There should be three toasts and I could not think of another. Except possibly 'To sex!', which might be considered uncool. But Daniel thought of something. One of the reasons why I love him is that he can always think of something.

'To life!' he said exultantly. 'L'chaim!'

We drank to life, and Horatio brought out his present.

A thin calico cat trailed him from the undergrowth, followed by three fine kittens. Horatio sat down at my feet, licking an elegant paw and looking complacent.

Kylie and Goss pounced on them with cries of joy. They moderated these and soon were covered in kittens. The mother cat nestled into their laps. Between them they had just enough lap for one cat. Cherie immediately claimed the calico mother as her own as soon as we could find homes for her kittens. That shouldn't be too difficult. They were very cute.

'They can't be yours,' I said to Horatio. 'You are no longer that way inclined. How on earth did she get up here? And what has she been eating? Who fed her?'

'Him,' said Trudi, pointing to Horatio. 'I find rat tails. He bring rats every day.'

So that was where the Mouse Police's rats had been going. Horatio would not hunt for himself, of course, he might disarrange a whisker or chip a claw. He was just wandering down to the bakery, borrowing some of the Mouse Police's nightly haul, and then springing from balcony to balcony up the building to feed the mother cat. Whose kittens were certainly no offspring of his. Why had an unrelated ex-tom cat done this?

'These are mysteries,' said Meroe. And they were. The only mystery destined to be left unsolved. And that was a nice, gentle, quiet mystery. The only type that I have any intention of being involved in again. I thought of the dead boys, the furious hatred of the old man, the smooth calm of Lestat. Not nice. Not going to do that again. Memo to the universe re Corinna Chapman as an investigator: I quit.

Recipes

Muffins

The secret of muffins is a hot oven, a well greased muffin tin and speed. You want to have all the measured ingredients ready on the table, fling them together, give them a fast stir so that they blend, then glop them into the trays and into the oven before they get depressed and sink. There is nothing to be done with sunken muffins except feed them to a pig or use them as mulch.

Plum Pudding Muffins

2 cups plain flour
1/2 cup sugar
1 1/2 teaspoons baking powder
1 1/2 teaspoons bicarb of soda
1 cup chopped candied peel, sultanas, chopped dried fruit
1 teaspoon of cinnamon
pinch of allspice
1 beaten egg
1 cup milk
2 tablespoons melted butter
1 tablespoon rum or brandy

Heat the oven to 300°F. Spray the muffin tins with oil. Mix all the dry ingredients together in a large bowl. Mix the egg, milk, butter and alcohol together. Pour it all at once into the muffin mix, stir it with a fork and put it into the prepared tins. Bake for about 15 minutes until they smell cooked but before they are burned on the bottom.

Herb Scrolls

Yeast is a living creature. If you heat it too hot, it dies. If you let it get too cold, it will die. If you want to capture some wild yeast, chop a handful of sultanas and leave them in a jar in warm water until they start to froth. That is the beginning of your mother of bread or starter. Don't do this unless you are prepared to feed it a cup of flour a day and otherwise to care for it like a mother. You can get the same results by adding a cup of rye flour and a cup of blood-heat water to a pint of real ale and leaving it in the sun until it starts to bubble. Water is blood heat when it feels neither cold nor warm in your mouth. Never put cold water in yeast or it will turn up its little pseudopodia and die on you.

If you just want to try the recipe, you'll need:

12 g sachet of dried yeast
500 g of plain white flour
1 tablespoon sugar
About 300 ml water (blood heat)
1 teaspoon salt
1 cup chopped fresh herbs

Mix everything except the herbs together for a while. If you have a mixer with a dough hook, use it until the dough has combined and starts to pull away from the sides. If you are using your hands, keep mixing until it does that. Flour is chancy. If it's too dry, add more blood-heat water. If it's too wet, add more flour. Flub it onto a floured board and knead until it feels elastic (this is one of those things you have to learn by doing, like sex or swimming). Then pat it out into a flattish rectangle like an unrolled Swiss roll. Cover it with a damp cloth and leave it to rise (sticking the whole thing in a clean plastic bag and putting it into a warm bed works).

Preheat the oven to 180°C. When the dough is all swollen, spread your herbs and a pinch of pepper on the up side, roll it up, and glue the seam together with water. Lay it on the bench and cut it into slices. Cook for about 10 minutes. Tastes gorgeous even if it's not exactly round or is a bit singed at the edges.

Happy Baking!

To receive a free catalog of Poisoned Pen Press titles, please contact us in one of the following ways:

Phone: 1-800-421-3976
Facsimile: 1-480-949-1707
Email: info@poisonedpenpress.com
Website: www.poisonedpenpress.com

Poisoned Pen Press
6962 E. First Ave. Ste. 103
Scottsdale, AZ 85251